Red C Publishing Presents...

The A-Z of Horror: S is for Slasher

DISCLAIMER: "This is a work of fiction. Names, characters, places and incidents are products of the author's imagination and are used fictitiously. Any resemblance to actual events, locales or persons, living or dead, is entirely coincidental."

Copyright © 2023 Red Cape Publishing

All rights reserved.

Cover Design & Interior Artwork by Red Cape Graphic Design

www.redcapepublishing.com/red-cape-graphic-design

Contents

One Person's Hero by Scott Chaddon	4
Therapeutic Nihilism by C.R.S. Ford	32
Sorority Slasher Summer by P.S. Traum	56
Last Resort by Barend Nieuwstraten III	81
What the Sonoran Takes by B.F. Vega	112
Slash Camp by Monster Smith	134
Framing Tina by Peter Hayward-Bailey	165
The Midday Matinee Massacre by Kay Hanifen	187
Birth of an Abomination by Roman Durkan	213
Old School by Ryan Day	234
Hide & Seek by Jason B. Edwards	269
Watch Me by Aisling Campbell	300
A Dying Art by Adam Holloway	323
Other Titles	355

One Person's Hero...

Scott Chaddon

Daisy Abbot turned and waved one last time to her date before he pulled away from the curb and drove off into the darkness. She was so happy and excited that she felt like skipping up the walk to her front door. She and Kyle had just concluded their fifth date. Every one of their dates, so far, had been wonderful. He managed to maintain a perfect balance between being a pure gentleman and a bad boy. After tonight, she imagined that they would be going steady soon and she looked forward to being the star basketball player's girlfriend.

Turning the key in the lock, she let herself into the house. Her folks had left for the weekend to celebrate an anniversary and had given her the responsibility of looking after the house while they were gone. It was the first time they had trusted her to be on her own for more than a few hours at a time, and she was not going to screw it up by breaking curfew or throwing a party. The nosey neighbors would blab anything they saw, or did not see, to her parents. She had been studious and responsible, and it had paid off. If she wanted to be given this privilege again, she had to follow the rules this time. Besides, who hires a sitter for a fifteen-year-old high school sophomore? If she messed this up, there would be no more chances for over a year. Closing and locking the door behind her, she hung up her coat, and made her way upstairs to her room. She glanced at the digital clock on her night stand. It was too late to call Marcy. Marcy's parents were even stricter than her own. They had started the practice of collecting Marcy's cell phone at bed time during the last semester of middle school, when they caught her texting a boy after midnight. Her best friend would have to wait until morning before hearing all the nitty gritty details of how she had allowed Kyle to get to second base.

After stripping off her clothes and dropping them in the hamper by her door, Daisy walked down the hall to the bathroom to get a shower. It was late, and she was too tired to take a bath. Open nudity was a rare freedom she could only indulge in when the house was empty. She silently thanked her parents for not producing a younger sibling. Marcy's little brother, Nate, never gave her a moment's peace or privacy. Retrieving a pair of towels from the hall closet, she entered the bathroom, turned on the shower, and waited to step in until it reached the right temperature. Once it was hot enough, she positioned herself beneath the multiple, pulsating streams of hot water. She moaned in relief as she let the water jets play over her back and shoulders. The hot water felt amazing as its pressure massaged her back and the steaming water caressed her skin as it cascaded down her body. She was in heaven.

***

Burt eased open the door to the master bedroom. The shower was loud enough that he could hear it all the way down at the end of the hallway. Standing in the shower, with the air handling fan running, his prey would be both deaf and blind to his presence. Despite this, he still moved as quietly and cautiously as possible. No point in taking a chance of frightening his target prematurely. After all, he had been watching her movements for weeks. Not that a high school student was difficult to track.

He had seen her for the first time while he was cutting through the community park on an errand. She was practicing stunts with her cheerleading squad. Burt was passing alongside a dense hedgerow when they had tossed her high enough into the air to make her visible over the vegetation, and Burt had seen her rise like an angel. From that moment on, he knew that she would be his next target, and all he could think about was her. Forgetting his errand, he found a good hiding place from which to watch his newest prey. He memorized her body in every detail, each move, the slightest gestures, and the melodic sound of her voice. When the mother of his obsession arrived to pick her up, Burt simply took down the license plate number, and later performed a simple search of public records, until he found out the girl's home address. After that, she had not been difficult to track and stalk, but then good girls were predictable.

He had been tempted to take her and her boyfriend as they parked and made out in his car, but Burt wanted her all to himself. As the water shut off, he crouched low just outside of the bathroom door, his knife in one gloved hand and the other open and poised to strike. When the sound of a blow dryer began, he relaxed a bit, but remained at the ready. Patience, after all, had its rewards.

***

Daisy stepped out of the shower, feeling clean and ready for sleep. Taking one towel, she damp dried her hair and then removed the excess water from her body. She used the second towel to finish tending to her waist length, blonde hair, before taking the blow dryer to it. Once her blonde locks were dry, she had brushed them, and wove it all into a single, thick braid. Her hair tended to tangle badly if she slept with it loose. She carefully applied skin moisturizer to her face and neck and brushed her teeth. Finished with her ablutions for the night, she dropped her towels into the bathroom laundry hamper on her way to the door. Her thoughts were still on Kyle and how good his hands felt on her as she turned the handle, opened the door, and stepped into the hall. The cooler air sent goose pimples all over her body.

Daisy had not taken two steps from the bathroom door when she felt a large, strong hand lock on to her left ankle. Immediately off balance, she yelped in surprise, tripped, and fell forward, her hands reaching out instinctively to catch herself. A sudden panic gripped her when the person who had seized her ankle jerked her up into the air and swung her ninety-five-pound body like a sack of potatoes, and slammed her, face first, into the hallway wall. As she bounced off the wood paneling and hit the floor, sparks floated in her vision, she could taste the blood that welled up from the gums of her shattered teeth and broken nose. She hit the wall hard enough to rob her of her breath so she could not even muster enough air to scream. Daisy barely registered what was going on when she was hefted into the air again and slammed into the walls and floor over and over. She felt her skin tear open and bones break with every impact. She could barely catch a breath between blows. Blood was everywhere, the hall was covered in it, and she felt as though something inside her had ruptured. The blood welling up in her throat made her gag and choke. It was difficult at best to draw a decent breath. After a particularly hard impact with the floor, the hand finally released her ankle. Daisy had been reduced to a heap of ruined flesh and shattered bone, lying in a weeping pile on the hallway floor. She was dazed, confused, and barely conscious. Her vision had only begun to clear when a massive hand closed around her throat and lifted her broken body into the air.

***

S is for Slasher

Burt enjoyed the hunt, catch, and kill almost as much as he loved the well-earned meal afterwards. He could feel the girl's struggles weaken as her body was slowly deprived of air. Her broken limbs, torn flesh, bruises, blood loss, and concussions had taken the fight out of her. Being careful to avoid stepping in any blood, he carried her down the hall, suspended in mid-air, to her room. He slammed her down on her bed and, just as she began to lose consciousness, he let up his grip and allowed her a few gasps of air. Burt smiled as he saw the slightest glimmer of hope in her eyes, then he pressed his blade against her sternum, just below the notch in her throat, pressed down, and drew the razor-sharp edge of his knife down the length of her abdomen, scoring bone and parting skin and muscle easily as her eyes bulged and she gasped, groaned, and writhed beneath his steady and practiced hand. The first slice ended when the blade ground against the bone of her pelvis. He made a second slice, crossways, making the two open gashes cross at her navel. The four fleshy corners bled freely and bulged upward as the first purple loops of intestine were slowly pushed up and outward. Burt tightened his grip again, pinching off her scream. She had managed to get a decent lung full of air. He was impressed. Her mouth moved silently and tears flowed as her eyes bulged outward until they looked like they might pop out of her skull. He held her this way as he pulled the veiny, red and purple loops of her intestines out, sliced them free at either end, and flung them aside. Burt delighted in how long someone could stay alive and conscious while they were sliced open and disemboweled. He had learned early on that the knife had to be as sharp as a scalpel.

Having more room to operate inside her chest cavity, he located her liver and excised it quickly and skillfully. Setting it aside, he could see the light in her eyes beginning to dim. He quickly reached up, into her rib cage, past the lungs, got a firm grip, and ripped her still beating heart from her chest before the last breath left her body. Knowing it would still take her brain more than a minute to die, he delighted in stabbing and slashing what was left of her body, knowing that her brain was still processing the agony until the very last moment as he ripped her body apart. By the time he was finished, she had been dead for over ten minutes. Burt was breathing heavily, covered in blood, and had become so excited by the act that he had climaxed and ejaculated in his trousers. Her naked body was reduced to ribbons of mangled flesh and had been partially dismembered. Bits and pieces of her had been strewn all over the room. He always felt an incredible physical rush during a fresh kill, but the greatest pleasure was yet to come. It was time to nourish his soul by feasting on her essence.

Collecting the heart and liver, Burt made his way to the kitchen. After removing the rain gear he wore to protect himself from blood spatter, and placing it in a garbage bag, he found some onions in the refrigerator and allowed them to sauté slowly as he sliced the liver and heart into narrow strips. He

S is for Slasher

quickly mixed a nice wine batter, dipped the slices of warm, bloody meat, and moments later his dinner was sizzling in the pan next to the onions. Allowing the meat to cook slowly, he set out a single setting of plates and flatware, and quickly retrieved a bottle of red wine from the cellar. He had broken into the house several times before, by disabling the garage door lock, and had already familiarized himself with the place. Once the meat was just right, he served up his dinner, sat down and experienced almost orgasmic spiritual sensations as he slowly consumed Daisy's vital organs. A kill always made him hungry and meat, after all, was best if it had been alive less than an hour before. He closed his eyes and savored each bite.

***

Two days later

Detective Gabriel O'Shea stood over what little remained of the Night Reaper's sixteenth victim. It had been, most probably, the fifteen-year-old girl, Daisy Abbot, who lived on the premises, but they would have to run a DNA comparative analysis to know for sure. The extent of the damage made any other form of positive ID impossible to determine. The scene, while gruesome in the extreme, only made O'Shea shake his head. The first five kills like this were so grotesque and vile that it had made him, a fifteen-year veteran on the force, nauseous to the point that he'd had to leave the crime scene to

S is for Slasher

puke. The following three, which were just as bad, had only made him sick to his stomach. After the tenth victim had been found, he discovered that he had become numb to the horror of it, though the nightmares were as vivid as the night of the first scene. The murders were so violent, bloody, and savage, that he imagined even Jack the Ripper would have had to turn away in shock and disgust. Exiting the bedroom and stepping into the blood-soaked hallway, he stopped the lead forensic tech.

"Please tell me you found something, Burke," said the detective, "anything at all."

"Sorry," said Burke, "but, so far, it looks forensically just as clean as the other crime scenes. We haven't found any hairs, fibers, footprints, or fingerprints that don't belong to the family. We are still looking, though."

"What was the point of entry?"

"It appears that he broke in through the garage door."

"This is his sixth garage entry. Were there any witnesses?"

"None. No one remembers seeing any strangers in the area and, as far as anyone knew, it was just another quiet night in the neighborhood."

"Damn! It was anything but a quiet night here. How about the kitchen? Was there anything there?"

"It's definitely him. Enough dishes and silverware for a single place setting were found in the dish washer, already cleaned. But he did leave the frying pan on the stove, as usual, with just enough trace material left behind on the carving knife and cutting board for a strong DNA identification. He wiped the kitchen clean of prints. We'll probably find that the meat in the pan was the liver and heart belonging to the girl in the bedroom."

"He always eats them both..." O'Shea swore under his breath.

"It would seem so. He does the same thing every single time. It's his signature."

"Arrogant bastard..." The detective paused. "Look, just get that report to me as quickly as possible, would you?"

"You can count on it, Gabe. You'll have it as soon as we've finished here."

"Thanks, Burke, this guy has got to slip up some time."

"Let's hope it's sooner rather than later."

"Amen." O'Shea knew that there was little he could do until forensics was complete and the autopsy finished, so he pushed his way through the crowd of reporters and looky-loos, repeating "no comment" all the way from the front step until he was safely inside his car with the doors shut. Damned reporters. The detective returned to the precinct to write up his preliminary report. Mr. and Mrs. Abbot, returning from a trip, had been so shocked when they discovered their daughter's body that the husband had needed to be heavily sedated when Emergency Medical Services arrived. The wife, a veteran combat surgeon working at the VA hospital, had suffered a shock but had been less affected, allowing her to make the call to 911. The

S is for Slasher

detective could not blame them for their distress. Discovering such a thing would be an unimaginably hard blow for anyone to take. He remembered Janice Cole, the elderly wife of Marvin Cole, the Night Reaper's eleventh victim, had suffered a heart attack and died at the scene. Their son had had to call in the deaths of both parents when he had sufficiently recovered from being violently ill.

O'Shea would interview the distraught parents in an hour or two, down at County General Hospital, when the sedatives started wearing off. The FBI had joined the hunt after the fourth killing, but, with the absence of any solid evidence, they were as stumped as the local police. They had profiled him as an "omnivore", meaning he had no particular preference for those he killed, a male most likely in his 40s or 50s and of undetermined race or cultural background whose hunting ground was the entire city and its suburbs. O'Shea, like the rest of the force, had been unimpressed.

He honestly did not envy them their job. He and the others were just local law enforcement, this kind of thing was supposed to be over their heads. This guy just made the feds look stupid. Doubly so, because they were also unsuccessfully hunting another serial killer, whose hunting area covered eight states. At least they presumed he was a killer. They had yet to find a single body, but O'Shea had overheard one agent updating another, saying that, according to blood spatter, the killer had used a knife, and, due to the loss of blood volume at each of the scenes, the victims could not have survived

S is for Slasher

the attacks. At the moment the score was 2 to 0 in the killers' favor.

At the moment, however, the feds were setting up roadblocks and surveillance. It was pointless. The Night Reaper had a two-day head start, he could be half way across the country, if he had even wanted to leave town. The FBI had already gone over the crime scene, and left, before the detective was allowed to investigate. All O'Shea knew was that this monster needed to be stopped. The problem was that no one knew just how to make that happen.

***

Six weeks later

Devin's eyes opened suddenly in the darkness. Instantly awake and aware, he sensed that something was wrong. Some disturbance within his home had disrupted his normally peaceful slumber. Sliding silently out of bed and into a crouch on the floor, he closed his eyes and concentrated. The only light in the room was the pale illumination of the half-moon outside, filtering in through the slats in his blind. The only light source outside of his room was the bulb at the top of the stairs, at the opposite end of the hall, which barely reached his door. These factors made his sense of sight all but useless in the near complete darkness. So, he focused on his hearing, listening for anything that might be disturbing the silence. A moment passed, then two, and then, there it was. He could hear soft footfalls as they padded slowly down the hall, toward his room. After only a moment, he determined that the intruder had come alone. Special Forces training, and three full tours of duty in the Middle East, had honed his senses to a razor's edge and he trusted them. Devin was the only member of his unit that had returned from duty without suffering from PTSD. It had mystified the physicians and psychiatrists. After all, he had spent all three tours on heavy combat duty and he was extremely good at his job. The lack of emotional trauma was neither a surprise, nor a mystery to Devin. He knew exactly why he seemed so resilient, but he was not about to share that information with the doctors. He had never trusted doctors in the first place.

Breathing easier, he determined that the intruder could not be the police. They were required by law to announce their presence, and, with his military record, no responsible department would ever send a single officer after him in the middle of the night, unless they really hated the guy. So, who would be dumb enough to come prowling around his home at this hour? He wondered if the intruder had been to the basement, probably not. Whoever it was must have decided to attack first and search later, there was no way they would have come up here if they had started down there and found his collection. God save him from idiots, home invasions sucked! Whoever it was would not catch him unprepared, and they were going to regret that they ever stepped foot in his house.

Reaching silently around, he slipped the eleven-inch hunting knife free of a sheath that was securely wedged between the mattress and box spring. He got to his feet and slipped soundlessly toward his bedroom door. The intruder, obviously a male from the weight and spacing between footfalls, was moving slowly and doing his best to be as quiet as possible. He was not being quiet enough, though. Devin positioned himself by the door and waited. He was ready.

***

Burt Casey was having the time of his life. The body of his work had become so infamous that the newspapers had given him a name. They called him 'The Night Reaper' and his specialty was keeping two steps ahead of the authorities and terrifying the public. A few more entries and his current scrap book would be full. Tonight, he was about to make his seventeenth kill. The authorities were baffled because he made a point of targeting everyone: men, women, children, the young, the old, the healthy and the handicapped from several different races and cultures. The FBI classified him as an "omnivore", he laughed to himself, that was a profile a grade schooler could figure out. All they had were generalities and his signature. Burt made their job harder by choosing his targets completely at random from all quarters of the city and suburbs. This one, for example, was perfect. He lived on the outer edge of town, not quite in the suburbs. This guy had made himself a perfect target.

S is for Slasher

Burt had literally bumped into him in a grocery store a month earlier and this fellow's reaction made an immediate impression. There was a look in his eyes, almost a challenge. It reminded him of a lion staring down a jackal. A moment later it was gone and the encounter over. He knew then that this was his new target. In the weeks that followed, Burt shadowed the man's every move from long distance, memorized his schedule and dug into his life, routines, and habits. He only lost track of the guy twice, something that had never happened before. However, each time he managed to catch up with him again at his house eight to ten hours later. He had no idea how the guy could slip out of his surveillance, but it did not matter as long as he caught up with him again. His research revealed that his new target was ex-military, lived alone, and worked from home as a day trader. He had no wife or children, no girlfriend, no boyfriend and no social interaction on or off the internet. Surreptitious questioning of the neighbors, disguised as a real estate broker, revealed that he was a quiet, withdrawn man with polite manners and a kind demeanor. This guy was practically begging to be killed in his sleep and might as well have offered up his heart and liver to be eaten. It was, in Burt's mind, an open invitation. The best part was that the body would not be found for weeks, or maybe months, after the kill. Unlike most of his hunts, he had been unable to gain quiet entry to the home to have a look around. The high tech locks his prey had installed were specifically chosen

S is for Slasher

to be pick proof. Burt supposed that PTSD was the source of so much paranoia. The guy was, after all, ex-military.

The time had finally come, and Burt's lengthy surveillance was about to pay off. He knew that the target's bedroom was on the second floor of the north side of the house, so he had chosen a small, ground floor window on the south end of the building to make his entry point. A glass cutter, a sheet of fly paper and a pillow ensured a silent entry into the house. He struggled at first, but eventually managed to force his considerable bulk through the narrow window frame and set down, feet first, on the concrete floor of the laundry room. He checked the window frame to be sure he had left no trace. Aside from the sound of a small dog barking somewhere outside, all was quiet. He took a quick look about, to be certain he was alone, and, seeing nothing, eased the unlocked door open. No squeaky hinges, that was good, Burt liked a well-maintained home.

Not being one to linger with a living body in the house, Burt quickly located the stairs. There was a single ceiling light shining above the landing, making things easy for him. He carefully placed each footstep over the open, load bearing stringer and moved slowly and silently up the stairs, taking one cautious step at a time. He would find his way to the kitchen later, so he could prepare his upcoming meal. Once at the top of the stairs, Burt eased his way along the hall as quietly as he could. His size, and the rain gear he was wearing, made this difficult at best considering the lack of carpeting, but little noises did not make much difference. After all, the target was sound asleep, and would be unable to hear him. Still, it was always better to be safe than sorry, he did not keep two steps ahead of the law by being careless. As he neared the door, he pulled the wicked looking, ten-inch butcher knife that had intimidated so many others out of its sheath. He grinned and licked his lips in anticipation of the kill. Slowly, he turned the knob and eased the door silently open. His brow knit and he frowned as he glimpsed the vague outline of an empty bed where parallel lines of silver light shone down on it from the window. Where was his prey? A split second later, the door was yanked open wide and immediately slammed closed again, colliding hard with his face, breaking his nose, and sending him reeling across the hall and into the far wall.

***

The intruder yelled in pain and surprise when the door crashed into his face, sending him staggering backward into the hallway. He was thrown against the opposite wall but did not fall. Devin, wearing only boxers, leapt through the doorway and onto his unknown assailant, slashing and stabbing. Was this guy wearing storm gear? It did not matter, plastic was not body armor. The man, however, was enormous and his thick arms absorbed Devin's first few attacks. The invader roared and threw him bodily into the hallway wall, knocking the wind out of him and forcing his knife from his hand. He bounced off the wall and landed in the middle of the hallway. Allowing his instincts to take over, Devin rolled to one side as the attacker brought his full weight down on the spot he had only just vacated. The sound of metal striking the hard wood surface told him that the stranger was using a large knife.

Lashing out with a foot, Devin kicked his attacker hard in the gut and was rewarded with the sound of the man sucking wind. He smiled knowingly. There was no body armor under the rain gear. As his would-be assailant gasped for a breath, Devin managed to get to his feet and locate his hunting knife, laying some eight feet away. As he maneuvered around the gasping form of the bulky intruder, he had just begun to reach out for his weapon, his fingers barely brushing the pommel when a heavy blow slammed into his side, he felt a rib give way as he was thrown forcefully into a wall. The intruder was incredibly strong and the pain was blinding.

The attacker lumbered toward him brandishing a large, broad bladed knife. Devin, still sucking in shallow, painful breaths, swung a clumsy kick at the man's left knee, which his attacker easily evaded, however, the feint forced him to change his stance and leave himself vulnerable. Devin took advantage of the opening and kicked hard, driving his heel into the man's unprotected groin.

***

S is for Slasher

Burt felt his eyes cross and his teeth clench as crippling pain lanced through his body. He doubled over and his knees threatened to buckle as he fought for air. When his vision cleared, it was just enough to see that his target had disappeared. Burt had just begun to turn around when he felt a blade cut deep across the back of one thigh, then his leg collapsed beneath him. He managed to twist about as he fell. His target had gotten behind him and Burt was down and bleeding heavily. Fear began to creep into his heart and doubt into his mind. Who was this guy? He was supposed to be some mild-mannered stock broker.

The slashes and stabs came at him in a blur of motion. Burt did his best to protect himself with his arms, but they were already damaged and could not stop everything. Stab in the gut, twist and pull. *This is all wrong*, he thought as he gritted his teeth. *This is not the way things are supposed to happen.* Forearm slashed open from wrist to elbow. How did a helpless victim suddenly become so deadly? Slash to the inner thigh. It did not take long before he started feeling lightheaded from the pain and blood loss. Stab to the left kidney. Burt shuddered and spasmed in pain as the blade was yanked free. Panic began to set in, and he started to lash out wildly, hoping for a lucky hit. Slash to the shoulder, stab to the gut. One of his frantic punches finally connected and he felt some satisfaction when he felt a bone break under the pressure. His would-be prey yelled out in pain, swearing up a blue streak. Burt wanted

S is for Slasher

to laugh at the man's pain but his vision was beginning to blur. The attacks slowed as his adversary favored his injured arm but did not cease. A deep slash across the gut disemboweled him. Burt's vision cleared enough to get a good look at the man's face. There was no fear, no terror, only savage determination. Eyes burned like coals, teeth clenched, not in pain but in fury, and Burt finally understood. He just laughed at the irony as the blade rose and fell over and over again. Then, just before everything went numb and the clammy grip of death seized him, he chuckled at his own joke, though the bloody froth that spilled from his lips made it difficult.

"It's always the quiet ones..." The darkness filled his vision and the cold claimed him.

***

Devin was about to get dressed and take himself to the hospital when the sirens and lights from half a dozen police cruises and just as many black sedans, came rushing up to his house, pulled into his driveway and stopped anywhere they could along the street. What in the hell was going on? Rather than going to his room, he stumbled down the stairs so he could open the front door before they could break it down. When he let the police and FBI agents in, he casually blocked the stairs leading to the basement while he directed the authorities upstairs before the paramedics could take custody of him. One police officer informed him that his neighbor, a Mister Henderson, while out late walking his dog, had witnessed someone breaking into the house through one of the windows and had called the police. A detective and an agent took his full statement. The paramedics eventually found him, assisted him to an ambulance, and assessed his injuries. Devin had watched the forensic techs come and go with their cameras and devices, and saw the coroner remove the body. Knowing it was evidence, he relinquished his hunting knife to a forensic technician who deposited it in a bag, sealed and signed it. His wallet and a set of his clothes were brought out to him so he would not have to stand out in the street wearing nothing but his underwear. Forensics made quick work of replicating the scene in his hallway and corroborated his account. He asked a favor and had an officer lock up his house and return the keys to him before the ambulance took him away to the hospital. The officer, seeing no reason to refuse, complied but made him promise to make the premises available for possible future investigation. Devin agreed and thanked him as he was lifted into the ambulance.

After being poked and prodded with fingers and needles, and following a battery of scans and x-rays for what remained of the night, it was revealed that he had suffered four bruised ribs on his right side, two fractured ribs on his left and clean break of his left humerus, not to mention numerous bruises from head to toe. The doctors and nurses were all kind enough to him, and he put on his politest face for them. Even though he had no desire to be in the hospital under these circumstances, Devin knew that the fastest way out of there was to quietly comply. After the FBI completed their interrogation, a detective named O'Shea paid him a visit to ask a few more questions. The detective informed him that the investigation had determined that the encounter was a clear-cut case of self-defense and he would not be charged in the death of his attacker. Devin was relieved that the investigation would stop with his attack, and he thanked the detective.

Late the next morning, after being bandaged, treated, and given a night's bed rest, he was given a reasonable bill of health, advised on how to care for his injuries, given a prescription for pain medications, and released. After a quick stop at the pharmacy, Devin was relieved to be home again as he paid the cab driver and went inside. Despite the rib brace and arm cast, this was the place he needed to be. He knew not to disturb the scene until the authorities gave him the go ahead.

The first thing he did was to check on the basement. Devin went down, through the study and into the library. Everything was exactly as it should be. He breathed a sigh of relief and returned to the ground floor. He made his way upstairs so he could assess the damage to his hallway. Devin made mental notes to repair the walls and buy several gallons of peroxide, bleach, stain and varnish to deal with the blood stains that ran the length of the hall, coated the ceiling, walls, and his hardwood floor. He had been informed by the police, during his stay in the hospital, that his laundry room window had been damaged in the break-in, so he added it to the list of repairs. He knew it would have to wait until the investigation officially closed, but one can never be too prepared.

Devin was just sitting down to lunch when the first knocks rattled his door. He looked out the window and was astounded to see a crowd of people gathered outside, holding up either cameras or microphones. When he opened the door, a dozen flashes went off in his face and half of the crowd started asking questions all at once, each trying to be louder than the others as he recoiled from the unexpected company.

"What in the hell is going on here?" he roared over the cacophony of overlapping questions. He immediately regretted it as his sore ribs sent stabs of pain through him. Everyone went silent in the wake of the outburst. Finally, one reporter spoke up.

"Mister Archer, Dave Simpson, Channel Twelve News. Were you aware that your desperate struggle for your very life in your own home brought an end to the reign of terror created by the serial killer known as The Night Reaper?"

"I did what? Oh, for the love of God!" He wanted to pull out his hair but his ribs throbbed and the cast made it impossible for his left arm, and pulling out hair with just one hand was simply pathetic.

"Mister Archer, do you believe your experiences and training in the armed forces were the factors that saved your life?" another reporter blurted out.

"Undoubtedly," he replied. "Now, if you'll

S is for Slasher

excuse me, I have to rake the carpet or something." He stepped back inside and closed the door. "Crap!"

The next day, the newspapers and media outlets went wild with the 'war veteran turned local hero' angle. Over the next couple weeks, as he healed, Devin was inundated with reporters, fans, and camera crews. Much to his gratitude, other local veterans arrived to help with crowd control. He ordered them pizza and beer for their aid and took time to be social and exchange war stories.

A week later, the letters started arriving, Devin's eyes widening in surprise as he read them. They were thank you letters, hundreds of them. Most were from citizens who were terrified by the Night Reaper, but several were from family members of the sixteen victims. These he kept. One contained a check for $10,000. Apparently one survivor had put out a reward for anyone bringing the Night Reaper to justice. Devin supposed that death could be considered a form of justice. He pocketed the check so he could deposit it later.

When the hospital was done with him, he had to attend physical therapy at the VA hospital to regain full function of his broken arm and improve elasticity in his healing ribs. On his third visit, he was approached by a doctor he did not recognize. She was thin, blonde, at least 150 pounds lighter, and easily a full head shorter than he was. She stopped in front of him, looked him solemnly in the eye and held out her hand. He took it and they shook hands.

"Thank you, Mister Archer," she said with a

slight tremor before turning and walking away. He caught a glimpse of her name tag. It read Linda Abbot, MD. Moments later, as he stared after her in confusion, his memory filled in the blanks and he understood.

***

O'Shea opened the report he was just handed and glanced over it briefly as Captain Logan walked up holding a rather thick file of his own.

"Is that the coroner's report on the body of the Night Reaper?"

"It sure is, Cap. Broken nose, concussion, severe bruising in the abdomen and groin, one burst testicle, twelve slash wounds and fifteen stab wounds. The bastard wore full rain gear, no wonder we didn't find any evidence. The doctor's report on the victim is almost as bad. No cuts but he was in pretty poor shape."

"I understand he was one big, son of a bitch," said Logan. O'Shea glanced at the report and did a double take.

"Holy Hannah! The guy was six foot eleven and 620 pounds."

"Archer's no slouch either; six foot two and 250 pounds of solid muscle."

"I wouldn't want to meet either of them in a dark alley," laughed O'Shea.

"It sounds like hell broke loose in the Archer house."

"Still, what kind of guy can take that kind of

damage and still kill his attacker? Does that seem odd to you?" asked O'Shea.

"Not really," said Logan. "Not once you've read this." He lifted the two-inch-thick file for O'Shea to see.

"What's that?"

"Archer's military history; Panama, The Gulf War, Somalia... A lot of it is redacted. The guy is an army captain, a green beret, Army Ranger with more medals than Patton. He has a twenty-year military career, eighteen of which was spent in heavy combat and the last two as a combat instructor. Discharged with full honors."

"Christ!" O'Shea's eyes widened as he scanned briefly through the file.

"The Night Reaper couldn't have chosen a worse target," said the captain. O'Shea nodded.

"And we're positive the Night Reaper is the body in the morgue?" asked O'Shea.

"Definitely," replied Logan. "When SWAT raided this guy's house, they found enough evidence to convict the freak ten times over."

"Even if homicide and the FBI will take a couple of blows over a civilian bringing down the serial killer, at least the public will be, and feel, safe again." It was Logan's turn to nod.

"We could lessen the collateral damage," said Murphy, the head FBI agent assigned to the case. O'Shea and Logan both jumped. O'Shea hated the way these guys just kind of skulked around.

"How?" asked Captain Logan.

"We don't come across with sour grapes," said

S is for Slasher

Murphy. "We get behind this guy Archer. Encourage his defense of his own home, and the laws that support it. Emphasize the war hero aspect. If we show solidarity and support, we share the spotlight a little and look less like butt hurt little girls."

"I think we can manage that," said Logan. "We provide a little hero worship and save the department a black eye. What do you think, O'Shea? You're the primary on the case."

"Sounds like a solution with no losers," said O'Shea. "Let's do it."

***

As soon as he was finished healing, Devin was given awards, expected to attend ceremonies and functions, television, newspaper, and radio interviews, and he was given the key to the city. Close behind that came the offers from publishing companies and television studios offering deals for autobiographies and movie rights. Unsure of exactly what was expected of him, he allowed himself to be swept up in it. After all, it could not last forever, and things would have to calm down sooner or later. He was assigned a writer for his autobiography, a second for the attack, and a screenwriter for the television and/or movies. Devin hired a lawyer to deal with the legal paperwork to make sure he got his fair share of the proceeds and arranged to have the screenwriter and autobiographer meet with him at a restaurant twice a week until the story was told

S is for Slasher

to their satisfaction. He also made a point of meeting the writer covering the attack at the same place; the fewer people that entered his home, the better. It was bad enough that the police had been in and out for a week following the incident, gathering trace evidence, taking photos, measurements, and such.

Devin hated being in the spotlight, preferring his solitary, quiet life, and remaining unnoticed by the people around him. He had certain needs that simply could not be met while he was in the center of the public eye and those needs were eating away at him more and more each day they went unmet. After four months had passed, and he still had reporters and groupies hanging on his every move, he decided that it was time to move away and start over, if he wanted any privacy. He would tell the media that he had tried, but he could no longer live with trauma associated with the house. They would buy that. In many ways, his private life had become the Night Reaper's last victim. He could not function while under the watchful gaze of the public eye. He was slowly going stir crazy. As he began house hunting in Atlanta, Georgia, his biggest dilemma was figuring out how the hell he was going to move the collection of twenty-three bodies he had hanging in the walk-in freezer in his basement.

Therapeutic Nihilism

C.R.S Ford

Molly manoeuvred with a half pirouette around the hooded figure in black robes. It reached for her scrubs and grabbed at empty air. Molly checked the hood with her free shoulder and raced off down the deserted corridor with Emily held deep into her other shoulder.

The smell of disinfectant was unusually thick in the air. Even Molly's hospital acclimatised nose wrinkled at the heavy smell. With the right medication and care, the smell wouldn't have bothered Emily at all.

The terrible disease morphing her blood cells from their usual plate shapes into much more harmful sickle shapes made it so she was a child who belonged more in a hospital than she ever would at home.

The fathomless pressure of her deformed blood cells squeezed her chest between tectonic plates, while pulsing throbs of agony filled her joints with lava. An intense nightmare of pain brought on by a sickle-cell crises a week too early. The disinfectant smell filled her vice-gripped chest and pushed any remaining good air out. She choked on her own lungs in near silent fits of inward facing coughs.

The hood that should have been a dozen metres back down the corridor appeared in front of them. It grabbed with one hand while swiping at chest level with a curved knife, barely missing Emily and slicing through the arm of Molly's scrubs.

His black robes had a deep crimson lining that shone as if silk. It whipped up and around navy-blue scrubs and a pair of practical shoes. Two crimson snakes twisted around a staff wrapped in barbed wire were sewn into the robes with a delicate thread. A perverse interpretation of the staff of Asclepius that took centre stage on the front of the inky-black robe.

Molly crouched as she lurched forward. Deep and bright blue eyes blazed with rage through carefully cut and hemmed in a gold thread eye holes. Wide, masculine hands swung the curved blade through empty air far above Molly and the child.

Molly swung a leg in a circle and caught the hood behind his knees. He fell backwards. Molly's legs dug in and thrust her forward and down the corridor. She held Emily tight, pulling the little girl deeper into her shoulder.

The hooded figure was behind her and then in front of her, seeming to teleport the twenty metres from where it had been stood. The hood dug its sensible shoes in and bent down low as it reached for her. Molly dropped to one knee, spun into position, and propelled herself upwards into the hood's chest.

S is for Slasher

Her knee connected with his sternum. It made a loud and wet cracking sound. The hood fell backwards, yelled, and clutched its chest. Molly landed on both feet and sprinted away from the groaning hood.

The hood appeared in front of her. No longer suffering from a cracked sternum, he stepped out from a connecting corridor. He seemed to learn from his last two failures and blocked the path by holding up his dukes tight against his chest and widening his stance. Molly saw the opening. She held Emily's head with both hands and slid across the floor. A near infinite amount of polishings had worn the floors to a frictionless surface. One of the many reasons medical staff wear sensible shoes. She slid through the hood's legs.

The robes whipped up around her. As she passed, she took the opportunity to headbutt the hood in his scrub-covered groin. It cost her a few inches of slide but was amply rewarding in satisfaction.

The hood doubled over and dropped to his knees with a barely masculine and high-pitched scream of "bitch!"

Molly couldn't help looking back. The downed hoods were still trying to get up, spaced out in regular intervals down the corridor. The one with the cracked sternum wasn't getting up at all. He lay writhing and moaning and clutching his chest. The others were still struggling. The one she had checked was already on his feet and stumbling over his down comrades towards her. She used the wall to righten herself with her free hand and push her along her way.

Two hoods blocked the corridor in front of her, one with scrubs and sensible shoes under his robes, the other a whole head taller than the first and wearing expensive business shoes and pinstripe trousers. The shorter of the two inched around the taller hood, seeming to protect him from the nasty lady and little girl.

The smaller hood looked ready to party. His hands were up kick-boxer style, with half open palms face down and elbows at forty-five-degree angles. His left foot danced against the floor with little taps ready to kick out. The other foot remained firm to the ground. His blade was pressed between his lips, pushing the fabric of the hood deep into his unseen mouth. The taller of the two stood still and seemed oddly content to let the smaller guy do all the work.

The smaller hood rushed forward in a strange dance that fluttered him across the corridor and covered half the distance between them in a few seconds. He danced forward again and as he reached four arms' length from Molly she broke left and sprinted through double swinging doors into the kitchen.

As the door swung shut behind her the larger hood bellowed in a commanding voice, "You can't run forever, Doctor Davies."

Three hoods burst into the kitchen one after another and disappeared from view, leaving the taller hood on their own for a full minute before one reappeared, shaking its hood.

S is for Slasher

"How the hell is she doing that?" the lead hood asked, his commanding voice irritated to the point of violent frustration.

Molly lowered Emily to the kitchen floor a level beneath where they had gotten on the dumb waiter. Older generations had no problem accepting a rope fed food elevator in every kitchen on every floor, all connected by one long shaft that could fit a grown woman and a small child. When the younger generations inevitably took over, the dumb waiter was deemed a death trap and contractors were called.

Contractors, being the rare breed of cost-effective individuals they are, installed a sheet of plywood painted identical to the walls and clipped in place with cost cutting plastic clips and cheap nails. The board was easily removable once you knew it was there and easy to put back in place. All one had to do was pull at the barely visible seams and the whole cover came away, then hold on to the clips while inside and pull it back in place. The dumb waiter was made to carry large selections of cooking implements and heavy portions food; it was more than sturdy and easy to use for little hands with little fingers.

Children found it, because there aren't enough nurses in the world to keep a successful eye on a group of kids determined to wander. Fire safety laws insisted the kitchen was just about the only unlocked door in the entire hospital besides the ancient and faulty paediatrics ward doors. All the food and sharp instruments were safely locked away

S is for Slasher

in walk-in freezers and cupboards. As if this was going to stop a bunch of hospital-bored children.

They'd found it the same way children find anything - by accident while searching for food. The best kept secret in the hospital. It had been passed down through the paediatrics ward for the fifteen years since its happy accident of a discovery. The original finders were long gone, leaving the discovery to new little hands who revelled at the opportunity to slip from floor to floor.

Emily, deep in late-stage sickle cell anaemia, weighed a heart breaking next to nothing. Molly, whose now smashed to a useless piece of plastic and glass phone insisted she put in an average of twenty to thirty thousand steps a day, hadn't had the time to put on weight.

It wasn't an easy journey, by any stretch of the imagination. The rope burned her palms. The muscles in her arms received the most strenuous workout they'd had in as far as she could remember. However, it was doable. Even if she dreaded the climb back up.

She lowered herself out of the dumb-waiter and knelt beside the girl. Emily sat and whimpered between pressed lips. Molly stayed low as she moved across the kitchen. She kept one eye on the door as the other searched for water.

She picked up a plastic cup so fragile it crushed in her hand and pulsed the water twice until the cup held a small mouthful. She winced as the ancient pipes grumbled before giving up the surprisingly clear stream.

S is for Slasher

Keeping low, she moved back to Emily. She dug into the pocket of her scrubs and popped a pill from a strip. Pinching the pill between her finger and thumb, she used the same hand to hold the glass and her free hand to coax the girl from her pain induced deafness.

With a careful balancing of the cup, pill, and the girl's head, Molly slid the pill into Emily's mouth and followed it up with the water. She placed the lip of the cup against the girl's bottom lip and gently pushed. Very little spilled. Emily choked for a breath but quickly swallowed the water and pill.

"Sorry, sweetie," Molly said, sweeping the girl up in one deft movement. "We have to go through the bad place again."

Emily responded with a muffled moan of agony and buried her face into Molly's shoulder.

"Last time," Molly said more to herself. "I swear."

The bad place had been the cardiology ward. It was a peaceful sort of place with lilac walls and, for the most part, quiet patients. It had the same three bay layout as every other working ward in the hospital with lilac painted partitions separating each bay from its neighbours.

Molly had finalised her residency there and, up until that night, she had fond memories of the cardiology ward. It was there she had learned the most important lesson her medical school hadn't taught her; a nurse will always do it quicker and better, leaving doctors to get on with their doctoring.

S is for Slasher

She tried with all her might not to look into the bays. To not even throw a glance their way. She tried to remember the fondness. She tried to picture the ward the way it had been back then.

No matter how busy she kept her mind, no matter how many of the hoods she had to avoid, the vivid memory persisted. It plagued her every thought. The image floated around the front of her attention. As much as she wanted to ignore the bays, as much as she didn't want to look into them... didn't *need* to look... they were seared into her memory.

Each one of the bodies was burned into its own personal engram. Faces that should have died comfortable and at peace were contorted in the frozen terror of their final moments. The ones that had enough left in them to put up a fight were slashed across the forearms and face with multiple and deep lacerations. They too succumbed to the hood's blade.

Every last one of the hundreds of bodies piled ten deep in the cardiology bays had died the slow and painful death of a severed aorta. A perfect stab, not just through the heart, but carefully aimed at the aorta. Deep enough to sever it completely and no deeper.

Molly knew professional work when she saw it. That bothered her much more than the hospital-full of premature corpses. The idea that someone with a very high degree of medical training performed every last one of the hundreds of brutal murders was something her brain was having terrible trouble coming to terms with.

S is for Slasher

Multiple rippers, she reminded herself. The only way they could have moved all these bodies down to cardiology in the space of the two hours she had been evading them was if there were...

Molly froze in her tracks for a step. There had to be twenty. At least, even then she wasn't sure of her maths.

A scant few feet to her right an elderly man dressed in pyjamas had flopped over a pair of elderly women, both in faded nightgowns. His slowly necrotising chest wound leaked in a steady stream onto the women's faces, posthumously baptising them in the blood of the infirm. The slick blood created a layer of lubricant. The baptiser slid from the women and flopped to the floor, his lifeless form slapping against the gore smothered floor.

Molly jumped in her skin at the sound of the falling body. Both hands gripped the girl. She ran through the ward and out into the corridor.

She checked the corridor before running down it and elbowed her way into the fifth door on her left. Inside, she was met with a counter slicing its way through a heavy sheet of plastic glass. She headed to the door to the left of the counter and slapped Alice from Pharmacy's ID card on the lock.

The door beeped and clicked. Molly pushed it and entered the pharmacy.

She sat Emily under the counter, safe from view. She moved quickly to oncology supplies and scanned through them. She found what she was looking for and removed it from the shelf. She then moved to the general supplies and retrieved a saline IV bag and a handful of needles and syringes. With one last stop, she retrieved an asthma pump and a sulbutamol canister. She slid them into the pockets of her scrubs and held in the IV bag with the same care she would have held a dozen eggs.

Moving back to Emily, she knelt down and scooped the little girl back into her arms.

"Almost done," Molly said.

Emily tried to smile through gritted teeth and a scrunched-up face. The smile pulled at Molly's chest, swelling her empathy and bringing tears back to her eyes.

"We're going to be fine," she said to the pain-filled smile and wasn't sure she believed it herself. "Last stop. Then all this will be over."

Emily nodded through a strained smile so honest it could have only have come from a child. Molly was reminded of frail porcelain dolls. One heavy hand and the little girl would be shards.

She was not going to let that happen. She stood and beeped and clicked her way out of the pharmacy. She froze in the door and listened. When nothing made the slightest sound she spoke in a near silent whisper, said, "Last time. I swear," and, grabbing Emily's head with her hand and pushing her face deep into her shoulder, rushed through cardiology back to the kitchen.

The night was wearing on her arms. She pulled the dumb-waiter's rope with each new grip raising them another few feet. The rope caused deep friction burns that stung her palm and felt as if the skin were coming away. Still, she pulled. Still, she got them both to the kitchen one floor above the pharmacy.

Once in the upper floor's corridor, she stopped again. Her ears twitched as she heard faint voices from the far end of the corridor. She pulled back in through the kitchen door and turned her head to the clock above the sinks. She smiled and silently counted to twenty-six.

Every call button in paediatrics went off. A cacophony of beeps that Molly found oddly comforting. The voices at the far end of the corridor swelled in volume and then faded off to the far distance.

Molly checked the corridor once and ran with the last of her strength to the isolation ward.

The twelve-year-old boy holding open the door to the isolation room had such a relieved expression on his face it brought a sympathetic smile to Molly. He wheezed with heavy and laboured breaths.

"Nice job on the call buttons," Molly said.

Harry grinned from ear to ear and with difficulty forming his words around his trouble breathing said, "Was... easy... they're all... controlled... in the one place. Just like... you said."

"Everything else ready?"

The boy nodded, sucked in as much air as his handicapped breath would allow, said, "Are... we sure this... is going to work, Doctor Molly? Was... way too easy to set up."

Molly reached out a hand and held the boy's shoulder. Emily stirred and buried her face into

Molly's shoulder. "I couldn't have done this without you." She held her eyes to his. "You know that. Right?"

"I just pushed a few buttons."

Molly indicated to his handy work and said, "That's much more than a few buttons."

Harry's face flushed.

As he turned to lead the way, Molly said, "Harry?"

He turned back with all the grace of a gangly teenaged boy and said, "Huh?"

"You did well." She smiled, looked at his handy work once again, and said, "Real well. Well done."

Harry's exhausted smile spread out wide with air sucking lips and beamed far enough across his face it almost bisected his nose from his chin. He led the way to the far end of the ward and held open the door. Molly lay Emily on the bed.

"Harry?"

The boy jumped into action.

"I need you to get me a cannula, do you remember what that is?"

The boy nodded.

"Wonderful. And a giving set, please, sweetie."

The boy moved to the treatment room and returned with the correct implements even more out of breath.

"Wonderful," Molly said and set to work connecting the giving set's tubing to the IV bag and the bag on the IV stand. She then got to work checking Emily's arms. The treatment had left the poor girl with more collapsed veins than a seasoned

S is for Slasher

junkie. Molly pushed lightly in the crook of the girl's elbow before deciding the back of her hand would be far quicker and safer.

Once the cannula was firmly in place under the dressing, she attached the tubing to the open end of the cannula, injected morphine into the bag, and adjusted the drip.

Finished, she placed her hand on Emily's forehead and in the bedside manner that had made Molly such a successful paediatrics doctor, said, "Couple of minutes and all the pain will be gone."

Emily's weak smile burned a welcome hole in Molly's heart. She said, "Thank you, Doctor Molly. You're the best."

"My pleasure, little miss peach face." She fought the urge to pinch her rosy cheeks. As cute as they made her face, they were just another symptom of her disease.

Emily giggled once as the morphine took hold and drifted safely off to sleep.

Once she was sure Emily was asleep, she turned to Harry and said, "You've done amazingly. Now I just need you to keep way out of sight. If they see you…" She left the rest unsaid.

The boy nodded affirmative.

Molly held his shoulder once more and said, "I'm so sorry you had to go through this. I wish there was another way."

"Doctor Molly," Harry said. "Neither of us would be here if it wasn't for you."

Molly broke inside and rushed the boy with a tight hug saying, "You got a bright future ahead of

S is for Slasher

you." She gazed in his eyes, searching for a reason why he'd had to deal with so much in so little a life. Watching him struggle to breathe had her reaching into her scrubs pocket. She tossed the pump and sulbutamol his way. "I almost forgot," she said with a guilty frown.

Harry tore the packet open and fitted the contents to the pump. He shook it a half dozen times, placed it in his mouth and took two pumps with long inhales. Almost immediately his breathing returned to his control.

Molly said, "Wish me luck."

Harry threw his arms around her, pressed his face into her shoulder, and let himself cry for a few seconds before brushing himself off with a shake of his head and saying, "Go."

Molly exited the isolation ward and took her time making her way back to the last place she had seen a hooded figure.

It took eight minutes of careful wandering before she heard a familiar male voice yell, "I found her."

A second later, the voice appeared wearing hooded robes with a scarlet snake stitched into the front. He paced his way towards her. A pair of green eyes sparkled out from the carefully hemmed eye holes.

Another hood appeared from behind her and held her firmly in place.

The hood with the walkie talkie said into it, "We got her," with all the enthusiasm of a teacher's pet offering an apple.

"Do you have the children?"

Dark brown eyes scanned Molly as if she were hiding the children under her scrubs.

"No," he said.

"Hold her," the voice on the walkie talkie said, "I'll be right there."

Molly smiled into the dark brown eyes. Her best condescending smile. The one she used for special occasions and special occasions only. The one she wouldn't dare use in a hospital under normal occasions, but this was special.

Molly made sure the green-eyed hood still focused on the walkie talkie. She slipped the morphine syringe from the arm of the sweatshirt she wore under her scrubs, popped the cap, and injected a very visible vein on the back of the hand of the hood holding her. He flinched as if she had pinched him and looked down. Molly palmed the needle before he saw it. He gripped her tighter. Right up until the full force of the opioid hit him in his central nervous system and weakened his knees to collapse.

Instead of going with him, Molly slipped through his relaxed grip and performed a kick born in swimming pools and perfected in competition. It connected exactly where it should have and the green-eyed hood dropped to his knees, cupping himself. She slid the needle to her hand and inserted it through the well-tailored eye hole. It bypassed the emerald iris and slipped effortlessly into his pupil. He dropped the walkie talkie and screeched as he reached for the needle. Molly grabbed the walkie talkie as it clattered to the ground.

S is for Slasher

"You really should get better henchmen," she said into the walkie talkie.

Silence responded.

Molly said, "It's going to take a lot more of your..." she paused for effect, "testi-cult to take me down."

Molly could feel the hate through the silent walkie talkie.

Two more hoods barged through the doors at the end of the corridor and began sprinting towards her. She ran all the way back to the isolation ward.

She didn't bother checking on the children. She counted on the fact that they had taken up position in the private room on the far side of the ward. Judging by the slightly fluttering gap in the closed curtains and zero noise, they were safely locked inside with Emily out like a light and Harry waiting for his cue. She took position on the bed of the private room closest to the door, making sure to leave the curtains open and the light on. She put her feet up for the first time since she'd started her night shift and made herself comfortable.

The first hood came into view an eternity of slow, careful breaths later. Close behind him were three other hoods. Quickly followed by another four. Panic flooded Molly. She darted her eyes through the hoods. Counting again and again.

They hadn't all come to gloat.

There is no way there are only eight, she thought and pressed the remaining doubts to the back of her mind as the lead hood walked through the open door to the isolation room. One by one the hoods

S is for Slasher

followed their leader. Each one taking space in the tiny room until they were all stood facing her. Sharp, curved blades emerged from the folds within their robes. Eyes of all colours glared at her.

Molly brushed invisible crumbs from the lap of her scrubs and said, "Director Herrick."

The tallest grabbed hold of the tip of his hood and whipped it from his head.

"Doctor Davies." The inevitable frustration he must have been feeling was barely disguised behind the stoic demeanour of the director of the hospital. "You continue to be a royal pain in my proverbial." He stared deep into her eyes. "I applaud your resourcefulness, but your refusal to hand over the children is…" he paused and studied her eyes before saying, "…unfortunate."

Every muscle in Molly's eyes fought the urge to watch the door being closed behind the hoods. She drilled her attention into Director Herrick's eyes.

"What children?" she said in her most saccharine sweet voice, hoping the heavy thumps of her heart in her chest was only loud to her.

"Let's not be childish now, Doctor Davies."

"It's okay, Director Herrick. Given the situation, you can call me Molly," she said and forced herself into a straight face.

The hood to the right of Director Herrick stepped forward and produced his curved blade. Herrick placed a gloved hand on the hood's chest. The hood stepped back without hesitation and resumed his position at Herrick's right hand.

Molly clocked his shoes and said, "You doing

S is for Slasher

alright there, Doctor Andrews?"

The hood's eye holes shot to Herrick, who sighed and made a whipping motion with his head. Doctor Andrews, Molly's direct superior, pulled his hood off. His face was a contorted mess of rage. He held the knife blade down. His gloves creaked around the handle. Herrick placed his hand on Andrews' arm as if holding him back.

"Doctor Davies?"

Molly yanked her stare from Andrews to the director saying, "Yes, Director Herrick?" in the tone of a child placating a teacher after being caught messing around in class.

"Where are the children?"

"Oh," Molly said and feigned ignorance with a finger to the centre of her chin, "which children would that be?"

Molly blinked twice to rid her eyes of the need to watch the heavy framed bed being rolled against the outside of the door. On the other side, Harry pumped both thumbs in the air and slipped around the corner into the next room and his handiwork.

"Don't you want to monologue?" Molly asked, firmly ignoring Harry.

Herrick said, "Not really."

Molly raised both eyebrows in response.

"Suffice to say," he began, "it's for the good of the hospital."

Molly remained silent.

Herrick's eyes flared hot as he said, "You've been a single blip in an otherwise flawless operation."

"Of mass murder," Molly said and crossed her

arms for effect.

"Euthanasia," Herrick corrected. "They were all sick."

"Well, yeah. That's why they were in a hospital."

"I have no interests in discussing the merits of refusing to help those beyond our ability to help."

"That's therapeutic nihilism, Director. It's literally in the Hippocratic oath." Molly kept her arms crossed across her chest.

"The Hippocratic oath is a relic from ancient Greece. It bears no standing in modern medicine."

"Are you serious?" Molly said and threw up her hands.

"This is bigger than you or I," Herrick said. "This is a matter of the survival of our society. Of our country. Do you really think this is the only hospital that needed a good purge? Do you really think our society could withstand the strain of so much infirmity? It's survival of the fittest, Doctor Davies. Even you should know that."

Molly's need to shrink back in revulsion had her gripping both hands into tight fists.

Herrick noticed the fists with a condescending glance and said, "This has been a hundred years in the planning, my dear Doctor Davies. There is nothing you or anybody else could have done to prevent it. It was coming, and..." he motioned around himself, "...now it's here and it's everywhere and..." he inhaled through his nose, "...it was flawless." He dropped his head as if finishing a sermon.

"And the staff?" Molly said.

S is for Slasher

"The worthwhile ones are home being well paid for their time."

Molly rolled her eyes towards the ceiling tiles and tried not to think of the fate of the less worthy staff.

"Do you see the authorities?"

Molly remained silent and still.

"We *are* the authorities." He let the information sink in before continuing with, "Have you not looked out a window, Doctor Davies?"

"I've been a little busy," she replied.

A sweet scent drifted through the enclosed room. Molly took a deep breath and let it out slowly. The sweet smell slipped into her nostrils and sent waves of relaxation through her.

"Did you know I was a competitive swimmer in my youth?" Molly said with zero sarcasm.

"And?" Herrick sounded as if he'd had about just enough of the young doctor's routine.

"Well," she said and slid an arm behind her.

The sweet smell swelled and filled the room.

"I was considering holding my breath," Molly said. "I can hold my breath for a really long time."

Herrick sucked in the sweet air through clenched teeth but didn't seem to notice it.

"But then I figured, we're in a hospital. So, why the hell should I?"

She brought her hand back to her front and slipped the portable oxygen mask over her nose and mouth. A wide smile broadened her features as confusion swept through the hoods.

"Enough of this," Herrick growled. "Get her!"

S is for Slasher

Four of the hoods lurched forward. Wicked sharp blades with nasty curves were aimed her way. Molly scrabbled up the headboard frame of the bed until she was standing against the wall with the oxygen mask still firmly to her face.

The two with the blades dropped first. One fell softly to the mattress and dropped into a snoring sleep. One smashed their face on the bed frame as they collapsed to the floor, his nose leaking crimson under the seam of the hood. The other two almost made it to Molly before passing out and collapsing to the sterile floor. Confused hoods whipped back and forth.

Reality dawned on Herrick's face as he opened his mouth to say something and inhaled a lung full of the nitrous oxide smothering the room's oxygen. He was the last to fall. A look of defiant hate smothered his stoicism.

Molly carefully got down from the bed and made her way around the bodies. The oxygen in the mask down to a few dozen seconds, she walked to the door and waited for Harry to let her out.

The oxygen level continued to drop as she waited for the lad. Panic rose from the pit of her stomach and smothered her chest. She scanned the ward on the other side of the windows. Harry was nowhere to be seen. The oxygen dripped away into her nose and mouth. It slowed to a crawl and gave up the ghost as the last of the life-giving gas made its way into Molly's lungs.

She held the last breath and dropped the empty oxygen on to the hooded bodies. She knocked on

S is for Slasher

the glass. Harry appeared, walking far too slowly out of the next room and into the ward.

A long, curved, and wicked sharp blade was pressed to his throat. Behind him, a hood led the lad with a hand to the back of the boy's neck while the other held the blade in place. Dark brown eyes scanned Molly and the surrounding bodies. The knife pressed deep enough into the skin to draw a little blood.

Molly banged a fist against the glass. It vibrated but remained intact. The dark eyes widened and then narrowed to slits. Molly pleaded with him and received nothing but hate in return. With his free hand, he removed his hood.

She knew him. Over the course of her career, Molly had worked every ward at one time or another. She knew every face that received their pay cheque from the hospital payroll and every regular visitor. Details were her thing, and there is no greater area of detail than the human face. The raging man with the blade to Harry's throat was a regular visitor. Usually escorting undesirables, even in his robes she recognised one of the many police officers that frequently graced Accident and Emergency.

His hateful expression broke into a grin as he watched Molly pound the glass with both cheeks puffed out like a hamster. Her face took on the scarlet flush of the oxygen deprived. The more she pounded the glass, the more oxygen her body diverted to her muscles. The red flush spoiled to a dark blue. Her lips puffed and darkening. Her eyes

S is for Slasher

pleading for the grinning man to let the boy go.

Serenity swept across his face. The grin dropped away to a dull smile. A simple blank stare with eyes flooded with euphoria. The blade fell from his loosened grip and clattered and clanged to the floor. A smile drifted through his lips and he fell as if a puppet with his strings cut.

Behind him a smiling and sleep-dopey Emily said, "Horrible man," before dropping the giving set's tubing onto the snoring man in his black robes and immediately wobbling and dropping to her knees.

Harry reacted quickly and pulled the bed away from the door. The isolation room's negative pressure surged the ward's clean air in through the open door. Molly lurched through artificial wind and grabbed as much clean air as she could. Emily reached out to her but couldn't bridge the gap between them.

Molly saw the little girl's gesture and held out her own hand saying, "I'm… okay," between deep lungfuls of breath.

She looked over to the downed hood. Emily's IV stand stood next to the body. The giving set tubing ran from the bag of saline/morphine mix into the hood's left hip. She had even reached up under the robes to insert it. It had been a miracle he hadn't felt it.

From what Molly could tell, the girl had managed to remove her cannula and insert it into his femoral artery. A one in a million chance. A god-honest miracle during a night of evil. Molly doubted the little girl even knew what the femoral artery was.

Unfortunately, she thought, *the hood was going to be fine. One hell of an opioid hangover, but fine.* They, on the other hand, still had to get out. There were more. How many more, she didn't know. She only knew there were more.

She pushed herself to her exhausted feet and scooped Emily into her arms. She held a hand out to Harry. He grabbed it without the slightest hesitation. Together, they made their way out of the isolation ward and to the nearest exit.

Harry tested the locking bar with a hesitant push. When no alarms sounded and the bar gave sufficiently, he pushed it open and the three stepped out into the night's air.

Hundreds of hooded figures in black robes stood waiting for them. They stretched the entire length of the car park. Shoulder to shoulder, each one brandished a wickedly sharp and curved blade.

Sorority Slasher Summer

P.S. Traum

"You're a great kisser." Emma slips her hand into my sweater. I guess she's done kissing. "God... you're so warm, Felissa..." She cups my left breast while her other hand rests on my thigh. A cold thumb rubs my nipple.

I can't help it, I let out a gasp. I hope it doesn't sound too excited; I like to try to play things cool. "You sure have cold hands, Emma."

"Yeah... I can tell." She pinches my nipple, which is already hard as a pencil eraser. Damn things always betray me. Emma knows exactly how to work me. I moan when she starts to twist and pull. "I'm so glad you don't wear a bra." She moves her other hand up onto my right breast. The girl eagerly kneads me like she's a desperate teenage boy.

"Hell... I don't really need one, do I?" It's nearly dusk, and the campus park is deserted. We're kind of tucked away among the rose bushes anyway. But I still look around self-consciously. The last thing I want is to put on a free show for some rapey frat boys. Still, there's something thrilling about getting felt up by a hot girl in public. I lean back on my

S is for Slasher

elbows in the long thick grass and let sweet Emma do her thing.

She kisses me again, deeply. "I fucking love your flat chest." She pulls up my sweater. "It showcases these luscious lovely perky nipples..." She moves that wet pouty mouth down to demonstrate just how much she loves them. Her long red hair tickles as it drapes over my sides. She places a palm on my lower abdomen as she licks and sucks, fingering my navel. I somehow manage to suppress a building moan.

She gazes up at me with that sexy coy expression. "This doing anything for you yet?" No way was I admitting I was already gushing. But another gasp leaks out when she slides her hand into my panties. When I feel her middle finger slip in, I squeal. "Uh huh... thought so." Emma unsnaps and unzips my jeans. I don't know how far she intends to take this, *in public*... but hey, fuck it. I really want to feel those wet full lips on my own swollen lips...

I smile and close my eyes in anticipation as I stretch out. But when I lift my arms over my head, I scream and jump up, accidentally shoving Emma's face.

"What the fuck?!" Emma had fallen back onto the grass.

I had felt someone's legs against my hands. Is someone stalking us? I back up and help Emma up as I point. We inch over to the bush and can see bare feet, and then shins and knees.

"Shit! Felissa... is that a dead body?" She grasps my hand. "Golly." I stride forward for a better look.

S is for Slasher

"Hey! Aren't you scared?"

Sure enough, it is indeed a sliced-up dead body, curled up under the bush. I know it's dead because the face had been flayed off of the skull. The hands were skinned off too. Just like all the others. Yet another gruesome victim of our unknown local serial killer. The news calls him a "slasher..." I suppose it makes sense, since the bodies usually are indeed covered in deep slashes. How has he not been caught yet?

"Fuck, Emma... The asshole's never dumped one on our own damn campus!" Police say none of the bodies were killed on the spot, and no one ever finds the faces and hands. I feel so stupid. We were out here lezzing around in a secluded patch of campus park, *at dusk*! No one even knows we came out here. That fucking body could've been me. Stupid. *Stupid, stupid, stupid*!

"Yeah, but so far every victim came from our university, right?"

"I dunno, mostly. Lately, I guess. Well, fuck... I guess we better go report this." I take Emma's hand.

"Zip up first..." She strokes my panties with a sigh.

"Did you really say 'Golly'?"

***

"Hey Fellatio! Those lips are looking good, girl..." He licks his lips as he stares at mine.

"Go fuck yourself, Josh!" I shout cheerfully with a smile and a stiff middle finger.

make mine feel...

"I hear that twerp Kevin's been bragging about some big date you have planned."

"He's not really the bragging kind, he's just excited." Emma's pretty kick-back, she doesn't get jealous or anything. "I would've gone out with him by now, but he wanted to wait for his birthday. Maybe the kid's a virgin or something..."

"I don't see why you don't get more out of it when you're with these guys, it isn't really fair to you. And you're kind of missing out on what they can really do with that thing..."

"Are you kidding? I get maybe an hour of foreplay, then while I go down on them, I slip my fingers in and take care of myself. Better than they'd be able to, I might add."

Emma held my face and sighed. "I wish you could get over what happened, though. Sounds like that fucking high school coach really fucked you up." Emma looked sad and kissed me.

"No, I told you, I fought back. I fucked *him* up pretty good. He'll never put it in anyone again."

"No... I mean he fucked you up mentally." She said it softly, almost a whisper. She stroked my face. "Things are going to get better. You'll see."

***

Kevin ran up to me panting, trying to catch his breath. "Fe... lissa... Two..." He put his hands on his knees and took a deep breath.

"Two what?"

S is for Slasher

"Two more bodies. They found them scattered all over the public pool, that..."

"What do you mean 'scattered'?"

"They're in pieces! All chopped up! Heads, hands, legs... This serial killer guy's going psycho, two at a time now, and all butchered up into little pieces... listen, Felissa, be careful."

"Yeah, no shit! Dude's been on the loose for like over a year now..."

"No, I mean it, watch where you go at night, don't go into town alone anymore, the stupid cops don't have a clue, or they don't care, I don't know. Maybe they're in on it."

***

"Welcome to Omega House!" Emma pulls off my blindfold.

"Hell... after *that* initiation..." I smile. I glance around the room. Emma wasn't kidding, these wacky girls are really, *really* into horror movies. Way more than I was, and I thought I was in deep. Movie posters, masks, replica weapons... even autographed photos from horror conventions. Even my obsessive nerdy brother didn't collect like this. We were both into the action figures and dolls, but it was mostly about the movies and music for me.

"Cool shit, huh? This is our library, see all the old videos and DVDs?" She points to the stuffed shelves. "I bet Patty could give you a run for your money, she's old school."

"Don't libraries usually have books?" I don't

S is for Slasher

know where they got an old VHS machine, or how they keep all this junk running.

"Don't be a bitch." She laughs and kisses me. "Come on, let's go join the others." She pulls me along.

"Don't I get to change back into my clothes?"

"Where's the fun in that?" She slips her hands into my robe. Of course.

We reach the movie room. The girls are laying around watching one of the *Texas Chainsaw* movies. I can't tell which one offhand, but that's Leatherface running around with his trusty chainsaw all right. Everyone's eating ice cream. Daphne throws me a pint of Double Strawberry. I guess they really have learned everything about me.

"Hey scream queen!" Rebecca hands me a spoon. "Did you like the library?"

"Cool hockey masks... A real Horror House." I bite my tongue... I hope it didn't come out as "Whore House." All of us get accused of being slutty as it is. Fucking haters.

"No... a Slasher Sorority!" Daphne waves a Freddy Krueger glove at me.

Melissa hugs me. "You're one of the Omega Girls now!"

There are less than a dozen of us, pretty exclusive, I guess. All types of girls, different races and sizes, but all kind of smart, or at least headstrong... Really, the only thing we have in common is we enjoy horror movies. Well, like Daphne said, *slasher movies*. Is "enjoy" the right word for it? A fun but safe thrill, in any case, like rollercoasters or weed or half-naked selfies...

I wonder how many of these girls are bi like me. Emma for sure, but she also really, really hates men. I don't blame her. She's had some bad experiences. Hell, we *all* have. That's the other thing we all have in common here. But fuck, that's probably every girl on earth.

On cue, Danielle shuffles over, she has a solemn look on her pretty face. She reminds me of another major thing we all have in common – that familiar haunted look in our eyes.

"Remember what we said, Felissa. It's not just fun and games. We're like the final girls in the slasher movies. We're survivors. Someday, someone will probably come after one of us. We have to be ready. We have to protect ourselves..."

"And one way is to study the movies and figure out what we would do if we were in that situation. I know. We have a real-life serial killer on the loose, so any one of us could be his next target. But damn, Scout, aren't these –"

"Extreme? Yeah... that's why they help, we have the advantage! We'll never have to encounter anything supernatural. No unkillable boogeyman. Men can actually die."

***

"What about Nancy?" Patty held up a DVD of one of the Elm Streets.

"No, the Freddy Krueger girls are a bad example, you don't fight that dream stuff in real life..."

Melissa smiled. "But he does have a realistic personality... he's a rapey piece of shit!"

"Yeah... most slashers aren't, that's one of the main things that makes them different from real-life serial killers..." Danielle stood up. She really understands the psychology of this stuff. "Who else? Who are the best?"

"Sydney Prescott is pretty tough and smart..." Rebecca loves those stupid *Scream* movies. Pretty low stakes when none of the main cast ever dies after six movies! "But my favorite is still Laurie."

Danielle freaks out. "Laurie Strode isn't even a true final girl! She's a fake-out! Dr. Loomis is the one who has to save her! He shoots Michael while she cowers on the floor crying!" Most of us hate Laurie.

"Dude, it's not exactly her fault..." Rebecca shrugs.

Rebecca can be stubborn. She's a big Jamie Lee Curtis fan. Not me, I can't stand her, and I hate her character, and all her sequels were stupid as hell and pointless. Hell, she died like three times! But I do really like the new "Laurie," Angel Myers in the Rob Zombie remakes. He fixed the character and found a better actress.

"But that's not the point, is it? Why are we watching these Emma?"

"To assess and analyze their survival techniques..."

"Why?"

"So, we'll never be some fucking asshole's fucking victim!" I can't help myself. I stand up and shout it. I get it. I know what we're watching is just actresses and stuntmen and special effects, but I totally get it. There are life lessons here. If you're a girl, you're always in danger. A specific kind of danger. Especially when you're young and pretty.

***

"You know... we don't have to... um, actually do anything. No pressure. I really meant it, I'd like to get to know you, Felissa." Kevin gave me a silly smile. "I really want to meet the real you, deep down..."

Kevin seems sincere enough. He's a little dorkier than I usually go for. But he's kind of cute, and he isn't very aggressive, he doesn't even seem confident, and I'm fine with that. He's wearing his normal casual clothes, no extra cologne or anything... so he doesn't seem to have any expectations of seducing me. Maybe it's true he's happy to just hang out, despite my reputation. But I find myself constantly glancing at his little bulge. I'm not sure if he's picking up on that. Well, maybe not *too* little...

"Hey, you want a drink?" Kevin stands up.

Hell no, I don't want a drink! I like to think I'm smarter than that! Red flag... even if it's dorky skinny Kevin. Never accept food or drink from frat boys, especially if you don't know them really well. And no alcohol unless your friends are with you.

"Naw... thanks..." I wave it off.

"Oh. Do you mind if I get one?"

S is for Slasher

"No, go for it." He heads for the door. "Hey, where are you going?"

"Hallway... that's where the soda machine is."

Soda? Vending machine? Sealed cans. No alcohol. Hell... me and my damn paranoia. Emma's been talking about going full lezzy. And with these new college friends, my sorority *sisters*, well... I don't know that I want to become a cliche man-hating feminist... And I can never trust my instincts. I'm usually wrong.

"Do they have Cherry Coke?" I check my pockets for coins.

Kevin laughs. "I think I can afford two sodas." He counts his quarters. "Well... barely." We laugh.

While he's gone, I unbutton my blouse halfway. From the right angle he should get a good glimpse. I kick off my shoes as he returns.

"Thanks." We crack open the cold cans. I lean back while he grabs a pad.

"Hey, do you want to see some embarrassing videos of me at the beach? I lost a bet and had to wear a pink bikini..."

Hell yeah! Playful I like... that's a vibe I try to go for but usually fail at! He sits next to me and holds up the screen, it's a good foot across. I sidle up next to him so our thighs are pressed together. The videos are pretty stupid alright, and I still don't get any sense of what he's packing. I've been leaning forward, and I know he feels the heat of our bodies. My hand's been resting on his inner thigh. I catch him looking down my shirt, and he blushes. So, I look down at his groin while he's watching me...

S is for Slasher

he's a bit plumper.

"Listen... Kevin... let me see it."

"What? That's *too* embarrassing. I'm kind of shy, Felissa."

I don't know if he's playing hard to get, or it's small or he has a weird one, or if he's really shy. Most college guys can't wait to whip it out.

"You don't need to be shy, dude. I'm sure it's great... and if I like it, you're probably about to get very lucky."

"Well... you show me yours and I show you mine. Classic rules. They go back to middle school, right? Maybe earlier. It's only fair, you know."

I sigh. "Kevin, you know *my* rules. I was straight up with you. If we hook up you can do probably anything you want to me from the waist up, but my pants stay on. Trust me, you'll be happy." I let my hand graze his swelling package, but I resist the urge to just grab it.

"You know, Felissa, it doesn't seem fair, if you get to see my dick but I don't get to see your pussy..." Now he has an annoying snotty expression.

What the hell! I don't want to push it. I know who I am and what I want, but I also don't want to come off as slutty. Straightforward is good, but so is classy... it's a fine line I usually screw up. His stupid arguing is making my head swim.

"Really, Felissa, you..."

The idiot's mumbling or something, he sounds muffled, I...

S is for Slasher

***

"Felissa!"

Emma's voice. Wait, when did she get here?

"Hey!" A cold wet cloth wipes my forehead. "You awake, girl?"

Awake? *What the fuck*?! I'm in my bed, on top of the covers. Emma is sitting next to me with a worried expression. I may be disoriented, but now I'm aware enough to panic.

"No, no, no... Fuck no!"

"Felissa, calm down, you're okay. We're –"

"Damnit! Emma, I didn't take anything! We were just sitting there talking! Not –" I'm sitting up, staring down at myself.

"I know, it's okay, Kevin called me right away. He said you blinked out on the couch so I ran right over. He looked worried."

"Yeah, I bet! Fuck, dude! No pills, no food, no beer cups, no chloroform, no ether, no –" I'm testing my clothes, tugging at everything trying to remember how it looked, blouse half-unbuttoned, shoes off, pants zipped and buttoned...

"Felissa, you weren't there very long. Did he give you any –"

"No gas, no skin contact, no... no anything, Emma! Just a Coke, a Cherry Coke, it was a sealed can! I opened it, he never touched it, it never left my sight... Why the fuck was I passed out?! What the fuck! Emma!" I feel tears in my eyes. I don't like this shit one fucking bit. "Do I call the cops? Campus security?"

S is for Slasher

"Well, don't panic, girl, I don't think anything happened. Kevin even asked me if we should call an ambulance. He offered to stay here after we carried you over. I sent him back." Emma shows me a thermometer. "You seem your normal self, let's think this over..."

"Damnit! Why me? Why does bad shit always happen to me?!" I feel like screaming. I think I will. I grab the pillow and scream into it.

Emma hugs me. "Felissa, please, calm down, I really think you're okay. Sometimes people pass out. Heat, allergies... hey, probably something you ate earlier. Maybe you were tired or stressed. PMS?"

I've already tuned her out. But she's right about one thing. I need to focus and think. I take a slow, deep breath and stand up. I close my eyes and try to let my body flow over me. I do feel normal. Nothing hurts. Nothing's numb or tingly. I smell normal. Okay. But I need to be sure...

"Emma, you know every inch of me. Certain areas better than I do. Examination time."

I start to slowly and methodically remove clothes and Emma sets them on the bed. Socks, blouse, pants. We both inspect them carefully. I take another deep breath and carefully peel off my panties. I examine them, feel them, smell them... Everything's normal.

"Okay Emma, check me out, be thorough." I open my mouth for her. Then she moves around me, staring closely head to toe. I lie down on the bed. Another deep breath. "Emma..." I close my eyes.

S is for Slasher

"Gynecologist time. Everything." I zone out a little.

By the time it's all over, I do feel a little better. Emma is certain I'm the same, safe and untouched. We debate finding a black light or something, but I think she's right. She even smells and tastes me.

"Well, Felissa? What's next?" Emma holds me and gives me a kiss.

"I don't know..." I'm still feeling pretty damn confused, and a little angry. "But it's better if I don't have to see Kevin for a while."

"Fair enough. We'll talk to him for you, okay? Just to be sure. But if it helps, you really weren't over there very long, when he called it felt like you had just left."

"Fuck, Emma... A killer's on the loose out there, and we have to worry about frat boys too? Along with everything else going on? What the fuck?"

"Welcome to womanhood, girl. Is it any wonder our role models are final girls?"

***

Daphne is feeling up my biceps. I'm soaked in sweat so I'm a little self-conscious when she moves to my lats. I shouldn't be too concerned, we're *all* sweaty, after all. There's something cool about being with my whole crew in the gym. It's not just that we're all in such great shape, or that some of us are so fucking hot. It's kind of...

"Empowering, isn't it?" Lisa must be some kind of mind-reader. Now she's feeling my arms too. "Damn these are tight! I can't believe how toned

S is for Slasher

you've become since you joined. It sure didn't take you long."

"I don't know, muscle memory, I guess. I was pretty damn strong back when I was a cheerleader in high school, I was more like a gymnast, really." I do a standing backflip just to show off. I'm such a bitch.

Danielle and Patty start whispering, and Amber joins them. They're looking at me and smirking. What the hell?

Danielle puts her fists on her hips while Patty waves everyone over. "What do you say, girls? We ready to vote?"

"Vote?" I thought I was already in! I've been in the damn sorority a while!

Daphne gives me a long, tight sweaty hug. I guess I've changed a lot, because it isn't gross, it's kind of sexy. Pretty damn hot actually. I glance at Emma guiltily. But she looks amused.

"We're proud of you, Felissa. You're strong inside and out. *And* you took our slasher studies seriously. Aced it all... a real pro. And you're tough and clever, a natural. A real badass." Daphne slaps my actual ass. Nice.

Emma comes over. "And I say we can totally trust her. I vouch for her." She kisses me.

Sharon rolls her eyes and shakes her head. "You're biased, nympho." Everyone laughs. "But I agree. She has my vote."

"Felissa, we already had a secret vote. It was unanimous. Now we make it official." Melissa walks over and grasps my hand to hold up my arm.

S is for Slasher

"You're already Omega House. But now you're final girl material. What say you, girls?"

Every one of them pumps a fist and yells out "Final Girl!" One after another, then in unison. I realize for the first time that no one else was in the gym, just our group. I'm not sure what's going on. Something feels weird. But I'm flattered, I can feel the love. It's nice to finally belong. Even as a cheerleader I was always an outsider for one reason or another. But this feels right. These strange girls feel like family.

"Yeah... Final Girls!" I shout. Uh oh... sweaty group hug!

***

"What the hell is this, anyway? Another initiation?" I'm blindfolded in Scout's car, she's driving, and Emma is in the backseat with me holding my hand. It's sweaty... is she nervous?

"Nope. That's passed. These are finals, girl..." Scout giggles.

Emma kisses my cheek. "Final exam time, Felissa!" She kisses me on the mouth, deeply. With the blindfold it feels really kinky. "I'm so happy for you, girlfriend."

"We're here, bitches! Time to get your gore on!" Scout ruffles my hair like I'm a kid. She's younger than me.

Emma helps me out of the car and we walk silently for a while. I can feel that we're walking in a field or something. We stop and Emma finally

S is for Slasher

removes the damn blindfold. I'm standing in front of a decrepit two-story house; it looks abandoned and dilapidated. The sunlight is fading into dusk. All the Omega sorority girls are standing there too, facing me. They're all wearing various degrees of sports armor like gloves and elbow pads, some with cycling helmets.

"Suit her up..." Jennifer points at me and the girls give me some stuff to put on or strap into. "I say Felissa doesn't need much... but give her goggles too."

"What the hell is this?" I don't know if I'm amused or scared. But I suit up all the same.

"Let's show her." Rebecca is grinning happily. She looks insane.

The girls drag a body out of the house onto the porch. It's Jason. Jason Voorhees from the *Friday the 13th* movies, machete still in hand, hockey mask and all. But it's a real human corpse. I can smell the death.

"What is this?"

Melissa kicks at the guy's head. "Remember Temple Carlson?"

I do. He's an asshole hotshot football player who was recruited out of our university into the big leagues last year. I nod half-consciously. A pretty big dude. Like Jason...

"He just date-raped a couple girls from Delta House. Rumor is he's been pulling that shit for years." Sharon spit on the corpse and stomped the crotch. "I was a high school freshman when he assaulted me in a park. He was wearing a ski mask,

S is for Slasher

so I never knew it was him until years later."

"Why is he dressed like Jason? How did he die?" I think I know what's going on now, but it's too crazy to believe. I have to hear it.

Danielle breaks it down for me. My head's swimming. This is surreal as fuck.

"Yeah... Yeah. Okay. Tell me again. Maybe dumb it down..." I sit down, right in the dirt with the dried-out dead grass.

"I think you get it, alright... But sure, why not. I guess it must be kind of a shock to a newbie. I forget that." Danielle sits down in front of me. Emma joins us and takes my hand.

"We target the worst ones, and definitely any piece of shit who's hurt one of *us*. We pick a slasher that best fits the asshole, and dress him up. We used to use stitches or nails, but it was kind of complicated and messy, superglue worked better. Mask, rubber weapons, whatever. But we can't let him have too much advantage, so we break his hands, sometimes fracture a leg or whatever. We lock him in the house with one of us and see who wins. Guess who always wins? If it gets too dangerous, we can always come in and help. Oh, usually the final girl has to improvise, but sometimes we hide a weapon somewhere for her, just to shake things up."

I shake my head. "Why would these scumbags play along? They have to know they're going to die anyway. And why aren't they worried about you framing them and going to jail or something?"

"Oh, I forgot that part, sorry. We threaten to

S is for Slasher

castrate them! Guys will do *anything* to keep their junk! Sometimes they get stubborn and try to refuse to attack the final girl, so we have to up the ante... We've only had one we couldn't convince, even torture wasn't working, so we just all joined in for the slaughter. Like a practice run. Oh, and they aren't allowed to exit the house, either... if they ever try to escape, we've got girls surrounding the house."

Lisa pipes in. "And now –"

"And now it's my turn..." I stare at my gloved hands. "Do I really have to?"

"You *get* to!" Danielle yells. She looks offended.

Emma strokes my face. "It's a huge honor, Felissa. And you can't imagine how cathartic it is! How satisfying..."

Sharon hands a tablet to Emma. "Show her."

"I have some bad news, Felissa..." She hugs me. "Brace yourself."

"Bad news?" Is she joking?

"I was suspicious of that damn little creep Kevin... I never dropped it, Felissa. I was looking out for you the whole time. And we finally got the proof..."

I feel sick to my stomach. I hope it isn't what I think.

Emma plays the video. A crystal-clear image. I'm sitting on Kevin's couch when he hands me the Coke. There we are looking at his stupid beach videos. But behind the big pad, the fucking creep very expertly drops something into my can. What a fucking pro. How many times has he done this? Just by touch he knows where the hole is. In like one second. There I am stupidly drinking my roofie. What an idiot I am. I watch myself waver and collapse. I don't even remember wobbling back and forth like that. It looks almost comical.

"I don't know if I want to watch this..." I look into Emma's eyes. Compassion. And righteous fury.

"Yes, you do. Like I always tell you, it'll be okay. You'll see."

Kevin lays me back on the couch and unbuttons the rest of the blouse. There he is unbuttoning and unzipping my pants. Off they go. He slides off my panties, slow and gentle. He leaves my socks and blouse on but opens the blouse to expose my chest. He drapes my left leg over the back of the couch and spreads my legs as wide as possible. He goes for his cellphone. Whatever's filming all this must be on his bookshelf, a hidden camera I suppose.

I close my eyes. I'm shaking, so Emma holds me. "It's okay, it sucks, but it's not as bad as it could be. Keep watching, Felissa..."

That little creepy punk holds his phone over my face, lingering there to emphasize that it's me I guess, then slowly moves it down, travelling all over my exposed body. Then he moves it closer when he comes back between my legs, and practically pushes it against me. Even that's not enough for him.

Emma kisses my cheek. "Don't worry, it's almost over."

Fucking Kevin reaches down to spread open my labia with his fingers while his other hand holds the

S is for Slasher

camera lens as close as he can. Then the creep leans down to get a good whiff of me, inhaling deeply and smiling at the bookshelf camera. He makes the "so-so" motion with his hand and shrugs. Then he tries to get a good shot of my starfish. He looks unsatisfied with the angle. So, he carefully flips me upside down onto my belly and spreads my cheeks apart for a clear view of my anus. The video abruptly changes. Now I'm watching the footage taken from the smartphone. Yup, there it is, the inside of my vagina in crystal-clear hi-def digital presentation. And there's the inside of my butthole... These are images I never thought I'd be looking at. Things not even Emma sees in our most intimate moments. The video ends.

I take a deep breath and close my eyes. "Emma... is there more? Did he –"

"No. That's it. He didn't... well, it was just for the video. I can show you the rest if you want. He dresses you and calls me."

"What a fucking creep! What, to get his jollies? So he can jack off to me every night?"

"No. Felissa... he sells these videos. You're not the only girl. We got all the names and all the videos when we interrogated him. I don't think he's even into girls. He's just a greedy rapey selfish piece of shit."

"Wait... other people have already seen this video?!"

"Probably... Yes. Sorry. Your pussy's in high demand. Guys have never seen it. You were number one on Kevin's list. We know he already sold it to

S is for Slasher

three assholes at school. Kevin claims they wouldn't post it online or anything, too valuable to just give away, but..."

"*Fuck*!" I'm furious. I don't think I'm scared or embarrassed anymore. Now I'm fucking pissed! "Hey! Why didn't you tell me?!"

"We just found out a couple days ago. We had to prepare fast. I knew you'd want to do this yourself." Emma squeezes my shoulder.

"Wait... so why Temple Carlson? What does he have to do with –"

"Nothing. We saved the body to prove to you this is real." Danielle shrugs. "Usually, we've flayed the body and dumped it by now."

"Why flay the hands and head?"

Daphne laughs. "Well, we don't want anyone knowing we're supergluing masks and rubber machetes to rapists, do we? And besides, without the face and fingerprints, it slows down the investigation. And it keeps people guessing."

"Wait... so there's no rogue serial killer at all... it's all you girls...?! So, all the slasher victims, this whole time they're all men? All of them?"

"Yeah, all rapist scumbags, every one of them a total piece of shit!"

"And Kevin? What about –"

Lisa points to the house. "In there, waiting for you!"

"You're fucking kidding."

Scout laughs. "Dude, you'll love this... we dressed him up as Freddy Krueger, the scrawny little fuck."

79

S is for Slasher

Emma squeezes my hand. "I know you hate Freddy."

I stand up. "And I hate goddamn fucking bitch Kevin even more!"

The girls cheer. Some pat me on the back or grasp my shoulder.

"Go get him, Felissa!" Emma hugs me. "Butcher that fucker!"

"If you run into any trouble, we'll be there. Have fun with it!" Sharon grins like a maniac.

I mull over what I might find in the house to use on Kevin. On "Freddy". I can't wait for him to attack me. I'm so going to kick his fucking ass! I hope there's plenty of broken glass lying around. I can always shatter a window... There's so much I want to say to him. And I have some questions. I hope he'll be able to hear me over his screams.

I march toward the old dark house as my sisters look on solemnly. A sisterhood of sorority slashers. Sacred avengers. We live in an evil world. Now I'm the one grinning madly. It's fine. Who needs sanity? Fuck it. I glance back.

"You know, there's an ex-high school coach we need to pay a visit to next week..."

S is for Slasher

Last Resort

Barend Nieuwstraten III

"Nothing quite says vacation like drinking a cocktail from a coconut," Ben said to Allison, sitting by the pool. He sighed contentedly and rested the hairy vessel on his hairy belly. "Though I feel a little guilty having rum added to it."

"Why's that?" Allison asked, licking the rock salt off the rim of her margherita glass.

"I feel like coconut water… fresh coconut water, fresh from a coconut, is the closest thing nature has ever come to producing an actual healing potion. I legitimately feel better after drinking it. Like it's restoring hit points. But adding rum to it kind of undoes-"

Allison groaned. "God, even sitting in the sun in a tropical paradise, surrounded by palm trees, you can't help but bring up video games. This is how badly you needed to disconnect."

"Hey, at least my drink's thematic. I look like I belong here in an island resort. I'm drinking from a coconut near palm trees while you sip your Central American cocktail."

"Again, this isn't a video game," she said. "Our drinks don't have to fit local cuisine."

"No, but video games are recreational, while margaritas are what *you* drink with your work gang. So, technically my mention of a recreational pastime while we're on another is less of an incursion than drinking a work drink is."

Allison smirked. "It's hardly a work drink. I can't do my job while drinking them."

"Point Ben," he stubbornly said.

"Points are a video game thing. Two points Allie."

"Adding points: accounting. Accounting is a work thing. Two points Ben."

"You just added a point," she scoffed.

"*I'm* not an accountant."

Allison laughed. "You helped with my tablet on the flight. That's IT support. Three points Allie."

Ben took off his sunglasses and pointed at her with them. "You requested that support. Fine, no further tech support for you for the rest of the trip. I'm on vacation now."

Allison smiled and licked more salt from the rim of her glass. "I can live with that if it means I'm a point up on you."

Ben smiled, shook his head, and took another sip from the coconut. "Not in hit points, baby," he said, tapping a finger on the hairy shell in his hand. "Not in hit points." He slurped the last few drops up his straw and stood up.

"You know they have poolside service," Allison reminded him.

"Not for what I need to do," he said, making her slightly grimace. "Though that would be the

S is for Slasher

pinnacle of luxury."

She gave a frown of disgust, but her shoulders and belly vibrated enough to give away her amusement.

Ben walked around the pool and found the bathroom. A long, tiled corridor, it was almost like a maze, turning right twice to continue to the men's down another corridor almost as long. His flip-flops echoed as they slapped against the floor with each step.

There was a single shower running as he entered a changeroom and looked for the urinal. There was a sobbing sound that caught his attention coming from the closed cubical. He pulled his head back, curious. It sounded like a child. He was about to shrug it off when the sobbing stopped for a moment.

"Is someone there?" a boy asked.

"Uh, well, yeah. Don't worry, just taking a pi... er, pee," Ben said.

"I think I'm stuck; can you help?"

"Stuck?" Ben asked, confused. He took a few steps closer. The door barely gave an inch of clearance from the ground, so he wouldn't be able to see anything unless he laid on the floor. The men's room floor. "Stuck on what?"

"No, stuck in the shower. The door won't open."

"Oh, you want me to go get someone?"

"Can you just have a go, mister? Please?" the boy pleaded.

"Well, it's locked from the other side. Your side. If you just turn the handle-"

"It broke off."

S is for Slasher

"Oh, that'd do it then." Ben patted himself down as he looked to the broad screw head under the 'occupied' status. "Okay, I just need something flat to turn it, then. He reached into his fanny pack and pulled out his multipurpose tool. "Heh," he said, triumphantly, "and Allie said I was stupid for bringing this with me." He unfolded a bottle opener with a flat top. Placing it into the groove of the screwhead it was a little loose but, on an angle, he could just turn the convex disc. The bottle opener slipped about, forcing him to make several instalments of the task, frustrating him as he'd yet to use the urinal. Eventually he shifted it around until the little sign said 'vacant' again. "Ha. Got it," he said holding up his multi-purpose tool triumphantly. He held up his other hand to high-five the boy on the way out, but when the door swung open there was a man in a wooden tribal mask. Frowning with wooden teeth and large, baggy, squinting eyes, its broad flaring nostrils were clearly the eyeholes.

The man grabbed him by the strap of his fanny pack and pulled him in, turning them around into swapping positions. Shoved into the stream of the shower, a hand went over his mouth and he felt several punches to his belly. It wasn't until he looked down that he saw a long blade flashing about in and out of the bottom of his eyeline.

He made to scream but the stabbing blade made its way up his body to his chest. By the time it occurred to him to fight back, he already couldn't breathe. He felt his bladder empty itself as he slid

S is for Slasher

down onto the floor. The man in the mask grabbed the multi-purpose tool as Ben's blood and urine circled into the drain between his legs. With one final plunge of the blade into his chest, Ben felt it fill with a sensation of pins and needles and his left arm go numb.

The masked man rinsed his blade in the shower and backed out of the cubicle, closing the door behind him from the top of it. There was clicking and scratching as the flat handle turned incrementally into a locking position.

The water poured onto Ben's legs as the room slowly went dark.

***

Catherine was perusing the gift shop with Sam, deciding on which fridge magnets to select. When she grabbed one, she looked to Sam who was staring at her with bulging eyes. "Yes," he said, anticipatingly. "They'll love that one."

She squinted at him. "Who will?"

He rolled his eyes, tortured. "Whoever that's for," he said, like a moaning child.

"You're not even trying."

"Just take one of each, or two of each, or whatever it takes to get as many as you think you need, and then pile them on a table when we get back and make everyone fight for the ones they want."

"I want them to be personalized," Catherine argued.

S is for Slasher

"They come from a factory. No one who made these had anyone in mind. They're all generic. They're all basically the same. No one will care. Fridge magnets are the primary thought-that-counts gifts. Now, let's do this later. I want to hit the pool while the sun's still up."

"It's hot enough here to swim at night *and* the pool's heated. You can swim here at four in the morning and the water will be perfect."

"Some of us would like to come back with tan. We don't all have your naturally dark complexion. Wait..." Sam shook his head. "Why would I want to swim at four in the morning?"

"Because pretty much no one else will be swimming at four in the morning," she said. "So that'll be the best time to catch the naked woman swimming in the pool."

"What naked woman?"

"Me, you idiot," she whispered. "So, start being helpful, or the naked woman will never come out to play."

"Oh, in that case..." He began pointing at different fridge magnets. "Steve, Ranjit, Terry, Lisa, Ludmilla, Zoltan, Li, Da-"

Catherine grabbed his hand to stop him. "I'll take that enthusiasm as a compliment. But I question the sincerity of the suggestions."

"Are you questioning my commitment to my colleagues?"

"The company only send a few of us. The least we can do is get a little something for everyone else."

"That seems like rubbing their noses in it. Very insensitive, Cat."

Catherine crossed her eyes at him, sighed, and scooped a bunch of random magnets. "I'll just go with your plan."

"*My* plan for the fridge magnets, *your* plan for the swim. Seems fair."

"Both times you get what *you* want."

"God damned patriarchy wins again," he joked, pulling a victorious fist in.

"Not if we get caught," she said. "A skinny-dipping woman on holiday's a playful bit of fun. But a naked man seen by anyone is an express lane ticket to the sex offender registry."

"Goddamned matriarchy wins again," he said, pulling a victorious fist in again.

"I thought that was you two," a female voice turned them around.

"Allison," Sam said, smiling. "If you're here to get guilt souvenirs for those we left behind, Catherine's already got the fridge magnet market cornered."

"No, I'm just looking for Ben," she said, looking about the store. "He went to the toilet like an hour ago, and I haven't seen him since."

"He must have needed to go bad," Sam said, with a playful grimace.

"I don't suppose you could go check the men's by the pool," she asked, with a gentle hand on his arm.

"An hour later?" Sam asked.

"Go check." Catherine elbowed him.

"Might actually be more," Allison confessed. "I fell asleep for a while there, and I wasn't exactly timecoding everything. We left our phones in our room and switched off."

"He's probably up in your room," Sam said, before Catherine gave him an authoritative look. He started backing towards the exit. "But I'll go check to see if he's waiting for someone to come wipe his butt."

"Thank you," Allison said, smiling.

Catherine stared at Allison's blue one-piece swimsuit, clinging to her plump but cute little frame. It had small frilly add-ons about the shoulders and hips.

"Did you buy that bathing suit in a place for kids?" she asked with a furrowed brow.

Allison smiled, putting her hands on her hips and twisted to show more of it off. "Yeah... Where else would I find something that makes me look like a mermaid?"

Catherine laughed. "Good point."

"Being small has its advantages," Allison said. "Especially with childhood obesity on the rise, giving me a little more space up top."

The pair walked to the counter where Catherine paid for the magnets, a few mugs made from carved coconut wood, and a couple of sarongs. They walked outside and waited in the sun, looking out to the nearby pool area.

"So, are all those included in the expenses?" Allison asked, pointing to Catherine's shopping bag.

Catherine shook her head. "No, the budget only covered the flights and accommodation. Probably could have squeezed more out of it if Tony didn't fly business."

Allison's face went bitter. "I was sat next to a screaming and kicking toddler, behind a full recliner, and in front of some giant with banana fingers playing memory on a touch-screen that he seemed to think was a *punch*-screen. Goddamned HR riding up in business? Their office already has the best view on our floor. Fuck," she whispered angrily through her teeth. "We could have had our whole department out here if he'd gone coach."

"Or stayed behind. We don't need a chaperone," Catherine said. "What, do they think-"

Allison elbowed her in the side. "Hi Tony," she said, as Tony approached.

"Hey, girls. Having fun?" Tony asked, smiling his dorky smile.

"Best work trip ever," Allison said.

"Yeah," Catherine added.

"Oh, well, try not to think of it as a work trip," he said, leaning and tapping his nose. "Unless Mister Taxman asks." He chuckled at his own joke, making it too awkward not to laugh along with him. "Though it pretty much is a work trip for me," he said, holding up a tablet. "As long as I crunch some numbers while I'm here, I can write this off with a little creative accounting." He winked and gave his throaty chuckle again. "Wouldn't have been able to bring all you guys and girls along otherwise. Shame we couldn't bring the whole department. We'll have to do a separate trip for them. Hopefully next quarter." He gave them a friendly wave and continued on his way.

"Quarter?" Catherine scoffed. "Man, that guy's racking up some serious business miles."

"So bullshit," Allison said. "HR is such a made-up thing too. People just kept dumping basic duties they couldn't be bothered doing themselves onto their secretaries who then started calling it a thing, then it became a thing, now they get paid more than half the office, and get all the biggest perks."

"I mean, it's kind of a thing. There're courses at university for it."

"There are also courses at university to learn fucking Klingon. That doesn't make it really a thing."

"I don't even know what that is," Catherine said.

"Yes, you do. Don't act like you don't. Everyone knows, even if they're not into that stuff."

Catherine smiled guiltily.

"Oh, you cheeky cow, I knew it," Allison said, jabbing a finger in Catherine's side, making her laugh.

"No sign of him in there," Sam said, returning from the men's changerooms. "Need me to check the ladies?" He shrugged.

Catherine squinted at him.

"He's probably gone to find something to eat," Sam suggested. "There is an all-you-can-eat buffet. He may have taken the sign as a challenge."

Catherine slapped his arm.

"What? I've had lunch with him. He's a

S is for Slasher

machine. I mean that as a compliment."

"In what circle is that ever a compliment?"

"Well, I mean, he's not thin by conventional standards, but he is for a man who eats as much as he does."

"That's true," Allison said. "It is sadly almost impressive. Ben eats all the stuff I only order just to Instagram."

Sam pointed to Allison for vindication.

"Right, well, I'll go look for him wherever smells good," Allison said, wandering off. "I'll catch you guys at dinner maybe."

"Alright," Catherine said, slapping Sam on the arm again. "Let's go take these to the room." She jiggled the bag.

"Is something going to happen in said room if I come with you, or do you genuinely need help carrying a bag that probably weighs less than your handbag."

"Oh, not with the handbag again. I *need* all that stuff."

"Really? You need four ChapSticks at any given time? What are you doing? Making out with the floor of every liquor store and supermarket cold room?"

"They're different flavours."

"The cold room floors?"

She smiled, annoyed. "The ChapSticks."

"Get some cargo pants."

"They don't make cargo pants for women."

"There are women in the army."

"Those are technically fatigues."

91

S is for Slasher

"But it still kills your handbag theory."

"No, fatigues are for women trained to fight for their country, while handbags are designed for regular women to keep their arms too busy to fight off sex offenders."

"Which brings us back to my original questions," Sam said, getting handsy.

"No," Catherine said, playfully pushing him away. "All that talk of food made me hungry."

"Meet you at the buffet?"

Catherine rolled her eyes. "Fine."

Sam gave her an assortment of quick kisses all over her face and giddily shuffled off in a reserved happy dance on his way to the buffet. She huffed, amused, and made her way to the elevator. At her floor, Catherine followed the corridor to their room only to find it wedged open with a laundry cart. She squeezed around it to find the bed perfectly made and tossed her bag onto it.

"Hello?" she said, looking around for the staff who'd made her bed. There was noise in the bathroom, where she hoped to go before heading down to watch Sam eat his own weight in shrimp. She knocked on the door. "Hello?"

"Come in," a friendly voice said.

Catherine opened the door and caught a white towel in the face. "This one for cart," the voice said, as she pulled the towel down to see a wooden mask. She was pulled into the room, off her feet, and flung headfirst into the toilet. With the seat up, her head smacked straight into the hard porcelain. The pain was such a shock that she slumped onto the cold

S is for Slasher

floor unable to even make a sound. The figure in the mask lifted her and tossed her into the bath face down, wrapping a gloved hand around her mouth. She felt a terrible shock to her lower back that spiked the pain in her head and made her legs go numb. She then felt a cold wet chunk of metal slide in under her chin and slice though the muscles in her neck as the tub filled with deep red fluid, pouring out about her face as air entered her from the wrong place. She choked and gagged as she was released and the door to the room shut, shortly before the bathroom door did. The taps were turned, and water started running over her shoulders, scalding hot.

The last thing she heard was the knife clinking loudly into the sink as that tap too was run to wash it.

***

Sam was strategically filling his plate at the buffet. He grabbed just enough of every single available dish to try each, so he'd know what to come back for. He looked at his plate with pride. So many colours, textures, and shapes, fit together like a culinary game of Tetris. He brought his bounty back to a table with enough seats for Catherine, Allison, Ben, Sean, who he hadn't seen since last night, and even Tony should he feel the need to grace the mortals with his divine presence.

Sam didn't know what half the dishes were. There was typical western food, with Asian and middle eastern infused experiments, but then unmistakeably local dishes. Fish cooked in coconut with some sort of the spinach, he thought, and potato, he wasn't sure. "Oh, oh, my god, yes," he said, eating it and waiting for anyone to show up. Though at the same time, if everyone else started showing up after he knocked out the first plate, he'd seem like less of a pig when he went back for more. Though Catherine would never believe for a minute that he genuinely waited for the others.

He was nearly through the plate when he saw Allison walk into the dining area. He waved her down. She approached wearing a sheer blue and white robe, which somehow still made her seem more formal that simply showing up in the blue swimsuit that could be seen through it.

"Do you have your phone?" she asked.

"Ah, yeah, why?"

"I still can't find Ben. Can you try calling him?"

Sam nodded while wiping his hands thoroughly on a napkin. He pulled his phone out of his shorts and gave Ben a call. The call went immediately to a message bank. "He's off-grid by the looks of it."

"Oh crap, that's right. We agreed to switch our phones off last night." She massaged her forehead. "I didn't see us getting separated."

"Have you talked to the front desk?"

"Of course."

"There's a lot of recreational activities available that he might..." he began to suggest as Allison cocked an eyebrow at him with her hands on her hips. "Right, well I didn't see anything on the

S is for Slasher

website about online gaming, so unless they have a vintage arcade room that they forgot to mention…"

"He wouldn't have left me by the pool like that," Allison said. "Well, maybe. But I'm still worried. I've got a bad feeling in my gut."

"Look, why don't you grab a bite to eat, just to make sure that bad feeling isn't hunger, and I'll call Catherine to check your room on the way down."

Allison screwed her face and reluctantly took his advice while he called Catherine. Her phone rang three times then hung up on him. He tried again and it rang out. A third time and it beeped at him, with a call failure sign. "What?" He instead decided to message her; *'Allie worried about Ben. Check room 3-12. Pls. Tell him to get ass to buffet before I eat everything.'*

He waited and only got a 'sent' confirmation.

A few minutes later, Allison returned with a plate. "What did she say?" she asked as she sat down.

"I think something's wrong with her phone," he said. "Or she's in the bathroom. She never takes calls in there."

"Nor should she."

"She does all her socials from there. What's the difference?"

"The lack of audio confirmation of a functioning digestive system?"

"That's fair," he agreed. "But I sent her a message and she didn't respond. So, I guess we wait."

Allison looked to her plate and shook her head.

"Well, if he's not here to help finish all the desserts I'm going to grab, after this, I'll flick him in the sack for making me waste food like that."

Sam and Allison ate their plates. Sam went back for seconds, as Allison picked a very photogenic collection of desserts. She arranged them for quite a while as Sam kept eating. She took photos from various angles, then finally started tasting some of them.

"I may need help with these," she said.

"Oh, nice collection," Tony said, hovering over their table with a plate full of food. "Mind if I join you?"

Sam and Allison both pointed to a spare seat. Sam couldn't help but notice he'd only grabbed about four different things. Sam scoffed internally, as the word 'amateur' sat teetering on the tip of his tongue.

Tony looked around the room after he sat. "Where's everyone else?"

"That's the million-dollar question," Allison said.

"Also, has anyone seen Sean?" Tony asked. "As soon as we got here last night, he seemed to slip off into the shadows, as it were."

"No, probably gone spearfishing or something unless there's some other kind of hunting or blood sport," Sam said. "Dude's always talking about doing stuff like that. Or wanting to do stuff like that."

"Right…" Tony said. "I always thought that was just part of his unnervingly dark humour. At any rate, I'm not sure they offer anything like that. I mean, maybe spearfishing. Somewhere. But not through *this* hotel."

"Well, I'm sure he's found some way to scratch that itch," Allison said, looking back to the dining hall entrance. "Seriously, where are they already?"

"Who?" Tony asked, seemingly struggling to keep up.

"Ben and Cat," Sam said. "Our better halves. Speaking of which, where's yours, Tony?"

"I couldn't well fly my wife out. She doesn't work for the company. This is technically a *work trip*," he said using air quotes. "I'm here on business, remember." He winked. "This is a *team building exercise*."

"Uh oh," Allison said with dread.

"Don't worry, I've whittled it down to a two-hour PowerPoint presentation on the last night."

"Can we be drunk for it?" Allison asked.

Tony sighed. "I guess."

Allison and Sam smiled at each other a moment before Sam glanced at his phone again. "I better go up and see what's taking Cat so long. If she's up there sorting out those fridge magnet souvenirs, I'm going to lose my shit." He looked to the others, standing up. "May I be excused?"

"You may," Allison chuckled. "I should probably go look for Ben while you're at it."

"Oh, we can split an elevator," Sam said.

"I'll just dine alone then?" Tony said, holding up a shrimp on a fork.

"Maybe we'll get a group together for dinner

tonight," Allison suggested.

"Yeah," Sam agreed.

"Uh… alright," Tony said, looking around at a table for eight at which he was now sitting alone.

Sam and Allison took the elevator to their respective floors and Sam returned to his room. He raised his eyebrows when he saw a 'do not disturb' sign on the door handle. Scanning his keycard, he opened the door and found the bed stripped of its cover. He checked the balcony and then the bathroom. Coming back out to the main room, he saw the bag from the souvenir shop on the floor, tossed aside. Something wasn't right about the bathroom he realised and looked back to see no towels in there. He smiled and went back downstairs to the lobby.

"Hi there," he said, approaching the front desk. "Did my wife come down here? Probably to complain about the lack of towels in our bathroom?" He held up his phone with a photo of her.

"Ah, no, sorry, sir. I haven't seen her," the young man at the desk said. "But if you need some fresh towels, I can have them sent up."

"No, no, well… probably yes. Room three-twelve. I think we need a bed cover too, but I'm just trying to track down my wife."

"Do you want me to page her?"

Sam held up his phone and shook it to remind the clerk of the last few decades of human history and technological advancements. "I hate to escalate things so soon but could maybe security just have a look at their cameras. I know she went up to our room around one or just before."

The clerk considered it, pushing his mouth to one side. "So, she's only been out of your sight for…" he looked to the computer monitor in front of him. "… just under two hours."

"Look, I'm not asking you to call the cops," Sam said, understanding how crazy he sounded. "But two hours of footage would take a couple of minutes to plough through on fast rewind. I mean, at least please ask the security guy. Please."

"Alright," the clerk said, gesturing for someone else to take his station while he led Sam down a corridor. "I'm not sure what the rules are, so you might have to wait out here, but I'll at least get our controller to speak to you."

"I appreciate this so much," Sam said, apologetically.

The clerk knocked on a small window in the wall and a large islander opened up, wearing a security uniform made rather practically of short sleeves and shorts. "Hey, what's happening?" he said in a friendly voice.

"We've just got a guest who's struggling to locate his wife," the clerk said. "She's only been missing two hours, and was last seen-"

"Sure, come on in," the security chief said, opening the black door next to the window.

Sam gave him the instructions as he got a friendly wave from another guard, looking at a collection of screens divided into several feeds of various cameras around the hotel. The several looking at the pool made him realise the four-in-the morning plan Catherine had was probably a bad idea. "You get many skinny dippers at night?" he couldn't help but ask.

"All the time. The night guys have a great job," the guard said as he rewound the corridor footage of the third floor that showed the entrance to their room. He went back and forth at different speeds, playing around with the settings. "Alright," he eventually said. "Cleaner comes in to collect room laundry, then your wife comes in, then laundry guy leaves with... bedding by the looks of it, then... nothing. Looks like your wife's still up there." He shrugged, fast forwarding for a bit.

"No, I went up there," Sam assured him.

"Oh wait. There's you." He paused the video of Sam going in to look for her.

Sam pulled his head back, confused. "What the hell?"

The guard started fiddling with multiple feeds, mumbling to himself.

"What are you doing?" Sam asked.

"Just seeing which cleaner that was, so I can ask them what they saw or if your wife said anything." He watched, pausing and running his finger along the screen where the timecode was, before going to another feed.

"You tracking him?"

"Tracking's a fancy word for it. It's pretty manual. But I'll find... man, this guy hasn't looked at the camera once. Wearing a cap. They don't normally... hmmm."

S is for Slasher

"What is it?"

"Well, he walked right past the laundry room," the guard said, leaning in towards the screen. "Where are you going, cappy-chappie?"

"What's going on?"

"Oh, looks like he's going to the waste room. Something must have happened to the some of the linen or towels. Still haven't got a look at his face though." He fast-forwarded for a while, shaking his head impatiently. "Doesn't look like he ever came out." He looked to another computer. "Roller door's been used a couple times today. Bit of a blind spot there on the feeds."

"Could we go have a look?" Sam asked, starting to get worried.

"Ahh... sure," the guard said, looking to his fellow guard. "Can you hold the fort?"

The other guard nodded, and the controller led Sam through the back-of-house passageways. When they got to the waste room, the guard's phone rang as he unlocked the door. "Yeah, can I help you?" he asked, and listened. "Ah, can they wait?" a voice on the other side spoke but it was too trebly and tinny for Sam to understand. The guard sighed. "Alright, tell them I'll be a minute."

"What's happening?"

"My kid's school. Sounds urgent. Don't know why they called the work number though. Ah..." he stalled, trying to make up his mind.

"If you want to go take it, I can wait in there. Maybe look around."

The guard crumpled his brow, not liking the

S is for Slasher

sound of it. "I shouldn't really..."

"It's a waste room. I promise I won't steal any of your soiled bedding or broken lamps, or other garbage," Sam assured him.

The guard smiled. "Alright man," he said, patting him on the shoulder. "Just don't touch anything with a warning sign attached to it."

"Got it," Sam said, pushing the door open as the guard went back down the corridor.

Inside it was dark, even with the few lights on. There was an array of dumpsters with colour coded lids, storage units, several doors, and switch boxes. He walked around and eventually saw the laundry cart from the security footage. It was empty when he got to it. There was a lower level like a loading dock with the roller door shut. Down there, there was another hard-plastic dumpster with a red lid. He crouched down to look inside then felt a sharp pain in both his legs, then both his arms. As he tried to push himself up, his legs failed him painfully and he fell onto his back. A man was standing over him wearing a wooden tribal mask and holding a large knife.

"Oh, fuck no," Sam said, and swung his arms at the lunatic.

The man in the mask cut Sam's forearm and the hand and fingers went useless at the end of it. He managed to grab the mask by the mouth and yanked at it, getting slashed on the side of the neck by the knife as he was kicked off the edge and fell into the open dumpster. The lid fell shut behind him and he heard his assailant swear under his breath. Then he heard footsteps scurry off, away from him.

With only one functional appendage, Sam fished his phone from the opposite pocket of his shorts. He switched on the flashlight feature as he found himself half buried in bedding and bloody towels. He grabbed a hand towel to wrap around his forearm, only to see Ben looking back at him. "Oh, Jesus," he said. "Ben." He went to feel his pulse, but Ben was cold. Pulling away more layers, he saw a whole host of meaty stab wounds. He then saw another body.

Catherine.

"Oh, fuck no. No, no," he said, dropping his phone to grab her and pull her close. It made him slip in deeper to the pile and he felt another head of hair. "What the fuck?"

He managed to reclaim his phone and shone the light on them. It was Sean, who'd been missing the longest. Everyone was there except for Allison and Tony. "What the hell? Why?" he whispered. Almost everyone from their group was here, dead. Except for himself, about to bleed to death, he realised. He looked to Catherine and felt little motivation to save himself, but even dead her face looked a little judgmental. It was as if she was lecturing him from beyond death to save himself. Using his one good hand and teeth, he tied a hand towel around the wound, but it was going to be a lot harder to do the legs. Still, one less wound to bleed out from, he figured.

The large red lid of the skip bin flung open, and Sam looked up. The figure jumped down and plunged his knife into him.

***

Allison leaned on the front desk. The clerk looked down at her. "Hello, miss, can I help you?"

"I was wondering if you'd seen my boyfriend yet?"

The clerk pulled his head back and held up a finger, as if remembering something, but then dismissed it. "Sorry, uh… what does he look like?"

"Oh," Allison said, realising her phone was switched off and in her room. She held up a hand for his height. "About this tall, pot belly, short but full beard, brown hair, blue eyes, answers to the name Ben."

"There are a few people here that kind of look like that," the clerk said. "But I don't think any of them have attended the front desk for a while. Where did you last…" he looked back, distracted as a tall islander security guard in short sleeves showed up.

"There's a call for me here?" he asked.

"Oh, sorry," the clerk said to Allison, holding up a gentle hand to placate her a moment. "Line three," he told the guard and turned back to her. "Sorry about that. So, uh, oh yes, where did you last see the gentleman in question?"

"Hello?" the security guard said on the phone.

"Well, we were at the pool this morning, he went to the changerooms, and he never came back."

"Hello?" the guard repeated.

S is for Slasher

"Would you like me to page him?" the clerk asked.

"Hello?" the guard said, pulling the phone away from his ear and looking at it, then the switchboard.

"If it's not too much trouble," Allison said. "His name's Ben Kowalski."

The guard hung up the desk phone and pulled out it his own from his pocket, shaking his head, and started thumbing through it while the clerk cleared his throat and leant toward a small microphone and pressed a button.

"Yeah, hello, is this Tompkins Public?" the guard said into his phone.

"Paging Mister Kowalski. Mister Ben Kowalski," the clerk said over the intercom.

"Yeah, I got a call from you just a few minutes ago," the guard said. His next few words were lost under the clerk's announcement echoing about the lobby and beyond.

"Could Mister Ben Kowalski come to the front desk in the main foyer, please."

"Well, that's what they told me," the guard said. "Don't know why they didn't call my cell phone. But either way, is my kid alright?"

"Could Mister Ben Kowalski please report to the front desk in the main foyer," the clerk repeated. He gave Allison a polite smile as he took his hand off the button and looked around.

"Well, someone called here from there," the guard said into his phone. He rolled his eyes.

Allison gave the security guard a sympathetic look when they caught eyes. He gave her a polite smile as well. "I don't know," he said to the person on the phone. "*You* rang *me*... well, okay, sure, now I did, but before that... okay, never mind. Thank you for your assistance." He thumbed the phone off and put it back in his pocket. The guard then looked to the clerk, the intercom, up to the speakers, then to Allison and pointed at her. "Are you missing a man by any chance?"

"Yes," she said, excited.

"Yeah, he's looking for you. I've got him out back in the waste room."

Allison crumpled her face in confusion. "What?"

"No, that's a different couple," the clerk said. "They're from three-twelve."

"Three-twelve?" Allison clarified. "Those people are with *us*. Different room, same trip, same group. Why are they in the waste room? Sam, yes?"

"You left someone unattended in the waste room?" the clerk asked the guard.

"It's not like he's going to steal our rubbish," the guard said.

"No, but if he eats thrown out food and gets sick, he might sue us."

"Don't worry, I'll go check on him," the guard said.

"Can I come?" Allison asked. "He's a friend of mine."

"What about your boyfriend?" the clerk asked.

"Well, I'll come back here if he turns up. But now I'm worried about Sam checking the bins for Cat."

"We don't serve cat," the clerk said, disgusted.

S is for Slasher

"No, his wife. Catherine."

"I don't' mind," the guard said, shrugging.

"Fine," the clerk relented.

Allison followed the guard through the back-of-house corridors until he opened the waste room door. Inside they saw a man in the blue cleaning-staff overalls holding a large knife. He jumped into a skip bin on a lower sub-level. Screaming and yelling came from the bin as the guard ran towards it. "Hey, you," he yelled, before grabbing his radio. "Emergency, emergency, code black in waste room. All hands."

Allison ran behind him as he leapt into the large bin and started grappling with the man. When she got to the edge, the guard was pushing the man into the corner as Sam lay there in a pile of bodies, bedding, and towels, bloodied with a knife in his belly. Allson saw Ben's face, Catherine, and even Sean. She couldn't help but scream.

"Fucking bastard," Sam yelled, while the large guard pulled the killer's arm up behind his back and pushed his face into the corner. He punched the man wearing the wooden mask in the back a few times until he went limp.

Another guard came running in as Allison collapsed to her knees and started crying. "What the actual fuck?" She sobbed, looking down at her dead and dying team.

"Oh my god," the second guard said, quickly pulling out his phone and dialling. "Yes, we need an ambulance and police to Sunshine Bay Resort. Got a man with knife wounds…" He stepped back to let a third guard past as he gave the address.

The third guard jumped down and helped the first with the killer. When they turned him around it was Tony.

"Tony?" Allison yelled. "Why?"

"Cutbacks," he said, as the head guard pushed him up towards the third guard and started dragging him out. Two guards pinned him to the ground, while the other started helping Sam with first aid. Allison recognised Ben's multi-purpose tool as it slid out of his pocket onto the floor.

"Cutbacks? What kind of psycho bullshit reason is that to kill everyone?" she asked, picking up Ben's multi-tool.

"Just the dead weight," Tony said, with his face pressed into the ground. "I've got numbers to crunch. KPIs to meet. Need to save the company money. I convinced the CEO I could bypass payouts and redundancies if we took those we wanted to get rid of on a company trip, that I would be able to convince you to all leave without issue."

"Without issue?"

"To save the company money," he said, as if what he was saying was reasonable.

"Think of it. Quarterly trips instead of layoffs. Tax deductions, write-offs…"

"What are you talking about? You killed Ben, you horrible shit."

"HR has a lot of respon-"

"HR isn't even really a thing," she yelled. "It's a made-up role, you view-hogging business-class flying piece of shit." She looked back to the skip.

"Where's that fucking knife?"

"Woah," the head guard said. "Better to leave that in, until he gets to hospital."

Allison looked to the tool in her hand and remembered Ben's long demonstrations of how fantastic he thought it was. She pulled out the blade from one of its handles. "Here's your fucking cutbacks." She dropped to the floor and started stabbing him about the neck and face.

"Woah," the guards said, getting off him to avoid the spraying blood.

"Who's the deadweight now, asshole?"

"Hey, hey," one of the guards raised his hand to stop her, but the other stopped him.

"Give her a minute," the head guard said. "There was a struggle… self-defence... all that. I'll ah… fix it in the report."

Allision stopped, already exhausted, while Tony was clutching at his bleeding neck and face, blubbing and whimpering.

It took her a moment to register what the head guard had said. "Really?"

"Yeah, but that should cover it though, love," the guard said, gently grasping her wrist to isolate the tool. "Maybe we just leave this on the ground, and we'll go sit you down somewhere."

Alison put the tool down gently, knowing how much Ben loved it.

***

An ambulance came to take Sam to the hospital

and police filled the hotel's waste room, asking staff and Allison questions. The police found Tony's tablet, linked in to all the hotel security feeds.

"I told them 'Admin' was a terrible password for a CCTV system," the head guard said, shaking his head.

The hotel manager offered to let Allison stay for as long as she wanted, but it wasn't much of a consolation without Ben. As beautiful a place as it was, it was now the place where he'd been killed. She was never coming back.

"I'm going to bankrupt the shit out of work," she told Sam by his hospital bed as she visited him before heading home. "Make them pay Ben and Catherine's families and us. Going to financially wring them out like a wet rag."

"I don't think they knew what Tony was trying to do, the lunatic, but yeah," Sam said. "Just for going along with a plan to save them redundancy payments."

"They may not have known, but I doubt they'd have had a problem with it. How the fuck are *we* the deadweight? If they don't pay out, I'm going to take a leaf out of Tony's book."

Sam shook his head. "Yeah, about that."

"The elephant in the room?"

Sam nodded.

"I went a little psycho there myself, I know."

"Understandable. He crippled me before I could do anything like that. Glad one of us got stuck in there, between you and me. For Ben, for Cat... even for Sean."

S is for Slasher

"Yeah. If I'm honest... in my heart of hearts, part of me wanted to do that for a really long time."

Sam nodded his head with a guilty half smile. "Listen. I'm going to be here a while. So, promise me one thing."

"What?" Allison asked.

Sam put his uninjured hand on hers. "Promise me you'll find a way to wrangle Tony's business class seat for yourself on the trip back."

Allison nodded.

S is for Slasher

What the Sonoran Takes

B.F. Vega

The sun beat down on the dry clay ground, throwing heat back up toward the sky as if the desert soil was trying to outwit the star which stole its water. No wind blew through the low shrub. No sound came from the cactus or rock piles. Everything with sense was hiding from the entombing heat. Or perhaps there was sound, small movements. Perhaps there had been warning but the heat was so complete, so omnipresent that it robbed not only the precious moisture from skin and hair and tongue, it also blocked sound waves and twisted light beams so that one could no more trust their own senses as they could a trapped snake, set free at their feet.

In this otherworldly heat and silence, it was as if the stranger had come from nowhere. They had struck so fast that at first the rest of them didn't realize what was happening. One minute Tony, the beautiful young man from the tour company who Leanne had been flirting with had been smiling at her from outside the modified jeep and the next moment the blood from his jugular was showering her in a rain of sticky life, which in the torridness of

S is for Slasher

the desert felt almost refreshing before her senses returned from their fevered hallucinations.

"Everyone back in the jeep" Arthur, the other tour guide, yelled. The rest of the group jumped back in beside Leanne, but the jeep had no windows and not even real doors.

Arthur turned the motor as the unknown killer, swathed in a sandy brown Tuareg and a full caftan of the same color, threw Tony's body face-first onto the hood of the jeep.

Leanne heard Arthur whimper like a little girl as the killer then jumped onto the hood and lifted the carving knife up toward the glittering light and heat of the sun again before plunging and hacking at Tony's neck until his head fully separated from his body. They all sat as if captivated by the carnage being played out before them. The heat dried Tony's blood as soon as it hit the baking glass of the windshield, a surreal twist that made accepting the reality of the atrocity harder.

"Arthur! Go!" Leanne yelled from her place in the back of the jeep and with her voice, it was as if whatever spell had kept them there this long had broken and Arthur gunned the jeep. The killer laughed as they hopped off onto the hard desert ground. The worst though was the thump and loud squishing noise Tony's body made as the jeep ran over it. Leanne looked out the back and, to her eyes, it seemed as if the shimmering heat swallowed the killer into the vast desert scrub.

When they got back to Apache Junction the police were already waiting for them. Leanne had called them from her cell phone the second that they had gotten into range. She watched the big search and rescue helicopter fly overhead as the local sheriff officers showed her to a place where she could clean up before giving a statement. Leanne was handed a blue jumpsuit and escorted into a shower stall.

"Please put your..." the female deputy had started, but Leanne was already putting her clothes into the evidence bag.

The deputy looked at her oddly before taking the bag and leaving Leanne to get the dried sticky blood out of her long black hair. It wasn't the first time that she had been covered head to toe in a stranger's blood, but by god, she had thought that the last time was really going to be the last.

When she emerged, she was shown to a room filled with her fellow witnesses. A deputy was bringing them sodas but she wanted water. It was July in the Sonoran Desert and even though the sun was about to set it was still well above 100.

Arthur walked in as the deputy left to get water. Arthur was also a very beautiful man, Leanne thought. He lacked Tony's charisma but there was nothing amiss with his lithe 6'2" frame or large wide green eyes. If pressed, she would have said that he was a mixed ethnicity of some form. His skin was too evenly tanned for the green eyes and sandy blonde hair to be purely European.

He sat beside her without looking at her or anyone else.

"I'm sorry about your friend," she said.

S is for Slasher

"I barely knew him," Arthur answered quietly. "I've only been working here for a month."

"Still, I'm sorry," Leanne said sincerely.

"Leanne Morningstar?" an officer called from the door.

Leanne nodded and followed the deputy to the room being used for interrogations.

"Please take a seat," the detective in charge said.

Leanne looked around her at what was obviously a conference room. On the walls hung enlargements of tintypes and silver prints taken at the very start of the photographic art form. One picture in particular caught her eye, and instead of sitting in the plush chair indicated she crossed to look more closely.

The picture was of the middle of nowhere. But to Leanne's trained eye it was familiar. The angle to the Superstition Mountains and the arrangement of saguaro.

"What's this picture of?" she asked the detective.

"The murder site," said a new voice from the door. "Or rather, that picture was taken when the owner of the Sonoran Silver Mine staked his claim. You can't see it, but there is a hollow just beyond the foreground where the mine entrance is."

"That's where the killer was waiting," Leanne said.

"It was, yes, Dr. Morningstar," the voice answered.

Leanne turned to the doorway. "I am retired, as I'm sure that you know since you took the time to look me up."

"Yes, I heard you had retired. I didn't have to

look you up though. You are Leanne Morningstar. I attended your lecture on distinguishing between ritualistic killings and cult killings for ritual."

"Is there a difference?" the first detective asked.

"Oh yes," the new person answered before pulling out their badge. "I'm Special Agent Jayne St. John and we need your help," Agent St. John said, sitting opposite her.

"I don't do that anymore."

"And yet, you of all people, the woman who brought the Paper Doll Killer to justice, just happened to be at the scene of a horrific crime."

"Coincidence," Leanne said, looking the agent squarely in the eyes. "I am on vacation. As I was driving down the freeway I saw signs for this place. I saw the tour company when I got here. I bought a ticket on impulse. There is no way that whoever did this knew that I would be on that tour. Ergo, you need my statement and my contact info and I need to get back to my hotel where they have air conditioning."

Agent St. John blinked slowly but instead of pressing the issue she sat back in her chair and nodded to the local detective. Leanne gave her statement then stood to go.

As she reached the door, Agent St. John said, "You are of course free to go…"

"But don't leave town?" she answered sarcastically. "What, are we in some sort of cop show?"

Agent St. John leaned forward on the table and didn't even look in Leanne's direction as she

S is for Slasher

answered. "No, I can find you no matter how much you are trying to lose yourself. I was just going to say that this is the fourth murder in the Sonoran desert of a male-presenting tour guide who was killed while leading a group of tourists."

"And?"

"And... this was the first time that the killer put on such a show. Usually, the killer strikes by slitting the throat and then laughs as the tourists run away. Why was this different? What could have been different about this group of tourists that the killer altered their ritual? Maybe they saw something or someone in that random group of tourists? Now, who, in that group, would a serial killer want to show off for?" At that, St. John pulled a case file from her briefcase and laid it at the end of the conference table closest to Leanne.

Leanne turned to leave but before she did she snatched the file then let the door slam behind her. She walked back into the room where the other tourists were waiting. Leanne took her old seat next to Arthur who had seemingly gotten a hold of himself while she was in the interrogation.

"I'm worried about talking to the police," he whispered to her.

"Why? Just tell them what happened. They might ask you to verify some things other people said. They will ask if you recognized the killer at all and then that's that."

"The police and I..." Arthur trailed off and looked away so that Leanne was staring at his sharp jawline and perfectly straight nose in profile.

"What were you arrested for?" she asked.

"It was a misunderstanding."

"It always is."

Leanne could see that he was about to say more but the officer came back in, called for Arthur, and let the others know that they were free to go.

"Look, Arthur," Leanne said, "here's my number. If you get into a bad situation, or if you need someone to talk to about this, try anyone else. But if all else fails give me a call."

"Thank you." He answered her with a heart-stopping smile that turned his ordinary green eyes into emeralds.

Kicking herself as a fool, Leanne gathered her things and tromped out to her rental car, throwing the case file on the passenger seat. She had lied of course. She didn't have a hotel reservation. Reservations made it too easy to be tracked down. She pulled up a reservation app and found something small and cheap nearby.

She could have afforded a nicer hotel, but in her experience, it was much easier for strangers to get by a bored concierge than the eagle-eyed clerks at cheap hotels whose jobs depended on knowing exactly how many people went into and out of a room. Once she had checked in, bolted the door, and made sure there were no bed bugs or dead bodies hiding beneath the sheets, she flipped on the local news.

There was nothing about the murder. She grabbed her phone and started searching the internet for Sonoran beheadings. The only thing she found was on an urban legend page linking recent deaths to the Flying Dutchman. A chill that had nothing to do with the AC came over her. How in the hell were these murders being kept away from the public?

She drifted into an uneasy sleep but was woken in the middle of the night by a phone call. She didn't recognize the number but instinctively answered it anyway.

"Hello?"

"Leanne? It's Arthur. I need help. I think that someone is in my apartment."

"Call the police," Leanne said as she sat bolt upright.

"I don't..."

"Arthur, this is no time to be stupid about..." But she stopped as she heard a door open and Arthur must have dropped the phone because all she heard was a scream.

Then whoever had entered must have picked up the phone and Leanne heard in a very hushed whisper, "Your move, Doctor," before the line disconnected.

Leanne immediately called the police and then called Agent St. John. Her first call went to St. John's voicemail so Leanne hung up and dialed again. This time St. John picked up on the fourth ring and promised to keep her informed.

Leanne hung up, but instead of going back to sleep she opened the file that St. John had given her.

The next morning St. John met her outside her hotel room as she was taking her bags to her rental car.

"There's been a development," she said. "Arthur and the other male tourists that were on your tour were all taken last night."

"Someone kidnapped four people in one night?" Leanne drew her eyebrows together. Quickly, she handed the case file to St. John and turned on her heel.

"Where are you going?"

"I'm leaving. I have no desire to be serial killer bait."

She got in the driver's side of the rental car and was annoyed when St. John got into the passenger seat, the file still in her hand.

"You can't just leave."

"I can and I will."

"What about Arthur?"

"That's your job."

"What did I miss?"

Leanne grabbed the file from St. John's calloused and scarred hands. She opened it, flipping through gruesome picture after gruesome picture until she got to the first picture of the entrails.

She turned the picture so that St. John could see it.

"You didn't tell me that they were being eviscerated and that the entrails were being used to make symbols."

"You weren't interested."

"You have to know what this symbol is," she said, flipping to the next picture.

"It's the symbol for woman. We figured that they

were trying to belittle the men they were killing."

"It's the astrological sign for Venus."

"So?"

"Venus is the morning star," Leanne said, pushing the folder back at St. John.

"We really need your help."

"No."

"Arthur needs you."

"I barely know him."

"That husband from Colorado that's missing? He has three little girls. Pretty blonde girls with blue eyes who…"

Leanne spun around. "There was nothing that I could have done to save Amy. Lillius had never struck the same family twice before. We had no way of knowing that he would do that."

Leanne took a deep breath and tried to banish Amy's eyes from her mind. She punched the steering wheel, the pain in her hand robbing the grisly image of its power for a moment. She heard herself asking, "What do you want?"

"Just come to the first scene with me. Tell me what you see."

"Just you and me?"

"Yes. Totally unofficial."

"Let's get this over with," Leanne sighed and turned off the engine of the rental. She grabbed her hiking pack and hopped out. She climbed into the agent's pickup and said, "Out and back then I'm gone."

An hour later they were in the middle of nowhere. The sun hadn't quite gotten to its full strength, but it was still hot enough that Leanne's eyes were already seeing the ground itself start to heave.

"We found the entrails first," St. John said, heading toward a spot just north of where the truck was parked.

Leanne wasn't paying attention. She saw something in the distance. Something that looked like a tall shadow. Humanoid in appearance, but with wider arms than normal and taller than the average person.

"What are you looking at?" St. John asked, startling Leanne as she had not heard the agent approach.

"I think it's a person," she said, trying to focus her eyes through the heat haze.

"I don't see anything."

"There, look." Leanne pointed. The figure shimmered out of view for a second and then back in.

"It's probably a saguaro. They can look a lot like a person in the heat."

But Leanne was already moving toward the dark figure. As she got closer she saw that it was not a saguaro. It was a human body nailed to an upright cross. Its severed head was on a little shelf between its feet and its entrails were laid out on the desert floor forming the Venus symbol.

"Holy Hell," St. John whispered.

Leanne saw with guilty relief that it wasn't Arthur but one of the other missing tourists. Something was weird about the symbol. The bottom of the 'body' of the symbol was an arrowhead. Leanne started walking in the direction of the arrowhead and saw another figure looming out of the haze.

She got close enough to see that another makeshift crucifix had been erected, this body was securely chained in place and intact. She quickened her pace when she realized it was Arthur. His naked skin was very pale despite his normal tan and there were third-degree sunburns on his shoulders, nose, feet, and genitalia. She took her hat off and put it on his head, giving Arthur a little protection. He made a slight noise and she was shocked that he was alive. She pulled her water bottle from its holder on her belt and gently tipped a little liquid past his parched lips.

St. John came up then. "Arthur?"

"Help me with these chains," Leanne answered.

Both donned thick gloves that were in St. John's pack and went to work trying to undo the chains. But they were secured into the wood itself and neither was strong enough to pull them free.

"We need help," St. John said.

"Yes. Give me your water bottle and multi-tool. Then go get us some help."

"I will be back as soon as possible."

"Be careful. There is a killer out there somewhere."

"You think they're still around?" St. John asked.

"Yes," Leanne answered before taking St. John's hat and putting it on her own head.

St. John hurried off toward the truck and Leanne

got to work with the multi-tool. She didn't really think that she would be able to get Arthur off the cross, but she needed to try. She knew that if she didn't get him down and out of the sun soon he wouldn't make it.

She dug around where the chain had been tacked into the wood. She was about to give up. It had been almost an hour and the sun was nearing its zenith. The uncanny stillness from the day before had descended on the Sonoran desert. Tiring herself out trying to rescue Arthur would get them both killed. She gave one last tug on the scorching chain, realizing that the killer wore gloves, not just to hide their identity, but because they used a metallic weapon to kill under the Arizona sun. She wondered if they had learned that lesson the hard way and had any scars to show for it.

She was surprised when her final tug bore fruit. She had loosened the chain enough that she was pretty sure that she could squeeze it around Arthur and get him free. She took a drink of water, forced a few drops down Arthur's throat, and got back to work. She succeeded in lowering him from his cross, though it had left even more burns on his body as the baking hot chains hit new areas of unprotected flesh.

Leanne opened the small emergency kit she kept in her hiking backpack. It didn't have much, but it did have one of those weird space blankets. She laid it out and drug Arthur onto it. She knew that they would have to find shelter and she couldn't carry him, but she could drag him with the help of the

S is for Slasher

blanket.

There was an overhang of rocks nearby and she started in that direction, hoping that it wasn't a rattlesnake den. Although that would be a more merciful death than the one facing Arthur right now.

When she got to the overhang she was relieved to see that at least something was going her way; it was actually a small cave, and she could feel the moisture from some water source inside it. If she could get Arthur into a cooling source he might survive. In the back of the small cave was a depression in the ground that was wet. Using her hands, she dug a little bit and found a small spring. She grabbed the multi-tool and dug some more until there was a small, very shallow pool of water right on the surface of the clay. She drug Arthur over and carefully slid him into the water, trying not to peel away any more skin from his burns.

She heard a noise outside the cave and stuck her head out to see if St. John had arrived. But the heat was so intense she couldn't see clearly more than five feet from the entrance of the cave. But she heard something that she couldn't see coming toward her quickly, rolling over the compacted clay. The thing didn't slow down until it hit the rocks beside her and bounced once.

Leanne was looking at the head of the male tourist from Colorado. In the mouth was a piece of paper. Leanne pulled it gently from the cavity and opened it.

Don't Move Doc, it said, and despite the heat

S is for Slasher

Leanne's blood ran cold.

Leanne pulled back from the mouth of the cave. She knew that this was a bad position, but she couldn't leave Arthur and he couldn't move by himself. She was going to have to wait it out.

She looked around at what she had with her, but there was very little. Her backpack had another bottle of water, a few granola bars, the first aid kit, and a flashlight. She also had St. John's multi-tool, but she didn't think it was going to help much.

As she sat contemplating, there was a slight groan behind her. She hurried over to Arthur. His eyes fluttered and she hoped that he would stay unconscious. The pain he was going to be in would be excruciating.

He started groaning some more and she knew that hope was dashed. She took off one of the leather gloves and stuffed it in his mouth as he began to scream. It was better for everyone if the killer didn't know that Arthur was alive. She dug a little more water from the ground, soaked one of the bandages from the kit in it, and bathed his forehead, hoping to both bring down his temperature a bit and give him a little comfort.

His screams lessened and his body stopped convulsing in pain as she continued to bathe his brow. She removed the glove and poured a little more water down his throat. He coughed a bit but swallowed it and lapsed back into unconsciousness.

Outside nothing stirred. There was not even a hint of wind. No lizards or snakes could handle the ground when it was this hot and they too were

S is for Slasher

somewhere hiding from the sun and those that would do them harm. She checked her phone. It was past two. Why had St. John not returned? Had she not made it back to her truck? Leanne was pretty sure that she could backtrack out of the desert to the nearest town, but not without some kind of cover from the twin deaths of sun and psychopath.

She stuck her head out again to check on her surroundings, the heat haze thicker than any fog from some Victorian ghost story. She closed her eyes and listened hard. In this stillness, she should be able to hear any movement, but there was nothing. She opened her eyes again and for a moment thought that she saw a black figure shimmer in and out of vision again. She did not want to be right about that and quickly pulled herself back into the cave. She knew there were six hours until sunset. After sunset she could slip back to town. If she survived until then.

At four she heard rattling in one of the bushes outside the cave entrance and something struck the ground hard. She waited until it was quiet again and went to check.

It was an arm. She recognized the Rolex the tourist from London wore. Tucked under the band was another note. She grabbed the note then flung the arm back toward where she had last seen the dark figure. She heard a distant laugh and scurried back into her cave.

The note said, *You won't make it until dark. Like that little girl never made it to school.*

Leanne felt sick. She stuck her head out of the

cave and vomited on the ground away from their hiding place. She heard laughter the whole time. She re-entered the cave and saw that Arthur's eyes were fluttering. Putting everything else out of her mind, she went to sit beside him and repeat the ritual of washing his forehead.

This time he did not scream out, and when she poured a little water down his throat he swallowed it without choking.

"Leanne?' he whispered softly.

"Yes. I'm here. Don't talk," she answered, bathing his forehead again.

After a few minutes, he asked, "Why?"

"Why am I bathing your forehead? Because you have heat stroke. Why are you laying in a puddle of water? Same reason. Why are we in a cave and you're naked and covered in burns? Because some madman is outside this cave trying to kill us."

Arthur's eye's fluttered again and Leanne thought that he might faint again.

"Water," he croaked and she poured a little more of the small amount of drinking water that they had left down his throat.

"Pain."

"I know. I'm so sorry," Leanne answered, almost on the verge of tears.

"Not y--"

"Not my fault? No, but I think this is because of me."

Leanne looked at the note in her hand. Then, because she had nothing better to do until sunset, she started to talk.

S is for Slasher

"I used to be a Forensic Psychiatrist. I specialized in occult and ritualistic killings. Eventually, my work got noticed by the FBI. Then the Paper Doll Killer." Leanne got silent for a moment. Something someone had said recently flitted through her mind. It was gone as soon as she tried to grab it. "Lillius Newmanson was a pedophile. He kidnapped little girls and when they had "worn out", he made elaborate paper dresses for them. Then he put them in wooden boxes fitted with a plexiglass lid that he stenciled their names onto. He then returned them to their family's front doorsteps."

She could feel the tears falling and she felt Arthur move a bit. Then his hand was laying on hers. She smiled through the tears.

"We thwarted the kidnapping of one little girl. So he took her little sister. Amy was four. He didn't leave her on her parents' doorstep; he left her on mine with a big bow and a valentine card." Leanne took a moment to quell the sickness the memory always brought. "Long story short, he had attached to me. He tried to stab me, the sniper across the street took the shot to save me. I still remember the taste of his blood and brain matter in my mouth. I swore it would never happen again." She looked down, her tears truly falling now. It was stupid, she couldn't afford to lose that much moisture.

"Tony," Arthur croaked out.
"Yes, what about Tony?" Leanne answered.
"Tony Sin…"
"Tony sinned?"

"No... Tony... Sinji..." Arthur was losing consciousness again.

But with her stomach knotting, Leanne realized what he was trying to say.

She poured some water into Arthur's mouth and headed to the cave entrance again to test her theory. She yelled out, "Jayne! I know!"

A loud mocking laugh answered her and the severed head that matched the arm hit the wall beside her. There was no note this time.

"Jayne. I'm right here! You could have killed me at any time on the way out here. Here I am, what are you waiting for?" She saw a movement in the heat haze. It looked like an amorphous spirit, but she knew it was a person in a caftan. She stooped down and picked up a rock, throwing it with all her might.

She knew that it would never hit St. John, but the laughter moved so she picked up a handful of rocks and started aiming just to the left and the right of the figure. The laughter lessened and the figure became clearer. She knew that it was coming closer to her. She threw again. This one made the soft thud of a hard object hitting soft material.

"You bitch!" a female voice called out.

"Me? You've been trying to summon me using other people's intestines. Who's the bitch? You didn't even have the balls to kill me when I was sitting beside you in the truck." She heard the movement and she ducked just in time to avoid getting hit by the head that she had last seen on the makeshift crucifix.

"You think you're so smart! You didn't figure it

S is for Slasher

out."

"Then why am I talking to you?"

"You let me leave with your only way out of this place!"

Leanne was silent for a moment trying to think. She heard a soft moan behind her and turned to look at Arthur. She knew that he wasn't going to make it until nightfall. But now that she knew who the devil was, it was just a matter of outsmarting her.

"Hey, Jayne. There are easier ways to get a psychiatric appointment."

"I'm not the crazy one here."

"The pile of severed heads at my feet begs to differ. So, what happened? Did your prom date back out and now you hate all men? You could just try Tinder or something you know, you're not that ugly."

"I am not ugly! Do you know how easy it was to get all these disgusting pigs out here?" St. John yelled, her voice rising in pitch.

"Sweetie, I was on the phone with Arthur when you kidnapped him. Don't pretend that you seduced them. Hell, what kind of a crap serial killer attacks their prey when that prey is on the phone to the best behavioral psychiatrist in the business. You're not only ugly, but you're also really stupid!"

Leanne heard St. John move again. She knew that her plan was working. If she could get St. John's emotions to take over it would give Leanne the upper hand.

"Hey, Jayne?" Leanne called out. There was no response. "So really though, what was it? Was your daddy mean? Did he say no when you asked for a pretty pony?"

"You have no idea what my life has been like. None! You with your uppity degree, going around pretending to stop harm. You couldn't even save one little girl! Do you know how many little girls I save with every man I kill? Huh?! All of them. They are all alike!" St. John ended this with a deep gulping sound that Leanne knew was indicative of tears.

Leanne crouched in the entrance of the cave. Now that St. John was emotionally involved in hurting her, the agent no longer moved silently. Leanne heard her drop from above and was ready to deflect St. John's knife using the nearest severed head.

The knife sunk deeply into the dead skull. Leanne kicked St. John in the knee.

St. John fell to the ground, trying to pull Leanne's legs out from under her. Leanne kicked her in the face. St. John caught Leanne's ankle and she fell, dropping the skull holding the knife. They both lunged at it. St. John's hand grabbed the hilt of the knife. Leanne had the little knife from the multi-tool, but she knew that if St. John could get the knife out of the skull, the little knife wouldn't be enough to stop the enraged killer.

Thinking fast, Leanne grabbed St. John's arm and bit into it through the caftan. St. John howled and let go of the knife.

"You want the knife?" Leanne asked.

She used the one leather glove she still had to

pull the knife from the skull and quickly turned as St. John lunged at her. Her hand came up, embedding the knife into St. John's eye. Leanne could hear flesh and muscle sizzle as the scalding hot blade dug deep into the socket. Using both hands and ignoring the agony of the burning handle in her one ungloved hand, Leanne pushed the knife with all of her strength until it broke through the eye socket into St. John's brain.

The killer cried out once and then didn't move again.

Leanne searched St. John's pockets for the keys to her truck. Finding them, she stood up and started pressing the alarm button. She heard the truck respond from somewhere to her left. She retrieved the vehicle and drove it up to the cave. She drug Arthur to the truck. It took her forever to get him into the cab, but she wasn't going to let him lie on the metal bed under the Arizona sky. Once Arthur was lying in the back of the king cab she cranked the air conditioner to full, took a swig from the bottle of whiskey she had found under the driver's seat, and drove off in the direction that she was pretty sure they had come from, leaving the body of the rogue agent for the Sonoran to claim.

S is for Slasher

Slash Camp

Monster Smith

Dear Mother and Father, I hope this finds you well and that you're both healthy and in good spirits. Camp is fun this year and I've been having a blast, although it's been a tad challenging if I'm being honest. Most of the people here are cool, and I even made a few new friends, believe it or not. However, things have gotten really strange around here recently and I'm writing this letter to you just in case.

You see, it all started a few days ago, though I'm pretty sure it goes back a lot further than that. But I can only tell you what I know; my version of what I've witnessed so far.

Everything was fine the first week; we played games and told ghost stories around a campfire, roasting marshmallows, making s'mores, and singing old traditional camp songs like "Kumbaya, My Lord" and "Jesus, Row Your Boat Ashore". Then, things suddenly took a turn for the worse, and nothing has been the same since.

I've been staying in cabin number nine, where all the other girls bunk, including the female counselors, of course. I was fortunate enough to

S is for Slasher

bond with a couple of the other campers, and we became fast friends – a crucial yet coveted part of the summer camp experience, or so I'm told.

Each morning we'd start our day by trudging down to the community dining hall where they served us a complete breakfast, providing us with enough fuel to keep us going throughout the daily activities they had lined up for us. Around midday, we'd take a short break and grab a quick lunch, and later we'd have a nice filling dinner, once the sun hid its face for the evening.

The food here is actually very good, although you'd never guess it as there aren't any five-star restaurants around for miles.

We were all laughing and goofing off at the table like usual – Angela Barker talking about kissing one of the boys the day prior, while her cronies, Sally Ray and Samara Yamamaura, nodded and confirmed the story like the guppies they are – when the rumor began to permeate. It spread like a forest fire on 'roids and hit our table like lightning. When it was all said and done, we could hardly believe what we were hearing.

Campers were gossiping like crazy, talking about a boy named Spencer Bradley who'd apparently vanished the night before, just after bed checks. He was a nice boy for the most part, shy and grounded, although a little negative if you ask me. I'd met him at the dance a week earlier, and he seemed like a nice enough fellow.

Most of the girls were scared to approach the boys and waited for them to make the first move, just like you see in the movies. They were nice and polite; mostly on their best behaviors, aside from a select few, and one of them even asked me to dance. His name was Charlie Ray. He was wearing a colorful tie with what looked like a very expensive suit, and he had a charming, engaging smile to go along with him.

Spencer Bradley had asked a girl named Tiffany Valentino to boogie down, and they seemed like they were having the time of their lives. She was loud and a tad obnoxious in my opinion, but it didn't seem to bother him. He grinned like a kid in a toy store, shaking his legs and tapping his feet to the beat as he busted a move while everyone looked on.

Not long after, the rest of the boys began escorting girls to the dance floor, one after another until the place was buzzing like a beehive. Ken Willis escorted Carrie Black and Daniel Rob took Brenda Yates. Matthew Cordell cut a rug with Pam Palmer while little Micky Myers burned it up with Ester Cole. There was something off about that Cole girl, I could feel it, but I couldn't quite put my finger on what it was.

A couple of the boys kept to themselves, hiding out in the dusty corners of the assembly hall while everyone else laughed and lived it up. One of them was named Mason Voorhees, an odd-looking kid who smelled something awful, as if he hadn't taken a shower or bathed in years. None of the girls wanted to go near him, it was a sad sight to see.

The other boy was named Teddy Krueger, a very strange boy who wore a glove on one hand and was

S is for Slasher

obsessed with knives for some reason. He wasn't like the other children, he was more of a loner who preferred not to fraternize with the other campers, if possible. He was happy sitting by himself, watching others out of the corners of his blank black eyes. If I didn't know any better, I'd swear he was up to something, the way he stared at us.

Anyhow, we all danced and partied until it felt like our feet would fall off, before heading back to our bunks for the night. There was a co-ed ball game the following morning, just after breakfast, and the Bradley boy was nowhere to be found by the time it came to hit the field. No one really seemed to be too concerned either, like he'd probably turn up at any given moment, although I'm sure more than a handful of us seriously doubted he would.

That night, after dinner, it was reported that one of the girls had gone missing as well. Her name was Jillian Robert, a quiet suspicious-looking girl who wasn't very fond of other people. Again, thinking it was nothing more than the two of them running off together in private to get a little frisky in the woods, no one seemed to care. It was strange for them to disappear as they did, but the counselors chalked it up to nothing more than raging adolescent hormones.

They told us that the pair of them would show up eventually and that it wasn't the first time something like this had happened. It was a bit of a regular occurrence apparently, just children being children. But, I had a sneaking suspicion that they weren't telling us everything. This wasn't the full story. There was definitely more to it.

Yesterday morning another girl by the name of Annabella Higgins was reported to have vanished without a trace, and the proverbial shit finally hit the fan. Panic began to set in and the counselors decided to put together a search party and comb the surrounding woods as best they could, utilizing whatever resources were available.

Everyone was asked to participate and instructed on what to do in case something or someone was found. Safety was their main priority. Three kids were already unaccounted for, and they didn't want to lose anyone else.

The plan was to head inside, gear up, and then everyone would meet up in front of the infirmary in an hour. From there we'd perform a tactical sweep of the entire campgrounds, from top to bottom. They had to be here somewhere, they couldn't have gone far.

As you probably already know, Camp Kadavar was built back in 1872 by a semi-wealthy man named Calvin Kadavar. He'd apparently inherited the land from his father, who had inherited it from his father, who got it from his father, and so on and so forth. Handed down from one generation to the next, if you will.

The rustic log cabins were made of sturdy, weathered white pine, most of them still consisting of the original lumber used to construct the place back in the eighteen hundreds. There are ten cabins in total; four are used to house the campers, one for

S is for Slasher

the Camp Director, one for the Infirmary, the cafeteria, the dining room, the rec hall, and last but not least the front office.

At first, the place touted only four bunkhouses, but six more were added throughout the years as it slowly grew to accommodate more and more residents over time. The place was originally intended to be living quarters for a rather large family of twenty-two; two parents, fourteen children, and six grandkids. However, suffering some unforeseen hardships and falling upon tough times a few decades down the road, the place was sold to a wealthy old Hollywood film producer who decided to give it a much-needed facelift.

There were two rows of three cabins that ran parallel with the lake, the other four structures creating an arch around the interior buildings like some sort of outdated, ill-conceived protection barrier between them and the surrounding forest. Off to the east was the overgrown baseball field and equipment shack, alongside the archery range. To the west was the fire pit, canoe shed, and repair shop, adjacent to the flagpole where campers and counselors convened first thing in the morning and each and every night to close out the day.

Dark dense woods flanked the place like an eerie army from beyond the dead, suffocating the area on all three sides. The fourth and only open spot untouched by the necrotic canopy of pine, was controlled by the slick shadowy waters of the stealthy steely lake that lay to the south. It was like an entity all in itself, or at least that's what it felt

S is for Slasher

like at times.

Large metal warning signs were posted on every individual light pole, fence, dock, and cabin door on the premises, informing boaters and swimmers to beware when participating in extracurricular activities while out on the water as it was strictly prohibited. Accidents were bound to happen, and there was no reason not to be fully prepared for them when the time came.

There was no lifeguard on duty and therefore patrons were left to their own devices when navigating the water; the signs said so themselves, loud and clear. Nothing had happened so far this summer – the first time in the history of the camp – but, if the stories we'd heard were true, it was only a matter of time before someone called in a code W69, possible accidental drowning.

Reports filed throughout the years seemed to collaborate the fact that there was at least one liquid-related injury or fatality a month, ever since the place originally opened. The first death dated all the way back to Calvin Kadavar's second youngest daughter, Katherine Kadavar, who unfortunately fell ill after secretly drinking the lake water for a week without anyone knowing, leaving her heaving her guts out until her insides were on the outside. It wasn't the most pleasant story, but then again neither were the majority of those that tended to circulate around the campfire.

That's one of the most tried and treasured traditions on campus, spinning yarns so terrifying your bunk mates won't be able to sleep for weeks, if

S is for Slasher

you possess the gift of gab, that is. Tales about creatures lurking in the darkness, homicidal campers searching for their next unsuspecting victim, and all other things that go bump in the night while you rest your eyes for a spell. It's really quite frightening if you think about it, which I'd rather not. Although sometimes I can't seem to help myself.

So, anyhow, to the north of Camp Kadaver is nothing but miles upon miles of green open woodlands, appearing to continue on and on forever like some never-ending painting from a world-famous artist that has yet to make a name for himself. It's very easy to get lost and turned around out here, especially if you aren't the average outdoorsman type. Campers were warned and cautioned about the potential dangers of exploring the uncharted woods by their lonesome. Enter at your own risk was the usual go-to deterrent.

At night you could hear dozens of different animals howling at the moon and rummaging around the forest floor, searching for something to catch their eye and tickle their fancy. It was a playground for the wicked, the sun methodically concealing itself behind a large monstrous mountaintop like some warped twisted game of hide and seek. You had to be on your best behavior when nightfall reared its ugly head, lest you'd find yourself offered up as the next link atop the food chain.

We all met up together an hour later as previously planned, fanning out in groups of five to sweep the surrounding campgrounds. Everyone was equipped with a flashlight and first aid kits were given to the select few who knew how to properly use them. They'd take all the help they could get, it was all hands on deck.

At about half past eleven o'clock, just as the counselors were about to call it quits and pack it in for the night, someone screamed, alerting any searcher within earshot to their unfortunate findings. Blood, bones, and clumps of matted hair were all that was left of the once lively individual, who now appeared glossy-eyed with one arm ripped completely out of the socket, lying discarded next to her.

The young, battered victim was that of Annabella Higgins, whose body had been discovered about half a mile from the camp, shredded like a slab of beef and left rotting under a decrepit old fallen log, a sight no one could possibly unsee no matter how badly they wanted to. One of those sad saps was yours truly. It was appalling. I felt bad for the poor thing. I really did.

Upon the horrific discovery of the mangled ravaged body, a curfew was instituted and immediately put into effect, hoping to curb any further incidents. The consensus was that an animal had attacked and killed the girl, leaving her mutilated corpse for the rest of the bottom feeders to scavenge and feed off of. The only thing was, there were no bite marks to be found on the body of the deceased.

It was like an invisible assailant had planned and

S is for Slasher

perpetrated the entire thing, yet there wasn't any evidence to back it up, except for the dead camper of course. The other two missing children were still nowhere to be found, those in charge expecting they'd make an appearance anytime soon. However, something fishy was afoot.

The next morning, after heavy contemplation, it was decided that camp activities would resume like normal, although there was nothing normal about it. There was a week left before the end of the season and no one wanted to disrupt all the work that'd been done up to that point. So, against better judgment, things continued as usual, despite the tragic circumstances.

That didn't last long, however, as later in the evening another kid turned up, this time in cabin number eight – the boys' bunkhouse. Spencer Bradley had indeed returned just like everyone believed he would, there was just one problem. He was as dead as a doornail.

A couple of the children had returned to grab a towel and don some swim trunks, looking to take a quick dip in the lake. What they found sent shivers racing up their spines. Hanging from the ceiling, suspended in mid-air by a handful of large grappling hooks dangling at the ends of half a dozen metal chains, was Spencer Bradley. Naked. And gutted.

Whoever had strung him up definitely wanted him to be found. Why else would he be displayed the way he was?

Those who saw it were forever scarred by the

S is for Slasher

macabre sight, unable to shake it, ultimately carrying the horrific image with them to their graves. His chest had been sliced open from groin to his sternum, and his fleshy pink skin had been flayed like fresh fish at a meat market.

Blood covered the floor like a barrel of sticky strawberry ice cream on a hot sunny day, and itty-bitty chunks of chipped bone and muscle littered the crimson cream like a layer of crunchy candy sprinkles. His sternum had been removed, along with all his internal organs; he was now just a hollowed-out husk of the boy he once was.

The smell was excruciatingly putrid and rotten, causing those in the vicinity to gag and nearly lose their lunches. Flies swarmed the chiseled steak statue like a McDonald's dumpster after closing time.

Why someone would do something so evil, so sadistic, was a new one to me. I mean, everyone has those deep dark feelings, or so we've been led to believe. But, acting on them goes against everything we're taught from a young age. Rules are there for a reason, and rebellion against such ordinances is typically not recommended, if one can help it.

I couldn't imagine the magnitude of mental detachment and unrelenting will it would take for someone to pull off such a repulsive act of artistic torture. It was a masterpiece, unlike anything we'd ever seen before, or since. There was simply nothing like it.

Worst part of all, someone had shoved a rusty old nail into his forehead like a pincushion, a crude little parting gift on his way out. It was like they were trying to send a message or something, only we had no clue what any of it meant. We were dumbfounded.

Three more kids went missing over the next couple of days, and things had gotten so bad, the camp director was on the verge of shutting the whole thing down and calling it quits for the first time in the history of Camp Kadavar.

Accidents were one thing, this was another. No one had ever been intentionally killed on the property before, at least not that anyone was aware of. The fear was so palpable, you could slice it with a scalpel.

If we didn't know any better, we'd have thought they were putting on an elaborate Broadway show. Only this was reality and not some slick sleazy low budget production put on in a pinch to turn a profit. No, this wasn't that at all. This was something entirely different.

His body had been peeled like a potato, his skin stretched as far as physically capable. Yet, he appeared peaceful, like he was taking a much-needed nap after a hard day's work. His eyes were forced shut, as if whoever had committed the crime couldn't bear to have the boy staring at him while he scurried about.

Whoever it was knew exactly what they were doing. Everyone was on high alert. The killer wanted attention, and by god, they got it.

People were scared out of their minds, clinging to their bunks like their lives depended on it. The

S is for Slasher

cabins had been locked down like Fort Knox, and no one was allowed to come or go. If we needed to use the restroom, it had to be in groups of three or more, for safety reasons.

The boys from cabin eight were momentarily relocated to cabin seven, where the rest of the male campers resided. They were forced to temporarily coexist, overcrowded as it was. There was strength in numbers though, making them less likely to be preyed upon; the more the merrier as people sometimes say.

As for the girls, we all curled up in one big circle, everyone frightened to the core. Promises were made to watch each other's backs and keep one another safe, but that's one hell of a tall task to ask of a bunch of whiny kids and young adults. People are fallible by nature, it's ingrained in our DNA.

All night long we heard strange noises and saw things move that weren't really there. I'm surprised anyone got any sleep; a few campers snoozed the night away without a care in the world.

Not me though, I was too afraid to sleep. Not after seeing what I saw with Annabella and hearing about Spencer. My head was too busy to let me catch any z's.

A few hours of boredom can kill even the most creative of minds, and we definitely weren't scholars to begin with.

It was the longest night of my life, waiting for daylight to make its heavily anticipated return. We needed to come at this from a different angle, with

S is for Slasher

fresh eyes and unbiased opinions.

Around three AM though, things began to get a little blurry, and the next thing I knew I was being shaken awake at the buttcrack of dawn. The majority of the girls were already up and nervously pacing back and forth in the room, attempting to rid themselves of the anxiety and apprehension brought on by the previous ordeal.

All of a sudden there was a knock on the cabin door, startling the crap out of us. Our hearts raced like the Kentucky Derby, everyone wondering if they were perhaps going to be the next unlucky victim. We had no clue who was rapping on the pine, and no one so much as moved an inch.

Staring at each other for what felt like an eternity in Eternia, everyone held their breath, hoping someone else besides them would muster up the courage to answer it.

Finally, one of the girls walked over to the window next to the door and peeked through the curtain to see who it was.

"It's Leslie Kernan," said Samara Yamamaura, through a face full of stringy black hair.

Everyone simultaneously exhaled, breathing a much-needed sigh of relief. Leslie was a nice, shy, respectful boy, there was no way he had anything to do with the two deaths. In reality, the killer could be anyone, but it was extremely unlikely he had anything to do with it.

"It's okay, girls. You can open it," said counselor Asami Aoyama.

She was a tad strange, but the girls seemed to

trust her more than anyone else, including the other three female counselors. As soon as the word was given, the bolt was unlatched and the door swung wide open. Leslie stood there in his war-torn t-shirt and overalls, looking worse for wear.

"It's okay, it's just me," he said, reassuring them as he stepped through the threshold.

"What's going on? Is everything okay?" asked Asami.

"Well, There's been a... how do you say... development, I guess is the best way to put it."

"And what do you mean by that?" asked Asami, scratching the side of her head.

"Has someone else been hurt?" asked Angela Barker.

"Umm, well, you see..." he said, trailing off.

"What? Out with it already," said one of the other girls, unable to take the suspense any further.

He grinned like a virgin on prom night as he entered the room, his left arm concealed behind his back. At first, it looked like he was about to magically produce a bouquet of roses out of thin air and profess his love for someone, but as he brought his hand around, the cabin erupted in screams of terror.

Girls went scurrying, scampering like mice scrambling for survival as the boy slowly crept toward them, knife in hand. He started to protest, but it was too late, the damage had been done. The blade gleaned in the sunlight as he brought it into view, causing one girl to faint and smack her head on the wooden two-by-four frame of the bunk bed, on her way down. She was out like a light before she even hit the dust-caked floor.

One of the other girls bolted for the door and Leslie reached out right as she did, snagging her by the crook of the elbow. She managed to slip free from his grasp like she was made of grease, and then plowed through the hard thick pine, busting her way outside into the bright blinding glare of the sun.

As he encroached further into the room, his knuckles turned pale white as he gripped the blade's hilt with gusto. The girls were absolutely terrified, hiding their faces under sheets, pillows, and anything else they could find as his head swung from side to side, barking like a wolf in a chicken coup.

A few ran for the exit, myself included, our legs carrying us as fast as they could out into the harsh unrelenting daylight. Screams continued pouring from somewhere inside the cabin, Leslie repeating over and over again for everybody to stay calm, saying he meant no harm and that he wasn't going to hurt anyone.

He just wanted to talk, that was all – or so he swore up and down.

One of the girls grabbed an old oar off the nearby wall display and ran at the boy, swinging it with both hands like a baseball bat. He bobbed and ducked under the weapon, just barely avoiding contact with what would have most likely been a knockout blow, had it landed flush.

Realizing the camper intended to do him harm, he reared back and let his fist fly, lifting the girl off her feet, sending her soaring through the air like a bullfighter at a rodeo. She crashed into one of her bunkmates, knocking both of them unconscious.

Another girl blitzed him in the haze of confusion, slamming straight into his shoulder. He stumbled backwards, his arms flailing like a vaudevillian act as he teetered between toppling over and staying upright on his feet.

Suddenly, Ester Cole charged Leslie with a knife of her own, using all her strength to try cutting the twisted twit to pieces and put an end to the mess. But of course, he was ready, sidestepping her as she lunged at him, gouging a chunk out of her shoulder with a crisp clean blade of his own. The girl got what she deserved, an eye for an eye and all that jazz.

Standing out in front of the cabin, we watched intently as chaos continued to rear its ugly head. I was trying to wrap my mind around everything, but I couldn't understand it. Why was this happening, and what was the reason for attacking us?

There was no real provocation for what he was doing, at least none that we could decipher. He was just a sicko with an itch to scratch, nothing more. Getting off on the depravity of others was something he craved. There was no actual need for it, but he couldn't help himself.

Another girl suddenly burst through the doorway, jostling me out of the trance I was in. For a few moments, everything was moving in slow motion, the bizarre incident unfolding right in front of me. Unable to stand still any longer, I turned

S is for Slasher

around and booked it, my legs moving as fast as they could go.

Those who'd managed to escape the cabin scattered like cockroaches in a kitchen, running in whichever direction they could as the screams continued emanating from inside. To a random passerby, it probably sounded like the surprise party of the year, only there was no party and the surprise was a six-inch blade of steel jammed into your guts for shits and giggles.

I had no idea what to do, but I didn't want to stick around any longer than I had to. I'd hoof it into the forest and hide out as long as possible, until someone came looking for me, or the police arrived. If I stayed quiet and out of sight, maybe no one would notice I'd fled the scene altogether, although it was a long shot, I had to admit.

Either way, I had to hurry. It was only a matter of time before the morning massacre was through, then he'd come searching for stragglers. Psychos like him didn't leave witnesses, it was common horror knowledge 101.

As I ran, I rounded the next cabin, hooking a left, heading past the dock on my way to the tree line. I could feel my heart beating in my chest; boom, bap, bap; singing like a choir of angels coming to take me away, ha ha. Things couldn't possibly get any worse, or so I thought.

But boy was I wrong. Dead wrong.

Looking back over my shoulder to make sure no one was chasing me, something suddenly caught my eye, causing my feet to trip over themselves. What I

S is for Slasher

saw sent me into a feverish frenzy, forcing me to ponder the fate of my own mortality.

There, lying face down in the murky undergrowth of the old decaying dock, was the young boy by the name of Mason Vorhees. From the looks of it, he'd been floating there for quite a while, his head bumping off the rotted wood over and over again like some sadistic melodic metronome; thump, thump, thump...

The skin that had settled at water level was slushy and gooey like a week-old bowl of soggy corn flakes that had sat out in the heat way too long. The droopy, soppy, pulp-like contents were separating into tiny little clumps of slop each and every time the body thudded against the dock. I nearly vomited, holding it back at the last second like a seasoned alcoholic after a serious New Year's Eve bender.

One could only imagine how long he must have floated here, swimming with the fishes like he was.

It took me a few seconds standing there, frozen in place, staring at the boy's badly decaying corpse before I noticed it. Just behind his ear was an inch-wide knife wound, which ran all the way across his throat, disappearing into the cold black water before reappearing on the other side.

I could only guess it's what some criminals may refer to as a Columbian necktie, of sorts. Although I'm no crime scene investigator, obviously.

Registering another scream in the distance, I instantly zapped out of it, pulling myself back to earth from my momentary mental lapse. Seeing

S is for Slasher

something so wicked and vile was entrancing and absolutely mesmerizing. It was hard not to stare. But there were bigger problems at stake, and there was no more time to waste. I needed to jet, like yesterday, and I turned to hustle toward the boys' bunkhouse.

Approaching cabin seven at a full sprint, something terrible began to invade my nostrils and I almost choked, my eyes tearing up from the noxious fumes. Long, hulking tendrils of thick white smoke suddenly twisted and danced all around me, threatening to suffocate anything in their path. I couldn't believe what I was seeing, the place was ablaze.

Flames lapped at the sides like a dehydrated puppy on a hot summer day. Smoldering embers gently caressed the bright blue sky, as if to greet it with a *Good morning, how do you do? If I may...*

I couldn't help but stare in amazement, watching the thing sizzle and pop like a pig on a spit roast. The fire roared with wild abandon, when all of a sudden something moved behind a window, making my skin crawl.

It looked like the silhouette of a young child with a bulbous head, who must have somehow gotten trapped inside the burning structure, unaware of its eerie portents of doom. I couldn't tell if what I was seeing was real, until it began crying out for its father.

"Daddddddyyy! Daddddddyyy!"

The voice was extremely familiar, and at first I couldn't seem to place it. Then, out of the blue, it hit me like a bucket of bolts and the hair on my arms stood up.

I recalled one of the boys at the dance who had pretty much hid from the others like a recluse, due to his unsightly deformed dome. It was easy to see that he desperately wanted nothing to do with the other kids, feeling like he was an outcast in a strange world. Only, we were all outcasts in some peculiar fashion or another, if only he'd known.

The kid's name was Vic Crowley, as far as I could remember. He was a weird one, no doubt about it. But it wasn't his fault. He was born malformed, his mother passing away while giving birth.

Raised by his father, he was a bit of a daddy's boy, if that was even a thing. Feeling the urge to help, I covered my face with my shirt sleeve and approached the door.

I could hear his pleas clearly now, calling out for his daddy yet again. It was absolutely heartbreaking.

Putting my palm up to the door to gauge how hot it was, I could feel the abrasive heat emanating from inside. Smoke swirled and swished all around me like a genie from a magic lamp. My lungs burned like hell as I accidentally inhaled a mouthful of fumes.

Something had to be done, and fast. There had to be another way in, there just had to be. If I didn't do something quick, the boy might not make it to see tomorrow.

As I searched for an alternative opening, I realized there wasn't one. The cabin only had one

S is for Slasher

door and two windows, one on each side of opposing walls. The only option was to break one of the windows and hope for the best, and I ran around to the side of the cabin, looking for something to use to smash the glass.

It took a few seconds before I was successful, but I noticed a pile of firewood sitting off to the left and immediately raced to it, looking for something to use. After finding a withered old hatchet stuck in a log, I stepped up to the window and braced myself for impact. Safety coming first, I yelled out for the individual to back away, that I was going to break it.

"If you can hear me, move away from the window," I screamed. "I'm going to bust it out! Here I go! Cover your face!"

I counted to three and hucked the hatchet through the pane, shattering the glass into a thousand pieces. Another scream came from somewhere inside and I immediately peered through the hole, hoping to get a better look at the situation. From where I stood, there wasn't much hope.

The boy must have been standing too close to the window, because in between puffs of thick intoxicating smoke, I was able to get a good glimpse of him, and he wasn't doing so hot. Like something straight out of a Stephen King novel, the blade of the hatchet had somehow struck him directly in the face, splitting his grotesque mug into two separate halves.

He screamed bloody murder as he stumbled backwards into the flames, his hair catching on fire

S is for Slasher

as he spun around in circles. He'd remembered the stop and roll part, but somehow he'd forgotten the drop portion. Not like it mattered one way or the other though, the poor kid was doomed.

Knowing there was nothing more I could do for him, I ran, deciding to try to recruit some help, if there was any. However, I knew finding someone in such an insane mess would be a chore all in of itself. And it certainly was.

As I tore off from the decrepit scene, I continued huffing it toward the camp director's cabin, hoping against all odds I'd find some kind of relief, some sort of assistance.

It was a crap shoot though, the place was empty, barren like the dirt-covered floor of the Mojave desert. It was extremely unsettling. Where had everyone gone? There was no one in sight. It was a bit jarring.

Then, as I grew near the west side of the property, I knew I wasn't alone. Lying in the middle of the fire pit, burnt to a Cajun crisp, was the charred and tattered remains of one of the boys. It was Teddy Krueger, in a red and green sweater – or what was left of it anyhow – along with a handful of long blackened knives sprawled out next to him.

Just as I was about to turn and high tail it out of there, a soft gurgling noise caught my ear, apparently coming from the badly overcooked cadaver. Focusing my attention on him, I suddenly became aware he was still breathing. Just barely.

"Oh my god," I said, kneeling over his body.

His crusty hat and dirty old sweater had both

melted into his skin, fusing with his flesh like a cheaply cauterized two-bit robocop. I had a hard time telling where his shirt began and where his torso ended. Not to mention the awful acrid smell of burnt tissue and bone. It was enough to make a grown man cry. Or anyone for that matter.

"You're going to be alright," I said, knowing damn well it was a lie.

Looking at me through deliquesced eyes, I got the feeling he wanted to tell me something. I don't know how I knew it, but there was something sincere and ardent behind those scorched forest greens.

I felt sorry for the kid, I really did. Hell, I felt bad for all of them, every last one.

"Don't worry," I said, "I'll get him for you. I promise I will!"

His lips – or what was left of them – began moving, the smallest whisper escaping through blackened teeth.

"What? What is it?" I said, leaning in closer.

His lips moved again, so little that it almost didn't register at first.

"I can't understand you," I said, leaning in even closer this time. So close in fact, I could feel the softness from his breath tickling my inner ear.

It took a few moments for me to understand what he was trying to say. But, once I did, everything went wonky and wobbly.

"It wasn't Leslie," he whispered. "It wasn't Leslie."

He must be delirious, I thought, shaking my

S is for Slasher

head. *He has no idea what he's saying. The fire no doubt caused some serious brain damage, that was all.*

But that wasn't all it was.

"I saw him do it though," I said, shaking my head in disapproval. "It was him."

However, something deep down told me that maybe I hadn't seen what I thought I'd seen. I never actually saw him stab anyone, and he had been saying that he just wanted to talk to us, nothing more.

"Check the cabin," he whispered through pursed lips. "Check the cabin."

Still unsure if I believed him or not, I knew he needed medical assistance. And stat.

"I'm going to go find help! I'll be right back," I said, cursing myself the second the words left my mouth.

Great. Now they're going to find you dead as a dingbat. Great. Just great, I thought.

As I got up and started to run again, I couldn't help but think of all the mindless murder and mayhem that had plagued our peaceful little camp over the last few days. How could this all happen? It was demented, demoralizing, and downright evil.

It didn't take long before I forgot all about it, however, when I came upon the next set of cabins. As I passed by the place, my gaze was drawn to an open door, where inside sitting on a couch in front of a tv playing the weirdest film I've ever seen, was Samara Yamamaura, her eyes missing from their bleeding sockets.

S is for Slasher

And, if that wasn't enough, sitting to her right was Ken Willis, dressed in his favorite black rain slicker, with a large ice hook stuck through the middle of his throat, sideways. They sat there together in a pool of their own blood, forever intertwined as one. It was devastating.

A few yards further lay three more bodies, each one riddled with multiple stab wounds and a bullet to the head for good measure. It was Amber Free, Brenda Yates, and Ester Cole, three of my bunkmates who'd run and escaped the attack at the girls' cabin a few moments earlier. They all looked like they had been caught by surprise. Probably taking a minute to catch their breath while trying to figure out a way out of this.

Before I knew it, I passed by another wide-open door, where two more bodies lay side by side on a carpeted floor, just inside the room. It was Charlie Ray and Tiffany Valentino, holding hands, fingers interlocked, face to face like it was some sort of suicide pact or something.

They looked peaceful, yet there was something off about them. I could just tell. Maybe it had to do with the creepy looking dolls sitting next to them, then again maybe not. Either way, I swear one of them was smiling and winked at me. But I couldn't be sure.

As I kept running, heading to the camp director's cabin to use the phone and call the police, something occurred to me. Someone was responsible for all of this, but I still didn't know who. Was it really Leslie, or perhaps someone else?

S is for Slasher

I didn't know what to think. I was so confused.

Nearing my destination, I came to a halt once again as I caught sight of another dead body, this one being the boy named Daniel Rob. He was sitting under a tree, its trunk serving as a backrest, his chest cracked open and exposed with thousands upon thousands of bees circling his head. They were busily buzzing about as they crawled in and out of his ears, nose, and mouth, hurriedly trying to settle into their new domain.

It was sickening, the incessant grating sound of the insects hard at work erecting their new comb inside their new home. I knew that if I somehow survived this insidiously wretched night, I'd never eat honey again. Not after watching the gore-soaked scene in front of me. I would have puked my guts out right then and there, had there been any left at that point.

Pushing on, I willed myself forward, running on wobbly legs until I finally managed to arrive at my target location. The door was shut and I banged on it as hard as I could, screaming for someone to let me in. After realizing the place was empty, I had no other choice but to risk it and break in, nothing but a slab of pine separating me from my lifeline.

I was about to kick it in, or at least try my hardest to do so, when it occurred to me to simply try the handle first. In the movies, people always leave stuff unlocked, and of course, the darn thing turned with ease, opening inward with a slow, ear-piercing screech.

You would have thought I was trying to raise the

S is for Slasher

dead the way the door creaked on its hinges, acting like an outraged omen of the slimy savage things to come. The shades on both of the windows had been drawn, casting the room in a deep, shadowy darkness and I ran my hand against the wall, searching for a switch of any kind.

A second later my fingers found what they were looking for, lighting the place up like the Fourth of July.

The phone was on the counter off to the right, plugged in over in the dining area, the internal layout of the cabin different from all the others, being the most luxurious space of all on the campgrounds. It was fit for a king, or the camp director, who I hadn't seen since the night before, now that I thought about it. Knowing every second counted, I shook it off and made a beeline for the old, outdated relic.

Like a flash I was there, receiver in hand, dialing as quickly as possible, hoping like hell I'd survive this treacherous summer camp. I was really beginning to hate this place, all things considered. I just wanted out of here, and now it was starting to feel like I'd be trapped in this godforsaken place forever.

While I stood there, waiting for the line to start ringing on the other end, I suddenly became hyper-aware that there was no dial tone. It was as flat as a flutist on rock and roll night at Carnegie Hall. This couldn't be happening.

Adrenaline on overdrive, I was mad as hell and began to lose it for the first time since all of this had

S is for Slasher

started. I'd held on as long as possible, but at what point is it all just a little too much? I couldn't bear it any longer. And then I finally looked out into the rest of the cabin, taking stock of my surroundings.

And that's when I saw it.

Sitting on the sofa, facing the only television allowed on the property, was snooty little Pam Palmer. Or, well... what was left of her, I guess. You see, her head was resting on the most eloquent high-end glass-top coffee table I'd ever seen, separate from its blood-stained body on the cushion.

Sticky yellow tissue oozed out the base of the skull, holding the head upright. It was like an elaborate horror movie scene, every tiny detail logged and accounted for. It was too real, too much to take, seeing her sitting there like the headless horseman from that old campfire fable.

Blood dripped from the glass and I screamed at the top of my lungs, unable to refrain any longer. The madness had taken control and I just wanted it to be over already. Without thinking, I'd inadvertently alerted anyone within range to my location, although I wasn't really sure how much it mattered at this moment.

Out of nowhere, there was a loud vicious bang coming from behind me, nearly knocking me out of my socks. Scared out of my skin, I frantically searched for somewhere to hide, not wanting to become another notch on the dead man's dead post.

As I surveyed the interior of the cabin, I noticed an old beaten and battered laptop, and I rushed to it like a kid on Christmas, hoping for some sort of

S is for Slasher

salvation.

Snatching it up, I booked it to the bathroom post haste, the only place left to hide from all this insanity. Soon they'd come looking for me – whoever was responsible for all of this – and there was nowhere left to run.

There was another loud bang, this time much closer than the last, and I knew I was in trouble. As quickly as I could, I hit the power button and turned on the computer, hoping to write this letter as fast as my fingers would fly.

And that brings us to now, as I sit here on this white porcelain throne, awaiting my feculent fate. Who could have guessed this is how it would end? Not me. Definitely not me.

So, in case something happens to me, show this to the authorities, they'll know what to do with it.

Wait… what was that?

I heard something…

There it is again…

Someone's coming...

I'm definitely not alone anymore. There's someone else in here with me. I know it.

Wait… I can see something...

No way…

It can't be…

It's…

It's…

But I thought you were…

No freaking way…

It just can't be…

Wait, stop… What are you doing…?

S is for Slasher

Don't come any closer!
What's that behind your ba…
No!
Stop!
Don't do that!
No!
Stop!
Please...
Please…

S is for Slasher

Framing Tina

Peter Hayward-Bailey

Kirsty zipped up her coat as the cold wind whipped around her, blowing her curly red hair about her face. She pulled her wild hair back and tied it in a messy bun as she walked at speed down the footpath. She just couldn't get used to these winter nights and she was now rushing back home as darkness fell. Kirsty couldn't face the wrath of her stepmother, because she knew that it would end in a big blow-out, where her dad would end up taking the bitch's side, and Kirsty would be grounded for the foreseeable future. She quickly looked left and right as she stepped into the road, crossing at a jog. She decided to take a shortcut through the park to cut out half the journey. It was creepy in the dark, but it would get her home before the last shreds of daylight faded, thus saving her from getting grounded.

Kirsty heard an owl hoot overhead, which was so loud it startled her, and she craned her neck, looking around to see if she could spot the elusive nocturnal predator. As she turned back to continue, she bumped into someone walking in the opposite direction.

S is for Slasher

"Sorry," she began to say, but the word got stuck in her throat as she immediately felt a burning sensation at her side. She looked down and saw dark red staining her top and looked up in horror as the figure that she'd bumped into advanced quickly on her. A hand clad in a black leather glove revealed the switchblade that had just slashed her side, as the figure grabbed her and began to repeatedly stab her in the abdomen. Kirsty began to cry out, and the attacker jammed the blade behind her windpipe and pulled, releasing a torrent of blood from her throat as the knife cut clean through her larynx, shredding muscle and sinew as it created a gaping wound that bubbled as Kirsty gargled on her own blood, trying to gasp for life-saving air that could not be taken in. She fell to her hands and knees and watched as the frosty grass underneath her began to flow with blood. She fell face down into the puddle of red, and as she started to black out, she felt the blade being forced into her back, over and over and over.

***

By Monday morning, it was all over school. The news of one of the most popular girls being slaughtered but mere minutes from her home was both thrilling and horrifying the other teens on campus. Rumours were already flying about who the killer could be.

One of the most popular theories was that it was an older boyfriend who had been given the brush

S is for Slasher

off.

"Did you know about any secret boyfriend?" asked Josh, sitting on the front steps leading up to the school. Josh was a tall, gangly teen who wore baggy clothes that seemed to make his frame even more noticeable. He had pale skin and sharp features that would have looked cartoonish on most people, but his pointed nose and strong jawline suited him. He'd been a friend of Kirsty's since starting high school.

"No man, you know she wasn't interested in boys. Dating anyone wasn't her thing," replied Tom, settling in beside Josh. Tom was Josh's friend, who tagged along on the outskirts of the friend group. He'd asked Kirsty out on a number of occasions, to the point where they'd had to have a word with him about boundaries and taking no for an answer. Tom was short where Josh was tall, and broad where Josh was lanky. They looked like a comedy double act paired together. He had cropped brown hair that was plastered down on his head with too much gel, piercing blue eyes that always had a bit of a wild look about them, full lips, and a nose that looked like it had been broken a couple of times. He wouldn't have looked out of place in an old gangster movie.

"I wouldn't put it past that bitch stepmother of hers. Get her out of the picture so she can have daddy all to herself," cut in Tina, a grim look on her face, and a razor-sharp tone to her words. Tina was almost as tall as Josh, but not half as wiry. She had a round face, with large brown eyes and a slightly

S is for Slasher

up-turned nose. Her face was framed by long, straight, black hair that she wore down. She had thick, winged eyeliner in the same jet black as her hair, with matching painted nails, and an equally dark wardrobe to finish her gothic look.

"That's cold, man!" laughed Josh, sweeping his blonde fringe out of his eyes.

"Yeah, well she is cold!" replied Tina, pulling her arms tight around her and gazing to the floor as if in troubled thought.

The bell rang and they all began to meander into the looming, grey building. What followed was a long assembly about staying safe, not walking out alone in the evenings, and messages of condolences for a bright young star that would no longer shine. There were some tears shed from the classmates that knew Kirsty, and some dazed looks from those who would rather be anywhere else.

For Tina, the day dragged along at a snail's pace, but she'd rather be here than sat moping at home and she felt like she had already cried out all the tears she could. Her and Kirsty had been close ever since Tina had transferred to the school a couple of years ago. When everyone gave the new weird goth kid a wide berth, Kirsty had made sure she felt accepted and had a reason to look forward to coming to school each day. After that, the pair had been almost inseparable, and had had many a sleepless slumber party sharing their innermost secrets into the night. This is why Tina thought that Kirsty's stepmother could be involved. The stories that Kirsty had told her about Joy's cruel streak could make her blood turn to ice just bringing them to the forefront of her memory. They used to joke about how such an awful, mean person could have a name like Joy. "The death of Joy" is what they'd nicknamed her.

When the final bell rang, Tina was already waiting at the school entrance for Josh, and inevitability Tom, to meet her for the walk home. They had been told that under no circumstances were they to leave school alone at such a dangerous time. As Tina began to make her way down the steps to avoid the surge of teens exiting the building, a black Mercedes came to a screeching halt in front of the school. Joy stepped from the car and marched straight over to Tina, her heels making an echoing clacking sound on the pavement. She wore a black pant suit, her short hair styled in a flat side parting at the front and pointed at the back. Her face was a red mask of fury.

"This is all your fault!" spat Joy, getting way too close to Tina and making her step backwards.

"Kirsty's father is in bits, and it's all because of you! If she hadn't started hanging around with freaks like you, this never would have happened!"

"This had nothing to do with being a "freak". She was murdered, this wasn't some kind of Satanic ritual or whatever the fuck you're thinking!" retorted Tina, trying to stand her ground. She didn't even see Joy's hand coming before the slap knocked her off balance and Tina fell to the ground.

"Don't you dare speak to me like that! I know full well you're all into weird shit, and my daughter should never have gotten mixed up with the likes of you! She might still be here then!"

"She wasn't your daughter! And don't you try to blame any of this on me! I love Kirsty! And I know all about what went on behind the closed doors of your perfect little world. And if anyone else did they'd be pointing the finger at you," Tina said as she wiped a trickle of blood from her chin with the back of her hand.

By now a small crowd had started to gather and, as Joy bared her teeth in a snarl and ran at Tina to hit her again, a teacher emerged from the crowd of gawking teens and grabbed Joy, telling her to calm down and ushering her to her car. As soon as this all happened, Joy immediately began to play the grieving mother and collapsed, sobbing into the teacher's arms.

At that moment Josh and Tom pushed their way through the crowd and Josh helped Tina to her feet.

"C'mon. Let's get you out of here and cleaned up. Don't worry about that psycho bitch."

Just as Josh had got those words out, Joy began screaming and pointing at Tina.

"That girl is poison! She's the reason my daughter is dead, and I want her removed from this school!"

The teacher carried on in vain trying to calm her down as the three turned and began to walk away from the school.

"Just ignore her," Josh soothed, "just listen to my voice and keep walking."

On the walk home, Tom was getting more and

S is for Slasher

more enraged, concocting all sorts of plans to get back at Joy, from slashing her tyres, to putting fireworks through her letterbox. Josh was still trying to be a calming influence and was talking Tom down from his criminal ideas. When they arrived at her home, an old-fashioned, red brick two-bedroom semi, Tina was exhausted and filled with a feeling of helplessness. If she'd fought back, she'd only have given Joy, and everyone else, a reason to ostracise the "freak" even more. Tina's parents were rarely home, and when they were Tina was mostly ignored, which right now suited her just fine. She told the boys that she just wanted to get cleaned up and turn in for the night. After convincing them that she was going to be okay, and telling Tom not to try anything stupid, they said their goodbyes. Now that she was alone, all she wanted to do was curl up and sleep. She took a long, hot shower, and changed into some pyjama pants and a vest, patterned with tiny *Star Wars* characters. She perched at her open bedroom window to light a joint, letting the chilly evening air wake her up a little. Tina let the smoke fill her lungs and held it there, until her head began to swim in the sweet, green haze. She released it with a long exhale out of the window and let her foggy thoughts drift back to her best friend. A tear rolled down her cheek as she put the joint to her lips again and began to inhale.

***

A hand, clad in a black leather glove, turned the

handle of Tina's front door. She'd forgotten to lock it on her way in because of all that had been troubling her thoughts, and it opened with a soft click. A figure dressed all in black crept into the dark house, moving around with the ease of someone who knew the layout of the place... someone who had been here before. The figure climbed the stairs slowly, deliberately, missing the steps that would creak underfoot. They crept towards Tina's room and slowly nudged the door open.

Tina lay tangled up in her duvet, snoring softly and sleeping heavily thanks to the weed. The figure took a moment to look at her, looming over her in the darkness. They stretched one gloved hand out towards her, holding a gleaming steel switchblade. The tip of the blade rested delicately against her face and the killer silently stroked it down her cheek. Tina stirred a little and brushed at her face, mumbling in her sleep. The figure retracted their arm and slowly backed out of the room.

The next bedroom belonged to Tina's parents and the figure stealthily entered their room next. They had both been drinking for most of the evening and probably wouldn't have woken even if the killer had stomped into the room. The leather clad hands picked up a throw pillow that had been discarded on the floor, and stood over the bed, staring down at the two sleeping bodies. They put the pillow firmly over Tina's dad's face and held it in place with one hand, while the other hand slashed a deep gash into his throat in one fluid motion. The blood began to flow freely from the wound and the bed clothes started to become saturated with it. The man's body began to twitch and convulse as the life quickly left it, and the killer moved around the bed, placed the now bloody pillow over Tina's mum's face and made the same cut, from ear to ear, opening a jagged crimson grin across her neck.

When both of them were no longer among the living, and the blood had stopped flowing, the killer silently made their exit from the house.

***

As the dawn chorus began to drift in through Tina's open window she sluggishly got up from her bed, shivering at the cold, wintery morning air that filled the room, and started to get ready for the day. After she had dressed, she headed downstairs to grab some breakfast before going to school. She looked around downstairs to find that her parents hadn't stirred yet. "Fucking drunks," she said under her breath and went to the kitchen to pour herself some cereal.

On her way to school she met up with Tom and Josh, and the three fell into step together with a comfortable familiarity.

"How are you doing this morning?" asked Josh in a concerned tone.

"We totally thought you'd ditch after all that shit yesterday," added Tom before she'd had chance to answer.

"I'm fine, it'll take more than a slap from the

S is for Slasher

wicked witch of the west to keep me down! Honestly, I'd rather be at school than moping about all day and baby-sitting my hungover parents. At least it helps keep my mind off things." Tom and Josh shared a knowing look.

"Yeah, well if that psycho shows up again I'll fucking take her down myself!" Tom jeered.

"Dude, you need to calm down. Getting yourself expelled and arrested isn't going to do anyone any good," Josh cut in, putting his hand on Tom's shoulder.

As they approached the school Tina looked out for Joy's car, and to her secret relief couldn't see it anywhere.

The school day started out in the normal way, the monotony of moving from classroom to classroom, being jostled and ushered on by the swarm of students, like zombies ambling to each class, zoning in and out of each teacher speaking in a tone that it seemed had been meticulously honed to be as boring as possible.

It was during third period History, when Mr Myers was droning on about some war that had happened long before anyone in this building was alive, when it all went wrong. There was a knock at the classroom door and the headteacher stepped in. He strode over to Mr Myers and whispered something to him with urgency. Mr Myers nodded and then the head beckoned over to the door. Two police officers entered the classroom and Mr Myers pointed at Tina. She sat up straight in her chair, mind racing with what could have happened now.

The officers both advanced on Tina, one to either side of her, and the first one, a burly, middle aged man with leathery skin and a buzz-cut, looked down at her and said, "Miss, please come with us."

"What's this about?" she replied, not moving.

Both of the officers put a hand on each of her elbows as if to move her from her seat.

"What the hell are you doing?" she spat, trying to shake them off. "Tell me what this is about!"

They looked at one another and an unspoken conversation took place between them. They pulled her from her seat and forced her hands behind her back as officer number two, a tall, muscular woman with blonde hair pulled back in a tight ponytail, placed handcuffs over her wrists.

"Miss Christina Greyson, you are under arrest for the murders of your mother and father, you have the right to remain silent…"

"What the fuck? My parents aren't dead! What are you talking about!?" Tina struggled in their grip and tears began to roll down her cheeks, leaving a trail of black make-up running from her eyes.

"… Anything you do say can be used against you in a court of law…"

"Please, I didn't do anything, my parents… they can't be…"

"… you have the right to an attorney, if you cannot afford representation then one will be provided for you."

Hearing her rights read out like this made the whole thing even more surreal, like it was some kind of crime show she was watching on TV. Tina's brain could not comprehend that her parents were dead, and that the police thought she had killed them. She didn't have a good relationship with them, but she could never wish such a thing for them. She seemed to go into a state of shock and stopped struggling and shouting over the officers. They began to walk her out of the classroom, flanking her on either side, as the teens in the class looked on, some horrified and others morbidly entertained.

***

In the police station, Tina was led into a small, grey room with nothing but a table and chairs, and one small window, high up on the wall covered by steel bars.

She was sat down at the table, and the officers left her there for a moment and stepped out. She had been un-cuffed when she had been sat down, and Tina absent-mindedly rubbed at her wrists while she still tried to make sense of what was happening to her.

The door opened and the officers walked back in, sitting down across the table from her. Officer number two put a folder down on the table and opened it.

"Quite a bloodbath you left at home," she said as she began to lay pictures out on the table. "What would make you do something like this?"

Tina tried to keep her eyes up, but they defied her and drifted down to the photos on the table. As

S is for Slasher

her mind processed what she was seeing, her mother and father side by side in bed, eyes closed, throats wide open, the dark colour of their blood covering them, drenching the bed, bile rose in her throat and tears began to sting the back of her eyes. She pushed the pictures away as she began to heave, tears streaming down her face for the second time today.

"Quit the dramatics. Tell us what made you slice up Mummy and Daddy. Were they mean to you? Ground you one too many times? Was it the heavy metal music telling you to do it? Or the disgusting horror movies you watch? We saw all the creepy and weird shit in your room, god knows what goes on in that head of yours."

Tina was taking deep breaths in through her nose, trying to calm the storm in her stomach.

"I didn't do this," she replied, her voice small and trembling as she tried to hold back sobs. She looked at the police officer through the tears welling up in her eyes. "I couldn't have done this. I've just lost my best friend; I can't lose anyone else."

"And where were you last night?" the other officer piped up, seemingly ignoring what Tina had just said.

"I... I was at home. I didn't even see Mum and Dad. They were out when I got in. And I had an early night, I'd had a bad day."

"We've heard all about the bad day," said officer number two. "Heard about you antagonising the woman who just lost a child!"

"That's not what happened," said Tina

defensively. "She assaulted me, I loved Kirsty."

Suddenly the door of the interrogation room slammed open and a glamorous middle-aged woman, with thick, curly ginger hair streaked with white and glaring green eyes strode into the room wearing a smart, charcoal pinstripe business suit.

"Please do not say anything further to my client. This girl had the right to legal representation, and you had no right to begin interrogating her without me present. As it stands, you have nothing with which to charge her at this time, and you cannot hold her."

She placed papers down in front of the officers. "Please contact my office and we can arrange the official proceedings, but for now, my client is coming with me." She beckoned Tina to follow her out of the room. Tina was so stunned she could only stare open mouthed as she stood from the table and gingerly followed this magnificent force from the room. She glanced at the officers as she walked past them, expecting them to grab her at any moment and push her back into the seat.

When they were exiting the building, Tina finally found her voice again.

"Who are you? How did you know I was here?" The woman turned to Tina, and put her hands on her shoulders, looking her in the face with a sympathetic expression.

"Christina, I'm Jess Bradford. I'm Kirsty's aunt, and I've been seeing everything that's been going on. Kirsty was very dear to me, and she used to confide in me all the time, even more so after her

S is for Slasher

mother, my sister, died. She needed family that she could depend on, and that would have her back. I'm just so damn sorry I couldn't have had her back that night!" Jess looked down and took a deep breath to stop herself choking up. "Kirsty told me all about you, and what you meant to each other, so with everything going on I know she would have wanted me to help you, and luckily for you I run my own law firm."

"Wow," said Tina, looking for an appropriate response. "Kirsty told me about you. I'm so grateful for this. Thank you so much, but what happens now?"

"Well, you can't go back home because it's a crime scene, and you can't leave town because the police will want you for further questioning, so for now you're coming home with me. You'll be safe, and I can work on your defence with you."

Tina's eyes had filled with tears again at the mention of her home being a crime scene.

"Can I get any of my things from home?" she asked hopefully.

"I'm afraid not, but we can pick up some bits for you to wear on the way. Come on, let me get you back, you could really use some rest."

Jess led Tina to her car, a sleek, blue vehicle that looked like some classic American muscle car. They stopped by a supermarket and picked up some clothes and a toothbrush for Tina, before continuing on to Jess's house. As Jess drove, Tina rested her head against the window, watching all the streets and scenery pass her by without taking any of it in.

S is for Slasher

She'd completely zoned out and drifted off to sleep. She was woken gently by Jess when they'd arrived at her place, a modern townhouse on the outskirts of the city, and she took her inside. She showed her to the guest bedroom where she had already laid out some towels and toiletries for her.

Once she'd showered and changed, Tina padded barefoot to the living room wearing shorts and a vest to meet Jess. Jess had changed too, and was now also in pyjamas, looking comfortable and at ease. She invited Tina to sit with her on the sofa and poured her a cup of tea.

"Right, we're not going to talk about anything heavy tonight, you're still in shock and you need some time to process. We're going to order some food, and then you can get some much-needed rest."

Tina just looked at her and nodded, lost for words and still feeling so grateful to this person for swooping in and helping her when things seemed like they couldn't possibly get any worse. They ordered pizza, and then Tina turned in for the night. She didn't know what tomorrow would bring, and her mind was a buzz of many different avenues of thought as she was claimed by a fitful and dreamless sleep.

***

As the hours drew on into the night, the menacing figure clad all in black silently entered Jess's house. She had left a window open slightly due to an unseasonably warm evening, which was

S is for Slasher

enough for the killer to gain access with ease. They were camouflaged by the darkness of the unlit home as they stalked slowly through the living room, running a gloved hand over the furniture as they went.

As the killer got to the top of the stairs, the bathroom door opened and Jess stepped out. The light from the bathroom flooded the landing and top of the stairs and she immediately laid eyes on the figure stood staring back at her through a black mask. They lunged at her, pulling out a flick knife that gleamed in the light. Jess screamed as she darted back into the bathroom, trying to slam the door to block the intruder's advance. They got to the door before she could get it shut and the force of their momentum knocked Jess backwards. She staggered and fell towards the bath. As she lost her balance her arms flailed to grab hold of something to steady her, but she grabbed the shower curtain and pulled it down with her, ripping it from the rail as she fell backwards into the bath. The killer seized this opportunity and grabbed at the curtain, wrapping it and tangling it around Jess so that she was fighting against it, unable to get up from the tub. The killer raised the flick knife and brought it down, piercing through the curtain and into Jess. She screamed at the burning sensation of the blade slicing through her flesh, and as she thrashed in the bath, becoming more tangled with the curtain, the knife came down again and again. Blood stains began to expand over the curtain and Jess's screams became weak sobs. When Jess became silent, the

S is for Slasher

killer stood and left the bathroom, wiping the blade on a hand towel on the way out and closing the door behind them.

Tina had woken with a start at the sound of screaming and had immediately thrown herself into action trying to protect herself. She pushed a chair up against the door and began to search the room frantically for something that could be used as a weapon. She was still turning the room upside down when someone began banging urgently on the other side of the door. Tina let out a sharp scream and jumped, turning to face the door with a look of sheer terror in her eyes. The banging came again, this time followed by a voice.

"Tina! Tina! Are you in there!? I came to check up on you, make sure you were okay, and then I heard screaming so I came in to help you."

"Josh, is that you?" Tina responded in a shaking voice.

"It's me, now open up. I got the killer good, I think he's out cold, so we'd better get out of here."

"We need to call the police and make sure Jess is okay," Tina said as she un-barricaded the door and opened it a crack to peep out. She saw Josh there, out of breath and sweating. She flung the door open and embraced him.

"It's already taken care of," Josh said. "Now let's go!"

She followed him out from her room and they began to descend the stairs. At the bottom, they turned into the living room. Tina froze as she saw a figure, dressed all in black, face covered with a black mask standing at the other side of the room, blocking the way to the front door. She turned to run and Josh stood in her way.

"Josh, we need to go! The killer is awake!" she said frantically, trying to push Josh back the way they had come.

Josh reached out one hand and shoved Tina back with enough force to send her off balance, knocking her off her feet.

"That's because I never knocked him out. I just wanted you out of your room, and you were more than ready to listen to anything I had to say when you thought I'd come to your rescue." he sneered.

"What are you talking about? What is all this?" Tina stammered, fear and adrenaline racing through her veins. She turned to the killer and he removed his mask, revealing the wild-eyed stare of Tom, a crazed smile pulling at his lips.

"Well, my good friend here doesn't handle rejection well," continued Josh, motioning at Tom. "So after Kirsty spurned his advances one too many times he wanted to teach her a lesson. The plan was just to scare her and rough her up, but things went a bit far, so we hatched a plan to pin it all on you. I must say that it didn't take much convincing to get everyone to believe that the freaky goth kid had snapped and gone on a killing spree."

Tina pushed herself to her feet, and threw herself at Josh, but as she flew at him he pushed her back down with ease, possessing more strength than his demeanour would suggest.

"This is insane," she said, fighting back tears.

"You killed Kirsty all because you couldn't take no for an answer!?"

"She wouldn't even give me a chance," snarled Tom, gripping his blade tightly. "I could have shown her how good we could have been together."

"Of course she wouldn't give you a chance, she was with me. We were in love, but she wasn't out yet, and now she'll never get that chance because of you and your disgusting, horny entitlement," Tina said, tears now falling freely down her cheeks.

"Ooh, plot twist!" laughed Josh, leaning against the door frame. "This is all getting very emotional, so we're just going to have to speed things along a bit. We need to make it look like you attacked me, and I managed to fight you off, tragically killing you in the process." He pulled a flick knife, identical to the one Tom was carrying, from his pocket and flicked it open, letting the sharp blade catch the light.

He raised his hand and stepped forward, but as he did a sharp, cracking thud filled the air. Josh's eyes went wide and he fell forwards, landing flat on his face, his body twitching slightly. Tina saw a claw hammer protruding from the back of Josh's skull, the claws buried deep into the back of his head. Blood was beginning to puddle around his head and bone shards were sticking up through his hair. Tina looked from the hammer to where Josh had been stood moments before. In the doorway stood Jess, covered in blood, breathing heavily and leaning against the doorframe, propping herself up and wincing from her multiple injuries.

S is for Slasher

Tom took in the scene with the crazed look in his eyes turning to blind rage. He let out a guttural scream and, knife raised, flew at Jess. Tina's adrenaline pumped as she took the opportunity to take Tom down, tripping him as he ran past her. The knife flew from his hand and, as he scrambled to retrieve it, Tina climbed onto his back, straddling him, and pulled the hammer from Josh's head. It came away with a wet sucking sound, and some brain tissue fell from it as she pulled it free. Tom tried to turn his head to look back at Tina and she brought the hammer down with an intense force onto his cheekbone, caving it into his face. He yelped and bucked as his bones shattered and his eyeball began to fill with blood and pop out from its socket. Tina raised the hammer again and Tom whimpered as it sailed through the air, breaking his jaw and splitting his cheek open. Broken teeth flew from the wound as Tina drew the hammer back for a third time. This time it landed in his destroyed eye socket, popping his eyeball like a peeled grape beneath it. Tom's whimpers and yelps ceased and his body continued to spasm beneath Tina. She raised the hammer a final time, spinning it to the claw side, and sunk it into the top of Tom's head. She rolled off him panting and crawled away from the gory scene on the living room floor. Jess collapsed to the floor, sliding down the doorframe, looking Tina in the eye.

"You're safe now. It's all over," she said through ragged breaths.

"But we just killed them," Tina said flatly, shock

taking hold of her.

"It was self defence. It was them or us, Tina, do you hear me? We didn't have a choice. I heard everything that was said. Their confession and their plans. Now I need you to go for help. They pulled the phone lines, so I need you to go next door and call for an ambulance and the police. Can you do that for me?" Jess still held Tina's eyes as she spoke. Tina nodded and pulled herself to her feet, leaving the carnage behind her and not looking back as she followed Jess's instructions.

Jess let out a heavy sigh, leaning her head against the doorframe and closing her eyes. It was over.

S is for Slasher

The Midday Matinee Massacre

Kay Hanifen

Ethel sat in the window seat of the Shady Springs Retirement Home's bus with her cane nestled between her legs. Mildred sat beside her, squinting at her phone and texting with her pointer finger. Ordinarily, she wouldn't give a flying fuck about the movie they were seeing: *Just Like Heaven*, a PG movie about a single father learning to love again after finding Jesus, but when she checked the movie schedule, she saw that the latest installment of the *Hack 'N Slash* franchise was playing at around the same time. The first one came out in the 1970s when she was in her mid-twenties. During that time, men would ask women to horror movies to give him an excuse to act all protective as she hid her face in his chest, but Ethel wasn't like those girls. She went to the original *Hack 'N Slash* on her own and loved every minute of the shocking violence and gore that had driven some of the men out of the theater to throw up.

It was hard being a widow with children on the other side of the country. She could no longer drive and most of what she did was dictated by the retirement home, something she chafed against. She

S is for Slasher

was an adult, so she should be able to make adult choices for herself, but those choices were becoming increasingly limited. So, she came up with a plan.

There were a few other horror lovers that she knew of. Mildred had suggested *The Haunting of Hill House* to their book club. The idea was rejected by the rest, but they still read it together and formed a fast friendship over it. She met Gary when she saw him reading a Stephen King novel. Greta had suggested the original *Hack 'N Slash* for the Halloween movie shown at the home. And Lewis, dear strange Lewis... she met him when he was telling scary stories to his grandchildren, regaling them with tales of ghosts that haunted the retirement community. Last Halloween, he'd somehow gotten his hands on a blood squib and pretended to stab himself at the dining center. He was nearly kicked out of the village for it, but Ethel thought it was hilarious. Together, the five of them became a little unsanctioned club that they liked to call the Horror Hounds.

"Which theater are we going to again?" Lewis asked.

"The Imperial on Main Street," Mildred replied.

His eyes widened. "You know that place is haunted, right?"

Ethel bit back a smile. She could do for a little horror movie pre-gaming with a scary story. "Is that so?"

"Hand to God." His gaze roved between the four of them, making sure that they were all paying attention. "They say that it was built over a cemetery, and you know that the dead don't like to have their rest disturbed."

"I get pretty cranky too if someone wakes *me* up," Greta interjected playfully. "I'd be doubly mad if my house was turned into a movie theater."

"Accidents and tragedies plagued the construction of the building. At least three of the workers were killed when a wall caved in on them, and there have been a number of suicides and freak deaths on the premises. When I was a kid, a teenager named Bobby Denbow killed himself in the projection booth, and another time, a reel caught on fire, burning the projectionist so badly that she had to get skin grafts."

"And they didn't think to close it?" Gary asked.

Lewis shrugged. "It's really the only theater in town. All the parents would have rioted if they had to drive an hour for their kids to see the newest movie. But I tell you, that place is haunted as all get out."

"Sounds like a perfect afternoon to me," Ethel said.

"What are you five talking about back there?" asked Nurse Mary, an overly bubbly woman who hid her sadistic streak behind a friendly smile and a pleasant demeanor. She didn't really care for the Horror Hounds and seemed to endeavor to make everything just slightly less convenient and just a little bit more painful for them. Ethel thought that she got off on the power trip.

Still, she smiled sweetly and said, "Just about

S is for Slasher

how excited we are to see this movie."

***

Greta stared longingly at Gary's profile. They'd had this connection for a while now, but neither seemed to want to make the first move. She understood why, of course. They both had lost their spouses of several decades and, even years after since their deaths, it still somehow felt wrong for them to act on their feelings for one another.

Ever since Ethel proposed that they sneak out of *Just Like Heaven* and watch *Hack 'N Slash*, she'd been fantasizing about him finally making the first move, the way he'd casually wrap an arm around her—maybe while pretending to stretch—and pulling her in close, kissing her lips and neck like she was once again a teenager hiding in the back of the theater for make out sessions. And maybe that would lead to more. She'd always thought she'd lose her sex drive when she got older, but it only seemed to grow. When her husband died, she'd invested in a number of handy devices that she never expected to want or need. But it still wasn't enough. She was—and pardon her French—horny and in need of living companionship rather than a machine's.

And judging by the way Gary stole glances at her, she could tell that he felt the same way.

The van pulled up in front of the theater's marquee, stopping to let its passengers out before venturing to find a parking space. Twenty people

S is for Slasher

shuffled out of the bus, walkers and canes scraping against the floor as they followed the second nurse, Alanna, like elderly ducklings. Unlike Mary, Alanna didn't seem to have much of a mean streak to her, making her well liked among the residents. With tickets already purchased, they simply grabbed their popcorn and drinks, ran to the restroom, and milled about the lobby. It felt strange to be going to the movies in a group like this. With the way that the nurses watched them, Greta felt a bit like a kid on a field trip, but without the nostalgia of getting out of school for the day.

She pulled out her pocketbook and got in line for the popcorn. It would be hell on her digestive system later, but right now she needed the comforting familiarity of a small popcorn, a Coca Cola, and a box of Sno-Caps chocolate.

"She's with me, actually," Gary said to the cashier before Greta could pull out her credit card. "I'll also have a small popcorn and coke, but instead of Sno-Caps, I'd like a box of Junior Mints." He said that last part with a wink. No one likes bad breath, especially when kissing another person.

The perky teenager at the cash register glanced between them, seeming to appraise them before squealing, "Aw, you're so cute! Coming right up, sir."

Greta winced at the almost patronizing tone but decided to let it go. The kid probably didn't mean anything by it. Besides, something else was on her mind. "I could have paid myself," she said softly to him, her cheeks blushing like she was a girl again.

S is for Slasher

He smirked. "You could, but a lady should never have to pay."

She raised her eyebrows. "So, chivalry isn't dead."

"Only if you spend your time around gentlemen like me."

"Here you go," the cashier said. Greta shoved the candy into her purse and grabbed her soda and popcorn, not bothering to wait until they were inside the theater before nibbling on it.

They joined with the rest of the group, taking aisle seats as far away from the nurses and as close to the door as possible, and making a show of getting settled. Greta, Mildred, and Ethel would leave first under the pretense of using the restroom together after the trailers started. Gary and Lewis would wait for the span of two or three trailers before following them. If anyone asked why they were at *Hack 'N Slash* instead of the movie they were meant to see, they'd just feign innocence and say that they got confused about which theater they were supposed to be in.

Ethel's plan went off without a hitch, and soon they were settling in for the opening credits of the movie they really wanted to see. Because this was a midday, midweek showing of a horror movie, the theater was practically empty.

***

There was something up with the group of seniors that called themselves the Horror Hounds.

S is for Slasher

Even with her pounding headache, Mary could smell their insubordination. Sure, they acted like sweet old folks, but she could tell that they were demonic, especially their ringleader, Ethel. She'd never met a more ghoulish old woman, and her influence was rubbing off on the other residents. Sweet, timid Mildred began talking back to Mary while elegant Greta began openly flirting with Gary, who clearly reciprocated. When Mary reminded her about the dangers of pre-marital sex, Greta replied, "It's not like I can get pregnant anymore," and then wouldn't talk to her about it again. Worst of all, though, was Lewis, whose mischief and scary stories grew more outlandish, effectively terrorizing the other residents. She looked forward to the day that Ethel would finally shuffle off the mortal coil.

Perhaps… she could speed it along. It would be a mercy, really. A quick end rather than the body and mind slowly deteriorating until you became a prisoner of a useless husk. Having worked with the elderly for the better part of twenty years, Mary had seen the horrors of aging firsthand, and even helped along some that were suffering… or those that were particularly bothersome to her. But why should that mercy be reserved just for the worst of the people in her care?

You should do it. End their suffering.

As the trailers ended and the opening credits began, Mary imagined the possibility of helping along all the residents in this room. She could easily overpower most of them, but not all at once. And Alanna would be a challenge. She was younger than

Mary, and fitter. If Mary wanted to put her out of her misery too, she would have to come up with a clever strategy rather than relying on her brute strength.

Another of the residents got to their feet, likely pretending to use the restroom when really they were headed God knows where.

There they go. One more resident to disrespect you, to throw your compassion in your face. They're all laughing at you, so you know what you must do.

Mary got up and left the auditorium, but instead of following the resident—who she recognized as Gladys—she headed to the employees only area. Guided by instinct, she slipped into the storeroom for the concession stand and grabbed a boxcutter. It wasn't much, but it would have to do.

She retracted the blade and shoved it into her purse before heading to the restroom. But before she left, she grabbed one last thing: a souvenir mask from the new *Hack 'N Slash* movie. It was an ugly, satanic looking thing, a mix between a scarecrow and a skull, but it felt right in her hands, and would feel even more right on her face.

Gladys was at the sink washing her hands when Mary approached. The resident gave her a polite smile. "I used to have an iron bladder, but now one soda leaves me peeing for the rest of the day," she complained. Yes, Gladys was a complainer. No matter what Mary did, she found something to whine about. If it wasn't that her food was too cold, then it was that her laundry wasn't done properly or that the sheets needed changing. And Mary, with

S is for Slasher

her subminimum wage job that truly did not pay her enough for all the literal and metaphorical shit she had to deal with on a day-to-day basis, just had to grin and bear it.

"I'm sorry to hear that," Mary said, pulling out the box cutter. Before Gladys could say anything else, she slit her throat, cutting a smile from ear to ear along the papery flesh of her neck. The old woman choked, grasping uselessly at the wound as her legs gave out from under her. As she expired, Mary dragged her to the largest stall, not bothering to hide the snail trail of blood that led to her final resting place.

It won't matter if anyone finds it. They'll be dead soon anyway.

She put on the mask.

***

Though the movie wasn't the best in the series, Ethel sat entranced by the screen. Honestly, these young actors and their self-referential script weren't doing much for her. Why did all movies have to be self-aware and referential these days? Why give all these winks to the audience? She missed when the characters in a movie could just *be* in the movie without having any genre awareness.

And here she was, complaining about how everything was better in the good old days. After listening to it from her parents, grandparents, and in-laws, she swore to herself that she would never be that crotchety old lady who complained about kids today. So much for that.

Still, it was a thousand times better than *Just Like Heaven* and watching gave her a rush of excitement that made her feel young again. The kills were good, and the slasher, Old Hackie, was as unsettling as ever.

Beside her, Mildred winced, covering her eyes as a nubile young cheerleader was cut in half by a chainsaw. Though she liked scary stories, she wasn't a gore lover like the rest of them. The killer jumped out, frightening the final girl, and Mildred jumped too, taking Ethel's arthritic hand in hers, and making her blush. She'd always found men and women equally attractive—and for the longest time, assumed everyone else did too—but had only started exploring that side of her in recent years. As she had gotten to know Mildred and bonded through their mutual love of Shirley Jackson, she'd developed something of a crush on the sweet, clever old lady. And sometimes, with the ways that her gazes and touches lingered, Ethel wondered if Mildred was inclined the same way.

Feeling a bit like a teenage boy, she pulled the old yawn and stretch trick before wrapping her arm around Mildred's shoulder. She leaned into the touch, resting her head on Ethel. Youth may be wasted on the young, but it's the old who willingly sacrifice their youthful hearts upon the altar of maturity. You're only as old as you feel, and right now, Ethel felt like a kid going on a movie date for the first time.

S is for Slasher

***

Lewis didn't like this. Not the movie. The movie was fun enough and a welcome break from the monotony of the retirement home. But he had this feeling in the back of his mind, a voice whispering that something was wrong and that he should flee while he still could.

He laughed to himself. Voicing this fear would do little but up his dosage of anti-psychotics. He already had a reputation for being the village oddball, so if he said anything, people would just laugh it off as the ravings of someone who's lost touch with the rest of the world.

But his mother was a cunning woman, and he'd been gifted with something like second sight, though not as powerful as her abilities had been. The moment he stepped into the theater, though, he was nearly bowled over with cold feeling of negative energy, a black hole that sucked all joy into it. Even those with the weakest of gifts should have been able to sense it, but everyone else went about their business buying popcorn and using the restroom before the movie started.

All but their resident Nurse Ratched, who glared in their direction with her signature scowl. She waited near the auditorium hall, her arms crossed and eyes narrowed, clearly suspecting that something was up. If he didn't look at her directly, he could see it—a strange, shadowy figure lurking behind her, whispering in her ear. He knew about the spirits at the theater, but this was much darker

S is for Slasher

than that. Something he'd only seen once when his mother performed a banishment on a home occupied by a demon. The sight of it whispering in Nurse Mary's ear made his stomach twist with nausea, forcing him to get out of the popcorn line. If he ordered some, he'd definitely throw it up, and it would be a massive waste of money.

The plan went off without a hitch, and they all managed to get to the movie before the opening credits had finished. He wanted to just enjoy the film, but he couldn't seem to relax. Something was terribly wrong, but he couldn't place his finger on what. In front of him, Greta and Gary passionately made out like two kids on lover's lane. Beside him, Ethel had finally found the courage to show Mildred how she really felt—at least, judging by the way they snuggled together. And here he was, alone as the fifth wheel and unable to relax because of a danger lurking somewhere in the darkness of the theater. It wasn't fair.

Get yourself some salt, he could imagine his mother saying. *Just in case you need it.*

He had seen saltshakers up near the popcorn stand. It wouldn't offer much protection against the dark presence, but it was better than no protection at all. But they couldn't just leave the auditorium. Leaving meant risking getting caught and ruining the whole plan. He wouldn't do that to his friends, not when this was something they'd been looking forward to for a while now. Besides, they were about a half hour into the movie, so they had an hour left. The other movie was two hours long, so

S is for Slasher

once this one ended, they would be out of their seats like Catholics at the end of mass to watch the last half hour of the one everyone else went to see. He could grab salt on the way to the other auditorium just to ease his mind for the final stretch.

Just as he'd made peace with this decision, it was ripped away from him. Someone in the theater screamed, and it wasn't a well-endowed actress running in heels away from the masked killer. No, this was real and seemed to be coming from right outside the auditorium.

The door to the theater burst open and the cashier who supplied them with popcorn came stumbling in, her hand grasping protectively at her side as the odor of copper filled the room. Lewis may have been a draft-dodging hippie, but he could recognize the smell of blood anywhere. The door swung open again, and someone wearing nurse's scrubs and an Old Hackie mask stepped in. The attacker raised a boxcutter, the stained blade glinting in the light of the projector.

"No, no, please!" the kid begged as her legs gave out from under her, forcing her to crab walk away from the killer.

"Get away from her," Greta shouted, throwing the popcorn. It sailed along the aisle before harmlessly bouncing off the killer, the popcorn spilling to the ground.

The attacker turned to face them. "I should have known," she said, and her voice was so eerily familiar.

It was the ever-sharp Ethel who figured it out

first. "Nurse Mary?"

***

Of all the people Ethel expected to snap and go on a killing spree... well, Nurse Mary wasn't that much of a shock, actually. She'd always had a sadistic side to her, something hidden under her bubbly demeanor.

"There you five are!" Nurse Mary exclaimed like she'd momentarily lost sight a couple of toddlers. "I should've guessed that you'd be hiding out here. Did you get the auditoriums confused? I know that they can be hard to remember, but this movie is wildly age inappropriate for you all."

Ethel couldn't help but roll her eyes. "I'm a grown woman, Mary. Nothing's inappropriate for me anymore." Out of the corner of her eye, she watched Lewis help the poor girl up and to the exit. She had to keep Mary focused on her. That would buy everyone else time to escape and get help. "Wait, come to think of it, there is one thing that isn't age appropriate: talking to me like I'm a toddler."

"You know my motto. Act like a child and I'll treat you like one," Mary replied. "Now, come on. Everyone here needs to take their medicine, and things will be much smoother if you all behave like I ask."

Even when she was young, Ethel was no athlete, but she had taken several self-defense classes through the years. It started as a part of her participation in the Women's Lib movement, but she found that she rather enjoyed martial arts, and it had saved her life several times. So, she kept up with it. As Mary drew nearer, Ethel shifted her weight onto her good leg. "Why are you doing this?" she asked, her fingers adjusting her grip on her cane as she dared to glance in the direction of her friends, most of whom having already escaped to the emergency exit on the opposite side of the auditorium. She forced herself to ignore them and focus on the woman with the boxcutter.

"Because I am so sick and tired of you five and your little Satan worshipping club," Mary replied, "and I thought that it was time to put you out of my misery."

Finally, Mary was within striking range. With a battle cry, Ethel raised the cane and struck her temple before Mary could properly attack her. She crumbled to the ground like a marionette with its strings cut, but Ethel wasn't stupid enough to assume that the murderer was dead. She'd seen enough horror movies to know that the killer always comes back for one last scare.

So, she raised her cane high above her and brought it down on Nurse Mary's head once, twice, three times. It likely wouldn't kill her, but it did give Ethel some measure of satisfaction. All those years of patronizing words and the assumption that just because she was older, she was a delicate glass flower that would shatter the moment she saw something vaguely scandalous. With a yell, she struck Mary one last time and felt the bones of her skull give. If nothing else, that would certainly kill her.

***

"We should get Alanna," Mildred said as they ran as fast as their creaky joints would let them.

"Dead!" the teenage girl sobbed. "They're all dead." She was partially propped up by Gary and Greta, and in the light of the lobby, the bright red of the blood covering her was stark against her too-pale face and white uniform.

Lewis patted Mildred's arm. "Go get the others. I have something I need to get." With that, he vanished to the concession stand.

Mildred nodded and ran as fast as her legs could carry her into the nearby auditorium. Along the way, she pulled the fire alarm, the flashing lights and ear-splitting screech interrupting the films. The small number of patrons filed out slowly, grumbling to themselves that they wanted a refund and apparently oblivious to the massive buckets of blood all over the place. Maybe they thought that this was just some kind of advertising stunt rather than something horrifyingly real. As she watched, she realized that no one filed out of the *Just Like Heaven* theater. They had to have heard the fire alarm but were either too stupid or too stubborn to move their sorry asses out of the fire exit.

"Alanna?" she hissed as she slipped into the auditorium. The odor of copper was stronger here and mixed with the smell of urine and feces. It was

S is for Slasher

enough to make her want to throw up all the popcorn she'd eaten during the movie.

A terrible feeling settled in her stomach; one made all the more eerie by the film still playing but to a silent audience. But still, she tiptoed to the nearest person she recognized, Steve Something-Or-Other, and shook his shoulder. He slumped, his body falling bonelessly to the floor.

Mildred screamed.

***

Gary picked up his head when a blood-curdling scream tore its way through the lobby. It could only come from one person.

"Mildred!" Ethel exclaimed, leaning heavily on her cane as she scrambled to the auditorium doors, leaving him and Greta alone with the hysterical teenage girl. Poor kid.

"Help me prop her against the wall," Greta said. "I want to see how hurt she is." They half-carried her there and broke her fall as she slid down, still sobbing. Greta took her hand. "Can you show me where she got you?"

The girl nodded and lifted her shirt, revealing a deep, oozing gash along her belly, her innards threatening to spill out. Greta hissed in sympathy and turned to Gary. "Grab the paper towels from the ladies' room. I need to keep pressure on this wound."

He hesitated. "Ladies' room?"

"Just go," she said, rolling her eyes. "No one will

S is for Slasher

care."

"Fine," he muttered. His chest hurt a bit—probably the greasy popcorn combined with the stress of the situation causing his acid reflux to act up. That didn't matter right now, though. What mattered was getting out of here alive.

A snail trail of red streaked into the handicapped stall of the bathroom. Feeling nauseous, his heart pounded, and breath came out in short pants as he followed it. He pushed the door open, revealing the slumped form of Gladys, her throat slashed into a second smile and her clothes soaked in blood. She stared blankly up at him with clouded eyes, the spark long gone.

The shock was like an arrow to his already weak heart, piercing it and stopping its rhythmic beating. He was dead within minutes of hitting the floor.

***

Greta kept her hand pressed to the girl's belly, wondering where Gary could have gone. She'd seen enough scary movies to know that even crushing Mary's head wouldn't get rid of her that easily.

But what could have made her snap like that? Surely it wasn't just them sneaking out of the movie. She was a bit like Nurse Ratched, but murder was a pretty extreme response to threats to her power trip. Maybe loony old Lewis wasn't so crazy after all. Maybe this theater was haunted, and the ghosts were using Mary to get their revenge. She almost laughed out loud at the thought. Now he had *her* thinking like an oddball.

The teenager's head began to nod as though she was on the verge of passing out and the fire alarm was so loud that Greta could barely hear herself think. She patted the girl's cheeks, trying to keep her awake. "Hey, hey—" she squinted at the name tag, her eyes struggling to parse the relatively small words. She really needed to get a better prescription for her glasses. Finally, the name came into focus. "Hey, Melanie, stay with me, okay?"

"I'm tired," she mumbled.

"I know, sweetheart, but you need to stay awake until an ambulance comes. Can you do that for me?"

She groaned, mumbling something incoherent about the displaced dead. Great. Apparently, the blood loss had become delirium. And where was Gary with the towels?

She patted the girl's cheeks again. "Uh, tell me. How old are you?"

"Nineteen."

"Are you in college?"

"Yeah," she replied, looking slightly more alert.

"What are you studying? If you don't mind me asking, of course."

For a moment, her eyes were focused on Greta. And then they gazed past her, widening as she said, "Frying oil."

Greta's final thoughts were something of a disappointment. She had hoped they would be profound and bring her an inner peace before passing on, but instead, she thought: *Frying oil?*

That is an odd thing to study.
And then her world erupted in agony.

***

Lewis gathered all the saltshakers he could carry. He would form a circle around his friends, one to protect them from the evil possessing Mary. His mother had taught him how to cast out demons, but it had been decades since he'd accomplished it. He was more than a little rusty. But rusty skills were better than no skills at all.

"Lewis…" came a rasping, mocking voice, "Lewis…" Mary staggered out of the auditorium, her mask bloodied and head misshapen from Ethel's blows. When she saw him, she smiled. "There you are, Lewis…"

He muttered a curse and ran as fast as his legs would carry him to the storeroom. Shaking the salt along the ground, he formed a line of protection in the doorway. Mama always told him that salt warded off evil spirits.

But still Mary lingered, taking off her mask to smile at him with swollen lips, a broken nose, and missing teeth. "You and your little cult are done."

"Then come get me," he said, taking a step back and spreading his hands wide, a cocky move. It might have been tempting fate, but he was certain that she wouldn't be able to pass over it.

Mary raised a foot as though she was about to step over the threshold, but then a troubled look crossed her face. She put it down and tried with the other foot. Still, she could not cross.

"Thank you, Mama," Lewis whispered up to Heaven.

Mary shot him a glare before walking drunkenly to the boiling oil used to fry the theater's chicken tenders. Heedless of the blistering burns, she dunked an extra-large bucketful into the oil before shuffling off to find another quarry.

Lewis let out a sigh of relief as he stepped over the line. Relief which became cold terror as not one, but two screams rang through the theaters. Shit.

Careful not to break the seal, he stepped over the line of salt and headed in the direction of the screams.

***

Dead. They were all dead. Mary killed all of them, including somehow overpowering the much younger Alanna. She must have been going row by row slitting throats, moving far too quickly for anyone to notice before it was too late.

Ethel was going to be sick. Mildred already had been, the odor of her vomit mixing with the rest of the awful smells. She never liked Mary, but she didn't think the nurse was capable of such absolute evil.

Mildred took her hand. "We have to get out of here."

Blinking and shaking herself out of her horrified stupor, they headed to the door, only to stop when they heard Greta's ear-piercing scream. "Shit," she

S is for Slasher

muttered, tugging Mildred to the emergency exits on the opposite side of the auditorium. This one should have led straight out, but the doors were locked. "What the hell? Isn't this a fire hazard?"

"I don't think it wants us to leave," Mildred said.

"It?"

"The theater. It wants us dead."

"Well, it can want the moon on a pizza pie for all I care," she replied. The auditorium doors swung open, and before Mary could emerge, Ethel hissed, "Get down!"

They fell to their hands and knees, Ethel praying that she'd be able to get back up again as Mary said in a sing-song voice, "Five little monkeys jumping out of bed. One fell into boiling oil and now she's fucking dead."

She watched Mary weave through the seats searching for them and began to crawl. Maybe if they got near the door, they could make a break for it and meet up with the others—the ones who were still alive, anyway.

She didn't want to think about the tackiness of the floor as she crawled, the way that her hands stuck to something damp and sticky that she wanted to pretend was spilled soda but knew better. The crawling made her knees ache something fierce, but she pushed through it. Aching knees were better than corpse knees. Mary kept singing and dancing through the aisles as she kept up her slow search.

Near the edge of the aisle, Ethel froze, waiting and listening. Mary had gone quiet. Did she know where they were? If she didn't, where did she go?

Fuck it. Her best chance was to get up and make a run for it. If all else failed, she could always break Mary's skull with her cane again. Using the empty seat to help pull herself up, she turned and found herself face to face with Mary's bloody mask.

"Found you," she said, slashing Ethel with the boxcutter. She raised her hands defensively, the blade slicing into the meat of her arm rather than any vital organs. With a cry, she stumbled, nearly toppling over the seats in front of her.

Like a mad Jack-in-the-Box, Mildred propelled herself upwards and launched at Mary, wrapping her arms around her, effectively immobilizing her as she thrashed about. "Get the blade," she gritted out.

Careful not to slice a finger off, Ethel twisted the weapon out of Mary's hands. Mildred let go, giving her the space to stab Mary in the chest, for all the good that would do. If bashing her head in didn't work, what would?

The stab wound stunned her, though, buying them enough time to escape the auditorium. The first of their group that they saw was Greta, though Ethel almost didn't recognize her at first. Her body was covered in third degree burns, her flesh the consistency of melted mozzarella. She was slumped over the body of the teenage girl, her eyes blank and throat slashed from ear to ear.

"Ethel! Mildred!" Lewis yelled. He carried with him a pile of saltshakers and a container of frying oil, the latter of which he was pouring into a circle on the floor.

"What are you doing?" Mildred asked as he took a lighter from his jacket pocket.

"I'm trapping the demon in a circle of flames. You two ladies use that saltshaker to make a nice circle for yourselves. It'll protect you while I exorcise the damn thing."

"Are you sure that'll work?" Ethel asked, already grabbing the salt.

"Ninety-percent." Both women gave him skeptical looks, making him cringe. "Okay, more like seventy-five percent. When you're the son of a cunning woman, you learn a few things. Make that circle big enough for all three of us. I have to be able to get there too for the ritual."

Ethel paused halfway through pouring the salt. "Wait, why don't you just stay in here with us?"

"Someone has to light the fire," he replied.

She handed Mildred the salt. "I'll do it. You're the only one who knows how to stop her."

"But—" Mildred began to protest, but Lewis handed Ethel the lighter.

"Make sure that she steps into the circle before you light it. It's the only way to trap her."

Ethel nodded and palmed the lighter. Just as Mildred and Lewis finished the protective circle, Mary appeared from around the corner. She stopped, tilting her head. "There you are. Tired of running?"

"You know how my knees are," Ethel answered. "They ache too much for that."

"So, you give up?" she asked, approaching slowly, like a cat stalking a mouse.

210

Ethel shrugged. "I've lived a long life. Come and get me."

With a howl, Mary lurched towards her. The moment she set foot in the circle, Ethel lit the lighter and dropped it. With a dull roar, the flames exploded around Mary, imprisoning her as Lewis began to chant.

Ethel raced to the safety of the salt circle, watching in horror as Mary's body levitated and contorted into positions that made her joints ache in sympathy. The air pressure in the room dropped like the prelude to a summer thunderstorm and Lewis's chanting reached a crescendo. His voice was strange, dissonant, like the sound of tuning musical instruments before a concert.

And with a crack of thunder, Mary's body contorted one last time and then fell still, the spirits animating it having now been banished for good. It landed with a dull thump as the sprinklers kicked in, soaking them as they clung to one another in awe. The sound of police sirens filled the air, their cue to get their story straight and find those patrons who had been evacuated with the fire alarm.

Gary had completely slipped her mind in the excitement until the ambulance wheeled him away in a body bag. Of all the deaths today, a heart attack from the stress seemed almost comically mundane, but it was probably the least painful way to go out of everyone that died. Ethel hoped that he and Greta could at least be reunited in heaven.

After they drove him away, Mildred spun Ethel around and planted a kiss on her lips.

"What was that for?" she asked, unable to suppress her girlish giggle when they parted.

Mildred smiled. "Life's too short to live in fear of what other people think," she replied, "and I'm not getting any younger."

Birth of an Abomination

Roman Durkan

Lit only by the last embers of dusk, a battered car sat with doors open amid gently swaying cornstalks, the GPS still babbling directions.

Dragged along the arid earth, a body clad in a Hawaiian shirt hung limply, feeding the corn with blood dripping from mangled limbs and fragmented jawbone. A single arm pulled it down the lanes of stalks, with glistening talons bursting out from splitting fingers.

"Because y'all be motherfuuuuuuckersss..."

Ahead, a barn sat among other worn structures beside the field. From inside, something thrummed like a deep heartbeat, something from below the foundations of the decaying wooden building.

Muscle sinew wormed and twisted around the clawed arm like writhing maggots, changing and shifting constantly. Some of it snaked down to the bleeding corpse below, as if to sample the torn and ragged flesh below it.

Impatiently, the figure threw it into the doors, and towards the pit dug inside. Red light gently shone from inside as the final vestiges of sunlight vanished away.

S is for Slasher

The thrumming continued, beating, breathing, rising with anticipation, like a living organ, a parasite worn into the earth itself.

"*So you motherfuckers, y'all better go and die... because y'all be motherfuuuuuckersssss...*"

Stumbling away, the form let the clawed hand reach up to adjust the pointed white hood hung over an askew head.

***

Twelve hours later

Dust rolled over the Midwestern road with all the slothfulness of a cloud on a windless day. On both sides, stalks of corn gently swung like a tire hanging from a withered oak tree. Dirtied by ground flecks of dried earth, a lone Toyota Prius slowly made its way, glinting under a cruel summer sun.

Keeping a nervous eye on both the fuel and battery meters, the driver wondered not for the first time just what he was doing in such an ass-backwards patch of nowhere. Perhaps it had been the traffic reports of that major pile-up on the interstate, driving him onto these cracked, gravelly tracks. Perhaps it had been the sudden confusion of the GPS as to where the hell he was.

Frederick Levi had always strived to be a level-headed individual. Growing up in a middle-class home in the Chicago suburbs, possessing a comfortable office job—all of it should have left his mind at ease. And yet, through it all, there had been

S is for Slasher

the vague, discomforting sense of being an outsider—something that, it felt like, came with being of a Jewish family. He was secular enough, indifferent to the news and debates always churning around matters of Israel and religion—but something, from comments at work to glances on the metro, had always bitten at his subconscious. Friends commented that he looked like a 'dweebier David Duchovny'. Jokes about foreskins. Such things that never seemed to end... he had for the most part done his best to ignore them, shuffling any response out of his consciousness.

And now, a friend, man by the name of Nathan Cornell, inviting him to meet for a weekend trip to Nashville, was no longer answering his calls. Despite being close enough, one of the few Frederick felt he could fully confide in, Nathan had only texted him the previous day to say that some accident on the freeway had diverted him. The same accident took Frederick to what he presumed were the same roads, but alone in these baking pathways he found nothing to make him feel any easier.

Signs hadn't been much help either. On the way here, he had passed two gas stations crumbled into nothing by a failing economy, left only as rusted carcasses boarded up and stripped of colour. Trying to find the owners of the vast cornfields around him had been a lost cause—probably they were just another corner of the immense megafarms that swallowed individual homesteads across the Midwest.

Dead businesses. Dead roads. Dead trees. Even

S is for Slasher

the corn seemed to barely survive under the sun, leaving bleached leaves crispy and the ears drained of brightness.

His eye caught what looked like the gated entrance to a driveway ahead—and not only that, a sign advertising 'GAS AND AUTO PARTS'. It looked as fresh as anything could out here. Pulling to the side, he eagerly scanned for any life, any fellow human that could point him to where he needed to go.

Stopping at the front of the driveway, he could indeed see a man reclining on a chair under a parasol near the stall, half-asleep and moving only to swat away buzzing insects. Some sort of mannequin appeared to be hung up on the gate behind him, too far off to be made distinct from here. Stopping the car, Frederick gingerly got out, shielding his eyes and coughing from the dry haze hanging over everything around him.

"Er... excuse me, but the sign said you sell gas..." he called outward, still hacking.

"Sure do." The seller leaned forward. "Shit, you drivin' one of them shiny-ass rice burners? City boy, ain't ya? Pappy worked in a motor shop back when there was motors worth selling 'round these parts. Business died, he died, this is all he left."

A dry, odd laugh sounded out as Frederick looked to some of the decades-old components laid out on the stall, before settling on the worn gas canisters lying by the side.

"Yeah... hard times for everyone... listen, I just need..."

S is for Slasher

His eyes fell on what had been mounted on the gate. He recognized it now. Some sort of dummy, partially stuffed with straw, with a party mask of former president Barack Obama awkwardly placed onto the head.

"I take it… I take it you're a…"

"Goddamn hater of that socialist uppity democrat." The man laughed again. "Country goin' to hell for decades, he was only what made it clear there was no turnin' back."

"But what about president… I mean, President Tru…"

"Shit, that guy? Just another fuckin' phoney. Ain't solving the *real* problems, you know what I mean. Out here, Republican or Democrat, don't make a difference to what folk like *us* actually want."

"And… what's that?" he murmured, settling his hands on one of the cans.

"A return to fine livin', eatin', and breedin'." A smiling response came as the seller shifted forwards. "But really, politics ain't gonna do that. Nah, what we have is a *real* solution…"

"Sorry, did you say breeding, or breathing?"

Frederick chided himself on the silliness of the question. Of course the man had meant breathing, it was all that logically followed…

Eyes widened as he looked up. Something was splitting down the seller's chest. A leering smile remained on his face as ribs protruded out through his vest like fangs—snaking tendrils, wrought from intertwined intestine and malformed organ, reached out along the ground towards him—

"Excuse this, city boy. But y'oughta thank me—you just got real good seats for the big event..."

Chortling, mirthful laughter echoed over the cornrows as Frederick was dragged back by pulsing appendages latching around his ankle, past the gate behind him. The next sensation that came was the dry, sickening taste of scorched soil blown into his mouth as he was forced down onto the parched ground. Struggling onto his back, he glimpsed other figures moving towards him, hooded, clad in white, as something shone from inside the decrepit barn within...

***

"Gentlemen... we have clearance. Satellite confirms these good ol' boys gathering around what looks like some sort of weapons stockpile. I think they just might be thinking they can outdo Uncle Sam in quantity of bullets. I think we oughta dissuade them of this notion."

Slamming a magazine into his cradled M4 rifle, Special Agent Gabriel Summers, of the Bureau of Alcohol, Tobacco, and Firearms, glanced to the heavily armed figures all crammed into the back of a military-grade armored transport. One designed to withstand attacks from rocket-propelled grenades and whatever else some insurgent all too happy to die for Allah was willing to throw at it. And here it was, being deployed against some rednecks dressed in bedsheets.

Truthfully, Agent Summers wasn't particularly concerned about whether these were jihadists or the Aryan Nations he was due to unload on. The ATF and the police forces it was backed up by happened to be better equipped than some militaries—so why the hell not use it? Waste was abhorrent to him—and full metal jacketed rounds could serve as nothing else when simply stashed in some damn warehouse.

"Sir, we're getting some distortion on the long-range radio." He could hear the voice of the driver coming in. *"Requesting advice, over."*

"Just keep going to the insertion point as planned." Summers shrugged. "Keep trying until you get 'em."

Either these yokels had developed strategic jamming or someone had done the AFT's communications shopping at a RadioShack clearance. Oh well. Meant less fuckwits breathing down his neck.

"Listen up!" Summers turned to the other agents behind him. "Main insertion point is coming up. As you may remember, expect heavily armed anti-government fanatics ahead. In other words, crazy-ass rednecks. Remember to maximize the cover in the cornfields, and on contact, you should…"

"Distortion's getting worse, sir… lost GPS… lost long-range completely… I can't explain it… not even picking up the long-band…" The driver came in once more. Summers responded with a confused expression. Seemed like these folk may indeed have been better equipped than the briefings indicated.

S is for Slasher

That, or someone had also bought the satellite itself at RadioShack.

"... consider these people unlikely to capitulate. Now just remember—there ain't no cameras out here."

Turning back to the driver, he tapped on the grating to the cabin.

"Tell the state police boys to remain at the alpha point. If these fuckers are jamming us somehow, tell them to get in backup after forty-five minutes. National Guard, drones, whatever. So long as they don't pussyfoot around."

A brief smirk crossed his face—he himself wasn't sure if it was the thought of actually needing to call in tanks on these pissants, or the satisfaction of pulling something without some prick on Twitter filming the whole thing. Either way, the boys seemed locked and loaded—all that he needed was a little entertainment to pass the remaining time.

One tap on the device in his pocket got just the thing.

"Whoa, thought it was a nightmare, low, it's all so true…

They told me, don't go walking slow, the devil's on the loose…

Better run through the jungle…"

On cracked roads and beside parched riverbeds, the ATF transports drove ever onward.

***

Frederick's eyes opened as a pulsing ache raced

S is for Slasher

through his skull like a jackhammer. The next feeling that came in was that of a reek—a vile stench, combining rotting meat with burnt, noxious remains. It took a few moments for his self to process the sheer nausea that grabbed him—like the sharpened digits of a corpse wrapping around his neck.

He glanced down. Something *had* been grabbing at his neck. Twisted, jagged bruises marred the skin there like a tattoo. Blinking with every heartbeat, he slowly looked up, still trying to parse his way through the cascade of pain.

Wooden walls, painted flaking red, reached up around him, surrounding a pit dug into the floor of what looked like some sort of barn. Hooks and chains hung from rafters overhead, while the walls—what he saw immediately jolted his heartbeat even further. Dozens of symbols, slogans, daubed markings of terrifying familiarity carved in or marked with faded crimson.

Symbols he knew all too well from his childhood lessons, from sobering stories from heavy-eyed grandparents, from news reports he had strived to desperately ignore. Swastikas. Twisted crosses. Imagery he couldn't begin to decipher…

And hanging overhead, directly over the pit… ragged bodies, in various states of decomposition. Flies festered and bred in pits of necrosis and rot, as bone protruded out from dried sinews hanging forlornly from carven limbs, like long-expired wares in a forgotten butchery.

The freshest of them all was wearing a

distinctive Hawaiian shirt, arms hanging out and desiccated.

"My god..." he wheezed, pulling himself forward—only to find rusted, prickling chains around both wrists. "Nathan..."

"Ah, there you are." A voice, the same from that stand, but strangely distorted, called in. "It'll begin soon, don't you worry."

"Begin... what will begin?"

"Down there, my friend... down there is what took grandpappy when he found himself all grey at forty... seeing his vitality seep away... all after he worked himself raising this here farm. Claimed it was Jews livin' on a farm a county over, to his dying breath. Trying to turn the white Christian man into a husk to feed their own rituals."

A strange laugh followed, as Frederick tried to clear his mind. He didn't know what the hell this... this man, whoever he was... was going on about... but he knew he had murdered Nathan. Hung him over there, and now...

"I don't think he was right about that, but it made a fine story. Story enough for me to see where the rest of the country could go. But, comin' back here... I noticed same thing happening to the rats and critters livin' in this here place... noticed also my own self... changing."

The figure finally moved into Frederick's field of view—white robed, nonchalant smiling face looking right down at him. His body was misshapen, talons hanging down from one hand, something quivering inside his mouth. Despite it all,

S is for Slasher

he kept on talking, almost in bliss from it all.

"I got me some of my pals and we began digging—found us... I dunno... this here rock, this stone... this thing down there... and we figured... if we feed it, it'll give us... something in return. Make us stronger. Purer. Better white men!"

"But..." Frederick glanced back, as he finally turned his head—others stood silhouetted in the barn entrance, some wearing pointed hoods all too familiar to him, but all similarly asymmetrical, letting bladed arms or bizarre pulsing growths hang from themselves. "You're... you're... not even human..."

"Human?" The Klansman—Neo-Nazi—whatever he was—turned sharply towards him. "And what do you know about human, city boy? You been around darkies, those fuckin' A-Rabs trying to tear down what we've built, too long? You know what we're trying to do here?"

Frederick paused. Something resembling rationality was coming back to him. They hadn't figured out his... background. Hadn't bothered to search his wallet... a one saving grace here.

"Trying to build a new army... one that's been blessed by what we've come across here... to take back America..."

"You... have you seen yourself?" Perhaps it was the debilitation he was going through. Perhaps it was the sheer absurdity of what he was seeing, like a demented fever dream—ranked with the hypocrisy, the stupidity, the callous ignorance of someone who had mutilated himself, murdered his friend—

Something was turning in Frederick's mind. Those efforts of being another meek middle-class good citizen, trying to ignore madness and cruelty as long as it stayed away from him... all of them fading away, from shock or otherwise...

"What's your name, good sir?" The warped Klansman took a step closer.

"Frederick... Frederick Wallace."

"So then... Freddy... you'll start to feel the effects soon... you see, for better white men to prosper, well, you can't make an omelette without..."

A sound like a motor clattering into overdrive cut through the air like a thunderclap, right before a string of punctured holes peppered along the opposite wall. Something hissed right next to his left arm—close enough for him to feel the minute splinters of wood scattered from the impact in the wall behind him.

Angered shouts rang out from outside the barn, as Frederick gleaned the sounds of shotguns being cocked and knives being drawn—he could see a gash torn across the arm of his captor, bleeding onto his crude white robes. There was no sign of pain as he made for the door, barking a string of barely coherent orders.

Feeling his heart strain itself under the sound of gunfire, Frederick looked down to see the chain holding his left arm broken.

Only an aged wooden plank in the wall remained connected to the other as he staggered upwards,

S is for Slasher

glancing to every corner of the charnel house around him...

***

Moving in a spearhead-shaped formation, a dozen armed AFT agents fanned their way through the cornfield leading up to the farm structures in the distance. An abandoned car, door torn open, had been found seemingly forced off the road nearby—Agent Summers had pegged it as another one of the disappearances that had turned the local authorities this way in the first place. Unless they found the body, it hardly mattered now. Only thing was to keep his M4 steady.

"Sir? You reading?" he heard one of the other agents shout over, tapping his earpiece.

"Negative. Radio's down—keep it tight," he called back. Ahead, he still couldn't see anything that could be strong enough for such a jamming effect—no towers or antennae. The thought vaguely troubled him—but the expensive ballistic vest and helmet he wore assured him in turn.

"Contact, one o'clock!"

He could see them now: white hoods, at the end of the field, with their pointed tips visible past the vegetation. Still in cover of the cornstalks, the ATF paused as he raised a hand. There was only a handful visible—but that barn... perfect place for storing weapons... arms... congregating a meeting...

And if there was no radio... fuck it. Not like they

S is for Slasher

had the time to wait for some jackass to run back and forth paging the governor. They were paid to neutralize these threats, they were given tens of thousands of federal money worth of gear to do so... time to use it.

"Team one, target the ones in the open. Team two... rake that barn. On my mark..."

A few moments for weapons to be steadied. A few more moments for triggers to be pulled and casings to spill out as he brought his hand down.

The fire echoed out across the field, as he saw two of the robed figures fall in the distance—the others, much to his surprise, staggered forwards, visibly wounded, but still moving.

"Targets still moving on the right—check your aim and..."

Shotguns fired into the air far ahead as he spotted something—something goddamn weird: a forearm, elongated as a mass of stretched glistening tendons, reaching out to pull one of the Klansmen along, propelling him forward into the field. Tapping the side of his visor, he steadied his aim, firing again.

Bullets cut through the deformed limb as the figure stumbled through the cornstalks—he could see more emerging from the barn, cocking weapons. Claws reaching out from under robes, extra appendages reaching from their backs, pus-dripping tongues licking out from beneath stained hoods and sheets...

"Fire at will!" he shouted. *"Everything in that direction has to die!"*

Some sort of degenerative disease? Bioweapons

stockpiling? Some hallucinogen they had laced the corn with? His thoughts rushed between the dire possibilities, and the question of how much fuckin' paperwork this was gonna take.

Clattering gunfire overlaid itself with the ever-closer bursts of sawn-offs, slicing through the surrounding cornstalks as the ATF dispersed. He glimpsed one agent tossing out smoke grenades as they bore down towards the barn—not that it would help them co-ordinate with the radio interference only getting stronger.

"*Motherfuckers!*" He could hear gargled shouts come in as he spotted flickers of white and torn flesh dart between the cornrows ahead. "*Gonna kill!*"

"Uncle Sam says hi," he growled. Ignoring the gunfire and shouts to his side, he fired his own weapon again, letting the bullets shred their way into the deformed hooded Klan freak now rushing towards him. Vestigial clawed limbs poking out of the chest flew away, as did spines of bone and malformed jaws sticking from beneath the bullet-riddled hood.

The last round in his magazine had been expended before the misshapen Klansman collapsed to the soil, coughing thick black mixtures of liquid gangrene onto the dust. Pushing past the dying stalks, he moved on ahead, trying to blot out the gunfire and chaos spreading out over the field.

Only a low, desperate, repeated muttering left his lips.

"*... run through the jungle...*"

S is for Slasher

Overhead, centered over the barn, the sky began to shift to an unnatural hue of crimson.

***

The air was reeking with a stench of cordite, smoke, and blood—crawling out from the loosened panels on the side of the barn, Frederick crept from obstacle to obstacle—behind the pickups dotted around the yard, and towards the house and silos that seemed to be the nexus of this compound. It felt no less safe—but all that mattered was it being further away from the flashes of white hoods and the exploding roars of shotgun barrels.

He moved to hide himself behind what looked like a tornado shelter—his shirt, smothered in dirt and dust, would help blend him in, or so he hoped. Surrounded by this madness, still reeling from whatever supernatural abattoir he had seemingly witnessed, all he could think about was that it was the same type of shirt he had worn to work, to family visits, to tiresome job interviews and soul-crushing car trips in traffic—

Once more, he inhaled deeply. Glancing over the side of the wooden shelter, he could glimpse figures emerging from the cover of smoke around the edge of the cornfields. Looked like cops, or National Guard, or something. Hard to tell the difference these days. And with their frantic, sudden bursts of gunfire, indiscriminately spearing through the dust and haze... he felt no reassurance from them.

Another deep breath. He could feel his mind

S is for Slasher

coming to a crossroads. One path to sink further into despair and oblivion, to sit here and weep, as mutant white supremacists and trigger-happy lawmen tore each other apart—the former likely to find him and send him on his way. Another path... one to look to these people that had murdered Nathan, probably many others, who talked of killing his people and so many others... and to stand up.

Slowly staggering upwards, he began to carefully open up the doors of the shelter, as something hit him. Peering inside, he could see a cache of weapons—shotguns, rifles, blunderbusses, crammed inside along with surplus ammunition.

A splintered piece of wood still hung off the chain on his right arm. This... and everything inside... was what he needed.

***

Seymour Abernathy, Grand Cyclops of the Midwestern Brotherhood of the Pure Aryan Anglo-Saxon Christian Crusade, felt only a vague numbing sensation from the bullets that had entered the talons growing out from his abdomen. In general, he had felt only a numbing sensation since he had dug up the... thing underneath Grandpappy's barn. He had taken the growths, the talons, the changes to him and his boys as blessings—and yet, even as feds moved to overrun his compound, he couldn't quite get that exhilaration he thought he'd get for all these years.

Him and the chapter had debated, as they felt the

S is for Slasher

bodily changes come over from every poor sap whose very essence they fed to that thing, just what the tarnation it was. A living thing, some fallen angel? Technological from—of course—Aryan civilizations gone past? Grandpappy, whose life it had also taken… thought it was a Jewish curse that had done him in. And even as Abernathy changed from this same power he too had wondered just what the hell he was truly dealing with, and if all this stuff he had convinced himself of wasn't just some desperate bullshit.

But talking himself out of it, that one day the thrill of a Klan uprising would be all worth it, had felt so much easier. Only, even the assurance felt fleeting, despite slogans and promises…

"You fuckers! White power!"

He discharged his shotgun once more into the body of another fed crawling out from the cornrows, as he darted to the side on strangely jointed, barbed heels. The boys also gave out their best battle cries and fighting spirit—but that same little annoying doubt that he was playing to the strings of something beyond him just kept on ringing in his skull like a persistent little skeeter.

Stumbling into his driveway, he found the rice cracker that dork they had chained up in the barn had been driving, still lying there. That wallet left on the dashboard had fallen onto the floor, in front of his eyes—he wondered, now, just why this attack had occurred after that little bastard earlier had arrived. *Perhaps*, he thought, *there would be a clue inside…*

S is for Slasher

Inside the vehicle, he willed one of his extra limbs to fetch the fine leather object, ignoring the smoke-choked clash behind him. Grabbing it with gaunt fingers, he tossed out the usual stupid membership cards, the gas station receipts—

An Illinois state ID. Frederick... Levi. Son of a bitch. So, the Feds had come for one of their own puppet masters. It all made sense now.

Turning around, he made for deeper into the compound, ignoring those Klansmen faltering around as bullets took their toll. This was something to fixate himself on—something surely to banish the doubt and those old feelings of desperate impotence.

"Levi! You goddamn little Kike! I'm comin' for you!"

***

He could hear them coming. Yelling the usual slurs and insults. Even as his father spoke of past oppressions and pogroms over childhood Yom Kippur dinners, Frederick had found it mostly distant, assured that nothing like this could affect his existence. Even in recent times, he hadn't wagered on being confronted by all the manifestations of hatred in this manner.

The automatic shotgun in his hands felt heavy, his hands around it clammy—but, as he leaned against the side of the house, he could feel all those now burning emotions crushed under apathy coming to the forefront. Changing him. Birthing him anew.

"Fucking little worm, you bought this on us, you little..."

Footsteps in the dirt came. Drawing in a sharp breath, he span around the corner, faced with a barely human-shaped mass of extraneous arms and mutilated bone bursting out from underneath those crude white robes—and fired.

He moved to the side as the Klansman lunged forward, ducking and weaving with speed he never thought he would have. As the first spent casing span onto the ground, he lunged forward, knocking the hideous mass off balance—it slammed into the side of the house, lashing back at him. Cuts appeared along his side—the pain was nothing.

Once more, he fired. The pain of the gunshot in his ear was also nothing. All that mattered was surviving this.

Only barely coherent, bloody gargles spat out from beneath the bent and twisted hood—as both main arms, clawed and stretched, lunged for him, Frederick lashed out in turn with the broken wood hanging from his chain. The sharpened edge slashed into just below the neck—enough of a distraction for him to level the shotgun between the eyes and pull the trigger. The head of the Klansman vanished, replaced by a massive viscid daubing of red and bone on the wood behind him, with tatters of cloth spiralling to the ground.

Frederick moved away, sliding fresh shells into the magazine from the bandolier he had picked up, moving to the corn ahead. He could see the distant

S is for Slasher

tips of pointed hoods streaming out from the compound, running away. The government forces would have their hands full trying to contain those already here, trying to make sense of what they'd find—but he wasn't going to let these ones slip away.

"*Malakh ha-mavet,*" he murmured briefly, before moving out for the cornrows. Above, the sky continued to shift to an unnatural shade of swirling red, as the buzz of what sounded like overhead drones passing rose and faded on by. He responded with only a momentary glance upward, before setting onwards.

He paused once more at the body of an AFT agent lying by the collapsed remains of a tractor on the edge of the cornfield. Expensive-looking body armor punctured at just the right points by a spread of shot. Hanging out from a gloved hand, a personal device still warbled out old song lyrics, just about audible over the distant din of the battle.

"*Over on the mountain, thunder magic spoke,*
Let the people know my wisdom, fill the land with smoke..."

Smirking dryly for a single moment, Frederick entered the corn, following the runners with all the unflinching purpose that now flowed through him.

The things ahead no longer scared him. There was no more meekness, no more doubt. Their hatred would not intimidate nor deter him, not from seeing that nobody like him need suffer their madness and cruelty ever again.

Time to finish what he had begun.

Old School

Ryan Day

A single thought occupied Roy's brain the day they let his ugly soul out of prison. One thought which had kept him strong through two long years of incarceration. The diamonds.

The robbery went from shit to worse, and there hadn't been five minutes to count the rocks before the heat had them burning rubber across the state. 'Them' being himself and his lousy partner, Mort. The pair made it to a creepy backroad in the ass-end of Nowhere, Somewhere, USA before luck upended another bucket of slop in the form of their engine blowing out. He'd long forgotten whose idea it was to bury the loot and return later, but that's what they did, drawing a crude map and tearing it in half. Insurance against an overeager party.

Three days later, Roy was picked up on an unrelated parole violation.

Fast forward two years and he wanted his diamonds.

Mort did a stretch himself as unrepentant scumbags tended to do – a weakness for booze and coke dragging him into one more scrape than he could weasel his way out of – but the state cut him

S is for Slasher

loose after six months. Roy found him crashing at a seedy crack den and they took the drive out to the forest-choked deadzone of Assford.

The intervening years hadn't been kind to Mort. Thinner hair and thicker glasses. Ruptured blood vessels gave him a ruddy St. Nick glow.

Roy fared better after twenty-four rounds with Chronos. He took a daily razor to his greying scalp and hours of confined exercise kept his body in solid condition.

'Did you bring your half?' Roy grunted, pulling the brakes on a narrow lane cutting through acres of dense woodland. It must have been fifty miles since they last saw another vehicle.

'Right here,' said Mort. 'And you?'

'It's safe.'

'Show me.'

'Right.'

Roy bent down, reaching between his feet. But, instead of producing his half of the map, he drew the small revolver hidden in his sock.

A deafening pop filled the car. The bullet punched through Mort's heart, arterial spurts painting the inside of the windscreen. A thick glaze dribbling down the glass and staining the moonlight Luciferian red on Roy's skin.

'I'm owed for those two years,' he purred, cold as ice.

Roy dragged his deceased former partner out through the passenger door and dumped him in a heap of twisted limbs. He took the crumpled half of map from the dead man's back pocket and felt good

S is for Slasher

about it. The spade in the trunk always had a dual purpose.

Mort's no-good carcass was lighter than it looked. Roy grabbed him by the ankles and hauled him deep into the undergrowth, disciplined enough to take care of garbage disposal before retrieving the diamonds. Better safe than sorry. He didn't bide his time for two infuriating years to get sloppy. If someone wanted to separate the rocks from his grasp a second time, they'd have to tear them from fists locked in rigor mortis.

The density of the trees and the totality of the night provided him plenty of cover to work, digging out clods of moist earth, the spade like a spoon tearing through sponge cake.

Eerie silence blanketed the woods, no chattering critters or restless owls to compete with the sound of shifting dirt. With riches on his mind, Roy gave it no thought. Excavating a shallow grave for his friend in perfect bliss until the distinct noise of twigs snapping like the dry explosion of popcorn kernels yanked him back into the moment. He stabbed the spade into the ground and drew the revolver from his waistband. Holding the gun in a crooked arm at navel-level, he scanned the periphery with three beady black eyes.

'Who's there?' he called to the darkness. 'Don't be playing with me. Get out of here unless you want a new airhole for your troubles. Do you hear me?'

The black void of the woods mocked him.

'Goddamnit!' he spat, wiping a film of sweat from the nape of his neck.

S is for Slasher

He got back to work. A jagged semi-circle of moon hung over Roy like an executioner's guillotine. Each star a voyeur, a cosmic eyeball peeping on human secrets. Maybe that alone was the reason he felt watched. Others might call it the guilt making his hair stand on end. But Roy had made a career of being vile and duplicitous, why should guilt bother him now? Spade in hand, corpse at his feet, he felt as guilty as a gardener planting a rose bush.

Between each scoop of damp earth, Roy craned his neck left and right, distracted by every fluctuation of the shadows, muscles tense, ready to empty the gun into the tree line and give any snoopers a nasty shock. But he kept the lump of cruel metal in his pants, reminding himself to focus on what was real. Beautiful sparkling diamonds.

Worms boiled from the crude grave where the soil had been disturbed, chopped into writhing pink spaghetti, mulched in with the fungal vegetation waiting to feast on Mort. Other creepy crawlies slunk from the undergrowth to investigate the sticky sweet slick of crimson pooling from the fatal wound.

'I'd say you deserved better, but you really didn't,' Roy said solemnly.

He left the spade stuck in the ground, unceremoniously kicking heaps of dirt over Mort with his boot.

Someone moaned.

Roy span on his heels, hand snapping to the revolver. Sweat greased the butt.

'Alright,' he warned, pointing the gun at a whole lot of nothing making a fool of him. 'I'll give you three seconds to show your ugly face before I fill you with lead! I'm not joking, asshole!'

Again, silence abused his ego.

Seconds ticked by, each a slow razorblade running the length of his spine, but no one appeared. No one made a sound.

Roy looked at the grave. All that remained of his former friend were the toes of his sneakers and his protruding gut. It seemed less funny now with paranoia chewing an ulcer in his stomach.

He thumbed back the hammer, choosing to confront whatever was lurking in the darkness teasing him. He'd already killed one person tonight and he was prepared to put down as many snoopers as he had bullets.

His eyes saw very little in the gloomy cage of woodland, but his ears were alert to every whisper of wind. His own footfalls crackled the undergrowth, but none joined the cacophony. A one-man band, his frantic heart played his ribs like a xylophone.

But the heavy breathing wasn't his own.

Roy stopped. There was no denying it. Someone was out there. Lurking.

'You better show yourself, you son of a bitch!'

Sweat oozed across his razor-nicked scalp.

'What are you, some kind of pervert?'

Dead wood crunched.

Roy blasted a panicked bullet into thin air.

S is for Slasher

If someone had shot at him, he would have immediately high-tailed it from the situation. An act no doubt very noisy. But, still, silence assaulted him like a psychic virus.

Maybe he was mistaken. Maybe he was losing his nerve with age. Maybe he was flat-out going loopy.

Roy sighed. A long juddering breath released through nicotine-stained teeth.

Then he made the mistake of turning around and came face-to-face with the most horrendous thing he had ever seen. More *thing* than man; a hulking, disfigured brute straight out of Lon Chaney's workshop

Roy couldn't breathe. Couldn't remember how. Trembling, he staggered backwards until the rough bark of a tree halted his pathetic retreat.

The Lurker held the spade aloft in one vein-engorged hand.

Roy opened his mouth wide enough to scream the nightmare away. Or attempt to. But the scream ended before it began. The Lurker drove the spade through his mouth, slicing both cheeks like Christmas ham, chomping through meat, tendons and bone until it met the solid wood of the trunk.

***

Cindy was a straight-A student but, today, distraction plagued her.

People almost always used words like "homely" to describe Cindy. She had auburn hair, kept neat

S is for Slasher

and straight in a center parting. Rosy cheeks which on a child would have been called adorably chubby. A dimpled chin and large, green eyes.

Cindy struggled to keep her focus on her schoolwork, ever drifting to the conundrum of her parents. They were fighting again. A more common occurrence every year, but this one seemed particularly bad. The kind of fight that spirals towards the big D-word.

Her mind slipped forwards through a multitude of scenarios, arriving at the point of contemplating which of her parents would remain at their nice middle-class house in their nice middle-class neighborhood and which would be stuffing their things into a suitcase and hitting the road. She would stay with her mom, even if that meant the heartbreak of leaving Cherrywood Drive. They lived close to school and close to her friends. Not to mention sentimentality. She made seventeen years of memories in that house.

'Cindy, are you listening to me? You're staring into space. Hey, are you daydreaming about what Steve's body looks like under that letterman jacket?'

Cindy resurfaced from the quagmire back to the classroom at Sleigher High.

Beside her, Angie had been having a one-sided conversation for quite some time. Angie, her best friend since third grade. Though a lot had changed in that time, not least of all Angie's body. She jumped the queue in development and had boys drooling after her since way before Cindy had any

S is for Slasher

idea what use boys could be. Those specific features, coupled with hair like a vibrant dandelion and dazzling blue eyes, made her the most popular girl in school. All the boys wanted to date her, and all the girls wanted to be her friend to soak up the attention by association.

'What *is* Steve's body like? Is he ripped?' Angie's mouth never stopped.

'I don't know,' said Cindy truthfully. 'We haven't got that far.'

'Tonight could be the night.'

'Tonight?'

'Don't tell me you forgot? The party?'

'Oh, right… the party. I don't know, Angie. I'm not sure I feel like going… Besides, my parents would never let me.'

'No way, you can't miss it! Forget about your parents – you're seventeen, you're practically an adult now! You know how to climb out of a window, don't you?'

Partying never appealed much to Cindy. The one and only time she drank a beer (supplied by Angie, of course) she made it halfway down the bottle before spending the rest of the night hurling over the toilet bowl. No part of her craved getting drunk, losing her inhibitions and making stupid decisions. She knew too many horror stories.

'I'll think about it.'

'Think quickly, because Steve is definitely going to be there and so are a bunch of drunk girls with loose morals.'

S is for Slasher

Cindy couldn't ignore Steve's popularity with the opposite sex, and she couldn't expunge the knowledge he wasn't a virgin.

The other kids wondered aloud why the school quarterback lowered himself to date a plain, academic girl. They called her wicked names, the worst being "challenge" because she didn't know what it meant and thus it came back to her in the small hours, twisted into cruel blades of her own imagining.

Whatever the truth of their relationship, Cindy fell for him all the same.

***

Cindy arrived home to the sound of vegetables meeting a grisly end on the chopping board. Vibrant red ringed her mom's eyes. She'd aged a handful of years in the past few weeks. Dad wouldn't be home for hours yet.

'Good day at school?' her mom asked with a forced smile.

Cindy's own gesture was just as fraught, averting her eyes. 'The usual.'

Not the time to bring up parties.

Most girls Cindy knew her own age had bedrooms bursting with personality. Or what they wished their personality to be perceived as. She lacked an aesthetic touch of her own; muted bedspread, pale blue walls and just three posters (David Bowie, the Beatles, and a Jane Austen quote.)

S is for Slasher

She kicked off her shoes and turned on the radio, the dial tuned to her favorite classic rock station. Then she sat at her desk to focus her brain on studying. It must have worked because the next time she looked up from her books was when the shouting started. *Dad's home.*

The pair of them were a slow earthquake; a grumble spreading through the house, building in intensity to full window-rattling tremors. The context and key points of tonight's verbal duel were lost amid the insults and accusations.

Cindy flopped onto her bed, clamping her hands over her ears. It helped a little. She thought about Steve. About his square jaw and the delicate hairs on his top lip which tickled her when they kissed. She thought about his piercing gaze and the way his powerful footballer's hands devoured her own.

Steve – every seventeen-year-old's dreamboat. The kind of guy a lovesick girl could imagine a future with. Two kids, a Labrador and a white picket fence.

The future seemed quaint and easy. The problems lie in the present.

She liked Steve. She loved Steve. But was she ready to go *All the Way*…?

Her parents found a second wind below, excavating arguments from days gone by. A greatest hits of hurt and recriminations. The opening act of an all-nighter, for sure.

Cindy sighed, defeated, and picked up her phone extension. Angie's number on speed-dial, naturally.

'Hello?'

S is for Slasher

'Hey, it's me. I've thought about it and... when can you pick me up?'

'Yes, bitch! I knew you wouldn't let me down. What have you told your mom?'

'Nothing. They're too preoccupied to notice me right now.'

'Still fighting?'

'Still fighting.'

'You deserve a night away from them. I knew there was a bad girl hiding away in there, Cindy.'

She laughed the comment away – the only thing "bad" about her were her Gym grades. 'If you say so.'

'Be ready in an hour,' said Angie. 'We're taking Doug's car. We'll wait for you at the bottom of the road, opposite the bus stop.'

Cindy hung up and assessed her current outfit. A grey sweater and blue jeans. The last casual social event she attended took place at a bowling alley. What did a girl wear to an illegal party?

An hour later, Cindy inspected herself again, this time with the aid of her bedroom mirror. Now wearing a loose white blouse adorned with lavender print, a plain black skirt, and knee-high leather boots (a rarely worn Christmas gift.)

With Angie and Doug waiting, she didn't have the luxury of marinating in her anxieties. She shimmied open the window, staring down at a much steeper drop to the manicured front lawn than she remembered. Exacerbated by nerves, she saw a perilous plummet, a one-way ticket to broken ankles.

S is for Slasher

Cindy took a breath and lifted one leg out into the open air, hooking her arms around the drainpipe running alongside the window. She descended slowly, jerking on petrified muscles. The relief when her feet touched solid ground was rapturous.

Paranoia urged her to hunker low to the ground, scanning her surroundings to make sure her parents weren't lurking in the bushes ready to spring out and bust her.

But the coast was clear.

Doug drove a sky-blue convertible, impossible to miss. His pride and joy. His baby.

Cindy hugged her best friend – noting how her neon-pink dress strained to contain her braless boobs – and hopped in the backseat. Released from the conservative confines of school, Angie teased her voluminous nest of blonde hair into an even grander tower of spun gold. Her lips resembled fresh slices of liver. Smokey bullet-wound eyes. Gold constellations glittering on her cheeks.

Painted like a Hollywood starlet, she gave Cindy a critical appraisal.

'Put this on, you look dangerously close to an old spinster.'

Angie held out a tube of lipstick. A bold earthy maroon.

'I don't know,' said Cindy. 'Won't it be too much?'

'*Too much* doesn't exist. This is your chance to blow Steve away. That's what you want, isn't it?'

'I guess…'

'Steve will think it's hot,' said Doug.

S is for Slasher

Cindy knew very little about Angie's latest boyfriend (and Steve's best friend) other than the obvious – he played football.

Full of trepidation, Cindy daubed her lips in the rearview mirror. The color demanded attention, for sure. She felt like she'd stuck a flashing light on her face. But if there was ever a night to be brave and bold, tonight was the night.

'Where is Steve?' she asked. Just saying his name sent a ripple of sparkly warmth through unexpected places.

'Already at the school,' said Doug. 'He went ahead to get the beers in with his brother's ID.'

'The school?'

'Yeah, the old abandoned middle school on the edge of town. It's been empty since way back. I guess whoever owns it now just left the place to rot.'

'A derelict school? It sounds like a death trap.'

'Nah, high schoolers have been throwing parties there for years. You need to relax, Cindy. Learn to cut loose.'

***

From the backseat of Doug's convertible, Cindy watched the middle school appear from the dense woodland like a flasher. Invisible one moment, suddenly presented in full glory the next. They parked amid the smattering of other cars gouging wounds into an old sports field. Heavy metal blasted

S is for Slasher

from the main building where most of the party had congregated.

Doug hauled a crate of beers under his arm, leading the way with a pretty girl on either side with all the confident swagger of someone used to being places he shouldn't, doing things he shouldn't.

Cindy trailed, fidgeting with her outfit as insecurity gave her a headache from the relentless mutterings in her ear only she could hear. Booze-sappy eyeballs seemed to challenge her sober gaze everywhere she looked. She needed to find Steve. She'd feel safe with Steve.

The school smelled bad. Damp and sweaty. When Angie told her about a big party, she hadn't pictured the spiderwebs wrapping everything like cotton gauze or the piles of cigarette butts and joint ends in every corner.

Doug thrust a beer can into her hand. She took it out of ingrained politeness but made no effort to pop the tab.

'Steve!' The rush of spotting him spiked her voice to an embarrassing pitch.

Cindy ran towards his golden halo of hair marking him out in the crowd. Embracing, their lips locked. Hers timid, aware of the bodies around them. His fierce, full of adolescent fervor. His tongue and breath tasted malty.

'You look hot,' were his first words.

The smear of dark lipstick she left behind stood out like a bruise.

Steve had swapped his usual letterman for a leather jacket. The aftershave on his neck smelled

S is for Slasher

like a lumberjack's cottage. The scent of both, raw and masculine, soothed her.

His lips assaulted her throat, mesmerized by lust.

'How much have you drunk?' she giggled.

'You're beautiful,' he moaned down her ear.

'You're sweet, Steve. Do you want to dance?'

'That would be one way to put it,' he grinned.

***

Angie and Doug showed their faces for all of five minutes before slipping away for some privacy.

'I saw a storage shed on the drive in,' said Doug.

'You want to have sex in a *shed*?'

'Why not? It's private and I saw the chain was broken on the door. I don't know what you want, Angie, we're not exactly going to find a four-poster bed, are we?'

Angie pouted, hands on her hips. Doug smiled – it was the pose she always struck before caving in.

'Come on,' he said, leading the way.

Just like he'd said, the chain lay coiled on the ground, a pile of rust-red links. The door stood ajar, offering a sliver of perpetual darkness.

'Do you have a flashlight?' Angie asked.

'Do I look like I have a flashlight? You never like doing it with the lights on anyway.'

Doug's fingertips probed the walls for a light switch, scraping trails through years of filth. His grasping hand came to a thin chain dangling from the ceiling. He gave it a tug and a sickly yellow glow filled the small space, exposing precious little

S is for Slasher

floor between the clutter of abandoned gym equipment.

Angie's flesh crawled. 'This place is horrid.'
'Quit complaining and get your clothes off.'
'You're such a charmer, Doug.'

Regardless, she did as commanded, slipping effortlessly out of her flattering dress down to nothing but her baby-blue panties. Doug raced to catch up and cleared space on a low unit. Angie sat back, cold lacquered wood biting her thighs, and beckoned him closer until their skin touched.

Suddenly, she flinched, pricking Doug's chest with her long nails.

'Ouch! What was that for?'

Her eyes were so wide her entire lids appeared to have receded back into her skull. A stare fixed over his shoulder. 'I think someone is spying on us.'

Doug turned just far enough to see the door, reluctant to leave his spot between her thighs. He'd left it open a crack to circulate air. He didn't see anyone.

'Do you want me to shut it?'

'No. I want you to go check. And, if it's some creep, I want you to kick his ass. That's what I want.'

'Really?' he groaned.

'Really.' Angie crossed her arms and pulled her thighs shut.

Doug huffed and grumbled. 'Fine.'

Shirtless, he dawdled towards the open door. Poking his head through the gap, he quickly scanned left and right.

S is for Slasher

'I don't see anyone.'

'Go *outside* and check.'

Doug clenched his jaw but said nothing, driven by the burning in his pants. Without looking back, he disappeared outside.

A minute passed. Then two. Doug failed to return.

'If this is some kind of game and you're trying to scare me, you can forget about having sex tonight,' she called out.

Worry froze into a solid boulder of anxiety in her gut.

'Doug! Stop being an asshole!'

She snatched her dress off the ground, furiously swatting at snotty strings of spiderweb. The coolness of the night nipped rigid welts all over her exposed skin. She wrestled with her dress, struggling to make progress against the cold, fury and fear.

Something kissed her bare shoulder. Instinctive fingers came away moist, smeared with black. Another drop hit the same spot, a dark crimson tear.

Angie looked up.

Overwhelming terror tied a knot in her throat, blocking the scream desperate to escape.

Doug hung over the edge of the shed, head limp and mouth agape. Grotesque pits of gore replaced his eyes, oozing the thick rain which continued to drizzle over her tanned skin.

Angie span away from the horror, wobbling on weak legs. Tears prickled her cheeks and rivers of

S is for Slasher

mucus plugged her nostrils. A sharp twig punctured her heel but she barely registered the pain.

When she saw the hulking figure watching her, the scream finally escaped, but broken and strained like a thousand violin strings cut with a sword.

The Lurker took a single menacing step forward and spurred Angie to action. She fought back control of her legs and scarpered any direction her feet could manage. An overgrown football field provided a wide, open space without obstacles.

Angie dared a single look back over her shoulder. The Lurker hadn't given chase, but it gave her little comfort. She ignored the long object in his hand and pumped her feet with every ounce of energy she could muster. Each step pounded the broken twig deeper into the underside of her foot.

She ran at full fury until a forceful impact between her shoulder blades stopped her dead. Confused, she stared at a length of steel javelin sprouting from her chest. Numbness spread through her limbs from the fatal wound and Angie slumped forwards. The tip of the javelin pierced the ground, propping her body at a slanted angle as she fell. Then she began to slide, squelching all the way.

***

Ernie Moss hated every single person at the party.

Granted, he didn't know each of them individually, but they were all part of the problem. He'd been the Sleigher High punching bag since the

S is for Slasher

day he stepped through its carceral doors. A scrawny kid prone to coughs and colds, violently enslaved by allergies.

Ernie was sick of it all. Sick of vulgar names and getting tripped in the hallways. Sick of wedgies and swirlies. Sick of stink bombs in his locker and dog shit in his shoes.

Ernie followed to the abandoned middle school with retribution in mind.

Equipped with a lighter stolen from his dad and a jerry can full of gasoline, he'd incinerate every inbred halfwit who made his existence pure misery. He chose a spot on the north side of the main building farthest away from the party. Time enough for his immolating vengeance to spread and grow before alarm could be raised.

He splashed gasoline across mold ravaged walls and doused sad rows of wooden desks, caustic fumes burning his nose and stinging his eyes. Rats and cockroaches fled from the shower of chemicals, the floor coming alive in writhing brown chaos. Ernie covered his mouth with his sleeve and sparked the lighter. A long blue flame, dancing, mirroring his ecstasy and adrenaline.

He tossed the lighter into the largest stinking puddle and watched flames race brilliant azure, shimmering like a tropical ocean. Greedy flames devoured the fuel, bursting into an orange crescendo, radiating an apocalypse of light and heat.

Job done, Ernie fled the school, out into the woods where he'd left his bike. But, returning, it was gone. The tree was definitely the right tree, distinguished by a face-like deformity in the trunk he knew he'd remember. But no bike.

Did someone follow him? How could they? He had no friends or acquaintances to blab his plans to. He moved invisibly through the world.

Some wasted loser from the party must have wandered out and stolen it.

His heart thundered, no longer pleasantly. Fear replaced the thrill of revenge.

If Steve or his cronies found out what he'd done, they'd kill him.

It transpired to be a short-lived worry. Something metal and ruthless wrapped around his throat, constricting and pulverizing his windpipe. His eyes bulged out of their sockets, blood vessels popping like burst waterpipes.

Red turned to black, but not before Ernie managed to recognize the weapon squeezing the life from his body as the chain from his missing bike.

***

Steve's lips were like wild animals. Breath hot and boozy, it made Cindy uncomfortable.

'Come on,' he moaned. 'I want to show you something.'

'What?'

'You'll see. Don't spoil the fun.'

The empty and decrepit school creeped Cindy out. As socially awkward as she was, the anxiety of straying too far from activity kept her in place. But she couldn't say it out loud, Steve might think her

S is for Slasher

childish. A little girl frightened of the dark. And he also might think she didn't trust him. She didn't want Steve to feel that way.

Angie ditched her for Doug, hardly being discreet about it, and nobody else in her circle of friends was invited. Angie had always been her social outlier. Realistically, following Steve was her only option.

'Alright,' she conceded. 'Lead the way.'

Steve licked his lips, salacious thoughts pulling his mouth into a knife-slash grin.

The journey couldn't have been far, but the claustrophobic atmosphere made Cindy feel worlds away from the party. She couldn't always be sure what she was stepping in, trying to reassure herself the occasional mushiness wasn't something grim. And failing.

'In here,' said Steve.

They entered a dank classroom. Cindy instinctively reached for a light switch but of course there was no power in the building. Educational posters lining the walls were visible in a silvery haze of moonlight permeating green and black filth clouding the windows. An obscene number of beer cans, some years old, littered the floor. The classroom reeked like a swamp in the height of summer.

Steve stood over in the corner, giggling. The pink-faced tittering of the heavily inebriated. The source of his mirth was a small cage, the inside choked with hoary sawdust like nicotine-stained

S is for Slasher

cotton candy. A tiny skeleton nestled within. A hamster.

'I guess when the school closed the class dorks forgot about poor Hammy,' Steve cackled.

Cindy didn't get the joke.

'Is this why you brought me here?' she asked.

Steve dumped the cage and pulled her in tight to his body. He kissed her hard enough to make her lips sting. His tongue punctured her mouth like a fleshy harpoon.

Cindy placed her hands flat on his chest, pushing space between them. It did little to stem his vigor. His fingers probed her thighs.

'No,' she said. 'Not here.'

'There're a million empty rooms. Pick one.'

Cindy gestured to their grim surroundings. 'Not *here*. Not in this horrible place. I don't want it to happen like this for us.'

'Geez, it's just sex.' The annoyance played in full color on his face.

'Maybe to you,' she said.

'I thought you loved me,' Steve pouted, turning his back.

The words hurt like a paper cut across her heart. She meant the sentiment and she'd never said it to anyone else. Not romantically. The words carried weight, but she wouldn't let it burden her into the obligation of sex before she was ready.

'Why did you even bother coming tonight?' he sneered. Unrecognizable. A malefic gargoyle.

'To see you.' Her voice was soft, quivering on the precipice of tears.

'You came here to make a fool out of me,' he spat back. 'You can be such a bitch sometimes, Cindy.'

The more he stomped her feelings into the dirt, the easier he made it for her to walk away. Bawling like a child denied ice cream before dinner. But she wasn't a commodity to be enjoyed at his convenience.

'Whatever,' she sighed, colder than death. 'I'm going home.'

***

Cindy returned to the hub of the party to find a deserted space with only the detritus of youthful recreation proving that the other kids were ever there. They'd even taken the stereo. She tried to remember when the music stopped. The sole sound was Steve's shuffling gait behind her.

'Where did everyone go?' she asked the emptiness more than Steve.

He shrugged and grabbed a beer like he'd come off a twelve-hour shift down the mines.

A door with a faded sign of a stick figure in a miniskirt clanged open and punched Cindy's heart up into her throat. The face that emerged was familiar. Black hair and black lipstick. A girl paler than moonbeams. Rita.

Noticing the staring audience of one, Rita quickly wiped at the stray flecks of white powder clinging to the fine hairs of her nostril.

'Oh, hi,' she said with a goofy smile.

S is for Slasher

'The accident happened when he was thirteen. His mother couldn't handle a husband who worked twenty-hour days and a complicated son, so she was out of the picture by then. I regret there not being anyone around to keep him straight. As it was, nothing stopped him cutting class whenever he liked. The way it happened was he got the ball he was tossing stuck up in a tree. He slipped and landed face-first on a spade I'd carelessly left propped the wrong way up…

'The injury left Ronald horribly disfigured, and his mind deteriorated from there. He never spoke another word and the smallest thing set him off in a violent rage. His body survived the accident, but not his soul.

'I've cared for him since that day, under heavy medication. Not much of a life, but we got by. Then, a few days ago, a report aired on the news about some kid cutting class who'd fallen through the rotten roof of a derelict barn and broken his neck. Paralyzed. Irreversible.

'The story made Ronald inconsolable, howling like no animal I've ever heard. I couldn't calm him, not even with the strongest meds all mixed up and thrown together. He knocked me to the floor and smashed the back door off the hinges.

'I knew in my gut he'd find his way here. This is where he should have been when the accident happened. I think, in his own twisted way, he's trying to save you all from his own fate.'

A long pause followed like a cassette running out of tape and reeling through nothing.

S is for Slasher

Then Steve laughed. 'That's the stupidest story I've ever heard. And it doesn't make sense. Who's cutting class, grandpa? It's the middle of the goddamn night and this dump has been closed for years.'

Ned sighed. 'It doesn't have to make sense to you so long as it makes sense to him. He doesn't think like an ordinary person.'

'If he's so dangerous, why didn't you send him to the nut house?'

'Maybe I should have. But he is my son and I love him. He lost everything, why punish him further? I wasn't strong enough to inflict the necessary evil and for that I'm sorry. But hate me later. You need to escape. Do you have a car?'

'I came in Doug's,' said Cindy. 'But we don't know where he is.'

Steve crushed his empty can and belched. 'He leaves a spare under the seat. I'll drive.'

Rita measured him up, teetering on the spot, cheeks flushed maroon. '*Can* you drive?'

'It's that or stay here with the maniac.'

'Please,' Cindy intervened. 'Save the arguing until we're safe.'

***

The other cars were gone – a drunken race to the chocolate tsunami on Main Street – just Doug's blue convertible looking anachronistic in the misty desolation.

S is for Slasher

with the ferocity of her grip. Inching closer until she was looking directly down the barrel at the Lurker's disfigured face. Her finger twitched.

But her conviction to finish the job came too late. The Lurker bolted upright where he lay and flailed his arms. The first knocked the gun away, the second sent Cindy flying through a tower of stacked beer cans.

Groggy, with fresh blood trickling into her eyes, Cindy crawled through charred debris. Raising her head to watch on helplessly as the Lurker lifted Rita up into the air and slammed her through a flaming table, igniting a hurricane of embers as her clothing and hair caught fire. Cindy screamed at the sight of her pale arm stuck out from the inferno, flesh dripping from the bone like wax.

Then the Lurker turned his attention to her.

Cindy scrambled towards the door left open on broken hinges by his entry, her lungs choked to pea-sized pockets by the smog. The gun lay on the threshold, glowing angelic from combined fire and moonlight. She grabbed it as she stumbled into the open air, numb to the blisters it seared deep into her palm.

She turned, raising the weapon with new surety, the silver sight holding steady between the Lurker's misaligned eyes. But she didn't shoot. Something better came to mind.

She shifted her sights, lining up the fire extinguisher fixed to the wall instead, and pulled the trigger.

S is for Slasher

A ball of brilliant yellow bloomed through the ground floor of the school, the force of the blast propelling Cindy several feet backwards through the air into a dense thicket. From her thorny bed, she listened to her tormentor's death wails as the school imploded around him.

And then she cried.

Cradled by the woods, alone but alive, she cried for a very long time.

S is for Slasher

Hide & Seek

Jason B. Edwards

It was Friday afternoon and everyone was sprawled out around Sophie's living room watching a DVD that Jared had brought. Jared and Iris had made out at last week's football game, and now the two of them were lying on the floor with their heads resting on the same pillow. Sitting directly behind them on the couch was Cat, who alternated between commenting on Jared and Iris' physical proximity and talking loudly over the movie itself. Seated next to her were Mallory and Cindy, who were currently passing back and forth between them a half-empty bottle of Diet Pepsi mixed with rum and laughing loudly at everything Cat said.

Sophie had claimed the recliner to the right of the couch, while on the other side of the room, sitting in a matching recliner, was Chase. Sophie could feel Jared's irritation building – Cat always made fun of the movies he picked, and for some reason he seemed surprised every time – but she was happy to see that Mallory and Cindy were distracted. For the past few weeks, both of them had been obsessed with the idea that Sophie had a crush on Chase, and they mercilessly taunted her for it in spite of the fact that Mallory had actually dated Chase for two months over the summer.

When the Diet Pepsi bottle was empty, Cindy rose to her feet, wobbled a bit, steadied, and asked Sophie where her parents' liquor cabinet was.

"My parents don't keep liquor in the house," Sophie said. "I told you that last time."

Cindy stared blankly at her. "Are you serious?"

"We've had this whole conversation before."

"Bullshit!"

Jared shushed. "This part is good," he said.

Cindy loudly shushed back. In a stage whisper, she added, "No part of this movie is good."

"Cindy, I think you've already had enough," Chase said, adopting the voice of a stern bartender. "I'm going to have to cut you off."

"Shut up, Chase!" Iris said.

"Make me," Chase said, with a wink.

"Come on, man," Jared said, wincing. "Don't do that."

"Oh, you want some of this, too?" Chase said, winking at Jared as well.

"Nobody wants any of that!" Mallory said, her words slightly slurred. "Trust me, Chase."

A tense silence filled the room, punctuated only by the score from the movie. It was the closest that Mallory had come to acknowledging her and Chase's relationship. No one was quite sure how he would respond.

"Exactly my point," Chase said. "It's a matter of supply and demand. If I lower demand on... all this," Chase gestured up and down his body. "The value goes up."

"Dude," Cat said, but she was trying not to laugh. "That's not how value works."

As the room filled with indistinct chatter and laughter, Sophie let her vision go out of focus. The 40-inch plasma screen television in front of her became a blur of sand, fire, and blood, while the sound of gunfire rattled out of her dad's surround-system. Her thoughts drifted back to a night two weeks ago when she took her dog Riley out for a late-night walk. She walked deep into the neighborhood, past the rows and rows of identical houses, until she came to a house with a bright yellow Hummer parked in the driveway. While Riley was pissing on the sidewalk, Sophie heard a quiet popping sound from behind the house. At first, she thought it might be a firecracker or some other kind of explosive, but when the sound repeated three times in the same rhythm, she realized it was a gun being fired, possibly with a silencer. She knew she should keep walking, but instead, Sophie just stayed there, standing on the sidewalk, staring into the impenetrable darkness of the forest, until Riley pulled so hard on the leash that she nearly fell over.

"Sophie, what are you looking at?"

It was Mallory's voice that brought her back to reality. Sophie realized she had turned towards the window and was staring out at the street.

Sophie smiled and tried to play it off. "I zoned out for a second," she said. "Did I miss anything important?"

"In this movie?" Cat said. "No way."

S is for Slasher

There was another round of laughter. Without speaking, Jared grabbed the remote of the DVD player, and pressed 'eject'. He stood up and walked over to the TV where he grabbed the disc out of the player and began putting it back into its box.

"Thank God," Cindy said. "I don't know how much more I could've taken."

Mallory and Cat laughed, but Sophie remembered how seriously Jared always took his movie recommendations and was not looking forward to having him sulk for the rest of the night.

"No liquor," Mallory sighed. "And the movie was a total bust. What are we supposed to do now?"

There was a moment of silence. Sophie saw her chance. "Do you guys want to go outside and look around the woods?" she asked.

***

The woods at the edge of Sophie's neighborhood were dense and dark. To some members of the group, they offered the chance to surreptitiously make out. To others, they offered only the threat of dirt, bugs, and the mild chill of mid-November in the South. Ultimately, everyone agreed to Sophie's suggestion for the same reason: it was something to do.

Sophie didn't let on that she had a destination in mind. She let them all think they were just wandering aimlessly, as they had done on numerous afternoons before. Cindy and Mallory, still punchy from the liquor, surged ahead, but Sophie managed

S is for Slasher

to keep them on track with the occasional course-correction. After taking a nasty fall early on, Cat had bounced back, no worse for wear, and was struggling to keep up with Cindy and Mallory. Iris and Jared, after a round of bickering that might have been playful or serious, disappeared together into the dark woods.

Chase hung back and walked side-by-side with Sophie. She wasn't upset about his company – she found his humor more amusing than annoying, which put her in the minority amongst the group. Every couple of minutes, Mallory would turn and cast an inscrutable look at the two of them.

At one point, they passed a row of trees with pink ribbon threaded across them, which Sophie recognized as a sign that the entire area would soon be demolished and replaced with new houses. She was surprised that development of the neighborhood was still ongoing – the houses on either side of hers were still empty, and she knew plenty of other streets in the subdivision were dotted with 'For Sale' signs.

It was on the edge of this area marked for destruction that she caught sight of their destination, though Cindy was the first to see it.

"Hey, what's up with all the shit over there?" she called out, before breaking into an awkward half-run, kicking up leaves and dirt as she scrambled up an incline.

Sophie started to shush her, but then decided not to. *Let her scream*, she thought. *Let them all scream, if that's how they want it.*

S is for Slasher

The rest of the group picked up speed and followed Cindy up the incline, while Iris and Jared emerged from the woods to rejoin the others, both their faces looking flushed.

On the other side of the hill was what appeared to be a makeshift obstacle course: a dozen wooden boxes stacked up along a stretch of flat ground in ascending order, old and half-worn tires laid on the ground next to each other, a rope ladder hanging from a high and sturdy branch, a series of wooden planks nailed between two trees, and most surprisingly, several lengths of barbed wire stretched between posts that had been nailed into the ground.

"Oh my god," Sophie murmured, lost in a quiet reverie. It was exactly how she had imagined it.

"Damn, Sophie," Jared said, "I didn't know you lived next-door to a fucking Ironman course?"

"Iron Man?" Iris asked. "Like the cartoon?"

"No," Jared shook his head. "It's like a, uh, race. A triathlon."

"But there's no room to race out here," Iris said. "This is only big enough for one person."

Jared groaned. "It was a point of comparison!"

Chase walked over to the barbed wire and crouched down next to it. "It's a low crawl," he said. "The Army uses these for training."

"Pft, right," Cat scoffed. "Like you know anything about what the Army uses for training."

"My uncle was in the Navy!"

"My point exactly," Cat said. "That's the Navy. Not the Army!"

While everyone else wandered around, kicking and poking at the various objects, Sophie walked deliberately across the entire course towards something she spotted at the other end. There was a stack of heavy branches that had been leaned up against a tree at the other end of a narrow clearing.

Sophie stepped out into this clearing, then looked back towards the area where her friends were playing. Affixed to the tree with two nails was a piece of steel, riddled with bullet holes, painted with the design of a target.

Hanging from the top nail was a small, golden cross on a metal chain. Without a moment's hesitation, Sophie took it down and looked at it. She ran her hands over the cross, feeling the shape of it with her thumb.

Sophie was shaken out of her thoughts by the sound of rustling behind her. She pocketed the necklace and turned around.

Mallory was there, standing just a bit too close, her breath sweet with alcohol and cola. "Did you know this was out here?" she asked.

"No," Sophie said, a little too quickly. "Why?"

"You don't seem surprised to see it," Mallory said.

Sophie shrugged. "Maybe I'm a little harder to impress than the rest of you."

Mallory narrowed her eyes at Sophie. She might have said something, but they were interrupted by a flash of light, followed by a scream of pain.

When Sophie turned, she saw Cindy rubbing her eyes and making a pained expression. "What the

S is for Slasher

fuck is wrong with you!" she yelled.

A few feet away, Chase was holding the digital camera he'd gotten for his birthday last year. Since then, the Sony CyberShot DSC-W1 had been a constant presence at all gatherings, big and small. Chase had a habit of getting someone's attention and then surprising them with the camera's highest flash setting. Somehow, Cindy was still falling for this.

"My bad," Chase said, grinning widely. "Didn't see you there." Before Cindy could respond, Chase looked over and saw Sophie and Mallory standing by the target. "What's that?" he asked, before blundering over to the tree. His eyes went wide when he spotted the piece of metal.

"Oh, sick," Chase said. "Hey, guys!" he shouted over to the others. "Come check this out! Target practice!"

At Chase's insistence, everybody else made their way over to the tree. As they were taking turns banging on it and shaking it, Sophie turned around to take another look at the stack of branches, but as she turned, she caught a glimpse of movement out of the corner of her eye.

Two words popped into her head: *not yet*.

"Guys," Sophie said. "I think we should head back."

"No way," Jared said as he scanned the horizon. "I want to see if there's any more of this stuff out here."

Chase nodded in agreement as he raised his camera and snapped a photo of the target.

S is for Slasher

Sophie took another look at the branches stacked around the trees. There were spaces in between them where she could see through to the darkness behind. In those spaces, she imagined that she could see the shape of a man, moving back and forth, watching them, waiting.

Chase positioned himself in front of the tree so that the target was directly behind his head. "Check it out, guys," he said, grinning. "William Tell!"

"Seriously," Sophie said. "The sun's going down, it's gonna get really cold. We should go back inside."

"That's not even what William Tell is," Jared said. "You need to have the target above your head. Plus you need an apple."

Chase laughed. "I'm not the only one who needs an apple, fatass."

"Fatass?" Jared looked down at his small gut, protruding slightly over his belt. "I think that's a little harsh."

"Fuck off, Chase," Iris said. "You're just mad because nobody wants to fuck you except for–"

"Please!" Sophie shouted. "Can we please go?"

Everyone turned all at once towards Sophie and she immediately wished she hadn't shouted.

"What's the big deal?" Cat said. "It's not that cold."

Mallory tilted her nose up slightly in a smug expression. "That's not why she wants to go back."

"Why, then?"

"Don't know," Mallory crossed her arms. "She won't say."

S is for Slasher

"So it's a secret?" Chase asked. "Now you've got to tell us." He was still standing with his head pressed against the metal target.

"Come on," Cat goaded. "Tell us."

"Who built all this?" Jared asked. "What's it for?"

"You might as well tell the truth, Sophie," Mallory said. She put her face right up in front of Sophie's. Bright green eyes, framed by long dark hair, with just enough baby fat to make her undeniably cute.

Sophie blinked and turned away. She couldn't look at Mallory's face for more than a few seconds at a time – any longer and she started having feelings that she didn't understand.

Sophie gritted her teeth. "Fine," she said quietly. "Let's just go, and I'll explain."

"Explain now!" Cindy brayed at the top of her lungs.

Sophie felt her breathing start to pick up. She tried to take one long breath to ward off what was coming, but she couldn't do it. After a few seconds, her vision was blurry with tears.

"Are you okay?" Cat asked, sounding genuinely concerned.

"She's just being dramatic," Cindy said. "She doesn't want to tell us!"

Sophie blinked and tears started falling down her cheeks. "Please, can we just go?" She was whispering now.

"Come on, guys," Chase said. "Let's get out of here."

S is for Slasher

Cindy sighed loudly and started stomping off back to the house. Mallory rolled her eyes and followed along. The others all waited for Sophie to take the lead, then followed behind her. At one point during the walk, Sophie stumbled over a rock and Chase rushed forward, taking her arm and helping her back to her feet. She accepted the gesture silently, feeling Mallory's eyes on her the whole time.

***

Back at the house, Sophie stood at her bathroom sink, staring at her own face in the mirror, studying the redness in her eyes, the puffiness in the skin below them. The tears had fallen in parallel tracks down her cheeks, cutting through her concealer. Sophie turned the cold water on full blast, lowered her head, and splashed her face with water until she felt her body relaxing.

She grabbed a washcloth out of the shower and used it to scrub away the rest of the makeup. After drying off, she took another look in the mirror. The acne she had been trying to hide was now more visible than ever, but she knew that reapplying it would take too long. She shut off the bathroom light and stepped outside.

Back in the living room, everyone was sprawled out, chatting quietly. As soon as she stepped around the corner, Mallory's eyes narrowed in on her.

"What happened to your face?" she asked.

Sophie pretended she hadn't heard her. "Sorry for

freaking out," she said. "I should have been honest." She took a deep breath. "Where we were just now is out behind my neighbor's house. His name is Nathaniel. He already lived here when we moved in two years ago. He... he actually saw us on the day we were moving in and he came to help us out, carrying boxes and stuff. He stayed and had dinner with us that night and then... he went home. And I've never spoken to him since then. But sometimes I'm at that end of the neighborhood, and I hear weird noises coming out of the woods... and I guess I wanted to know what was up."

At first, nobody responded. Sophie became highly aware of the fact that she was standing up in front of everyone. She shifted her weight from one foot to the other.

"I'm gonna get a soda," Sophie said suddenly. "Does anyone need anything from the kitchen?"

Nobody did. Sophie went into the kitchen by herself, opened up the fridge, and stood there staring into it, feeling the cool air against her skin.

She ran through her story again in her head. She had been careful about what she told them. She hadn't told them how she and Nathaniel had started talking when her parents were both inside the house. She hadn't told them how her dad had overheard their conversation, or how he started screaming at Nathaniel because of what he'd been saying and demanded that he leave their home at once. She didn't tell them about the fight that followed and how Nathaniel only let go of her father's neck when he saw that Sophie was crying. She didn't tell them about how she laid in bed that night, feeling the cool breeze blow in through her open window, listening to her parents arguing downstairs. And she certainly hadn't told them about what she found on her bathroom mirror when she woke up the next morning.

The fridge emitted a high-pitched chirp to let Sophie know that the door had been left open. She grabbed a Diet Pepsi out of the fridge and closed the door. When she got back to the living room, everyone else was in the process of moving downstairs so they could try out the Xbox 360 that Sophie's dad had recently purchased.

***

While the rest of the group was playing around with her dad's copy of NBA 2k6, Sophie was watching Jared and Iris. The two of them were off in the corner by themselves, sprawled out together on the bean-bag chair, talking in low, hushed tones. Their bodies were close together, and while they weren't actively kissing or fondling each other, it was obvious from his slightly stooped posture and the way he folded his legs that Jared was struggling to hide an erection.

Eventually, Iris got up and joined the rest of the group, leaning over the back of the couch to watch the screen. A few minutes later, Jared joined her. He flipped open his phone and made a facial expression that was too big to be natural.

"Missed call from my mom," he muttered. "I

better go outside and call back."

"I'll come with," Iris chimed in, affecting a casual tone. "I need some fresh air."

The two of them slipped out through the sliding glass doors. No one commented on their exit. Everybody knew what they were really going to do..

Iris and Jared followed the same general path they had taken earlier that day. They walked next to each other, not touching or speaking, but highly aware of one another's bodies. The sun had set behind a thick cover of clouds half an hour ago, and it was almost too dark to see. Before long, Sophie's house was out of sight.

Without warning, Iris turned, grabbed Jared by the arms, and pushed him up against the nearest tree. She pressed her mouth against his and Jared let out a small, muffled sound of surprise, but he quickly caught up with her, and soon the two of them were kissing sloppily and running their hands over each other's bodies. Jared slowly moved his hands down to Iris's ass, and when she didn't protest or signal disinterest, he squeezed it hard. Iris let out a small moan of appreciation as she pressed her body even tighter against his and reached up to run her hands through Jared's thick, brown hair.

After a few minutes, Iris reached for Jared's belt. When she went to unbuckle it, Jared froze up. His arms went slack and he broke away from the kiss.

"Whoa, whoa," he whispered.

"What's the matter?" Iris smiled as she continued to work the belt, still riding the momentum, hoping this was just a temporary case

S is for Slasher

of nerves.

Jared put his hands on hers, stopping her. "Maybe we should slow down."

Iris stopped smiling. "Why? Did I do something wrong?"

Jared shook his head. "No. I'm just not sure…" He trailed off.

As the passion faded and dried up, Iris felt her senses starting to clear. She realized for the first time how dark it was out in the woods. No moon, no light from the houses or the street.

"What the fuck?" Iris said. She took a step back. "You're not into me?"

"It's not that."

"Then what is it?" Iris put a hand on her hip. "What are you, gay?"

"I'm not gay," Jared furrowed his brow.

"If you're worried that your dick is too fucked up or small or whatever, I'm sure I've seen worse."

Jared blushed, but even though she was inches from his face, Iris didn't see it. "I, uh…" He stammered. "You have?"

Iris sighed. "Whatever. Let's just go back," she muttered to herself as she turned away from him. "What a fucking waste."

Iris started to walk away, but she stopped when she felt something cold and hard being pressed against her forehead. Before she could identify it as the barrel of a gun, the person on the other end pulled the trigger. There was a sound like a muffled thunderclap and the top of Iris's head split open, sending a spray of blood into Jared's face.

Jared let out a wordless yell as the hot blood hit his eyes. He didn't have time to say or even think anything else before the gun was pressed against his forehead and the trigger pulled a second time.

***

Back inside the house, Cat had wandered off on her way to the upstairs bathroom, and when she came back, she remarked on the size of Sophie's house, declaring that it would be a great place for hide-and-seek. Mallory, starting to sober up a touch but still very excitable, squealed at this prospect and insisted that they play.

Mallory had a well-documented love of the game and all its variants, going back to fifth grade when her family, new to town, joined Sophie's church. The two of them got along from the beginning, but it wasn't until they both attended one of the church's overnight lock-ins that they became friends, bonding during a game of 'sardines' where Sophie was the person chosen to go hide. Mallory found her right away and it took a full hour before anyone else joined them, leaving them plenty of time to sit by themselves, giggling in the dark as the strangeness of the situation wore away their layers of emotional armor until they were sharing secrets like lifelong friends.

From that point on, the two of them attended every lock-in the church hosted, until Freshman year when Mallory met Cindy and stopped participating in any church events that her parents

S is for Slasher

didn't force her to go to.

Because Mallory so loved to hide, she was always the first to call "not it." Sophie, anticipating this, called out shortly after her. Everyone else scrambled to get theirs in, ending with Cindy, who was a bit more drunk than Mallory. She scowled when she realized that she had been singled out and looked to Mallory for help, but Mallory, ever dedicated to the game, just smiled and shrugged.

"Should we wait for Jared and Iris to get back?" Sophie asked. She had the feeling they should all stay together, even if she couldn't say why.

"They're probably..." Cat said in a sultry voice. "Otherwise occupied."

"In other words, it'll be forever until Iris gets back!" Mallory punched the armrest of the couch. "Let's play now!"

After a little more hectoring, Mallory got everyone up and moving. Cindy gloomily followed Mallory's instructions to put her head against the far wall and close her eyes, but she balked when Mallory asked her to count to one hundred.

"What ever happened to counting to ten?" she asked. "I'm not doing one hundred. Thirty, maybe."

"You'll do one hundred and you'll like it," Mallory said, before she pulled her hand back and slapped Cindy's ass so hard the sound was like a gunshot. "Bitch."

"Goddamn," Cindy whined. "Not so hard."

Without any warning, Cindy started her count. Mallory, Cat, and Chase all ran up the stairs, whispering and snickering as they did, while Sophie stood motionless, staring at the back of Cindy's head.

Cindy's count passed twenty.

Thirty.

Forty.

When Cindy called out 'fifty,' Sophie turned and walked up the stairs.

When she reached the living room, Sophie cocked her head to the side and listened for any sign of the others, but apart from Cindy's droning voice below her, the house was silent.

Even though some combination of these same people had hung out at Sophie's house dozens of times, this was the first time they'd ever played hide-and-seek here. As such, she didn't think anyone had ever fully explored her parent's bedroom on the second floor – at least, she hoped not.

Sophie made her way up the stairs to the second floor, moving quietly now, in case Cindy was a better listener than she appeared. She tiptoed down to the end of the hallway and into her parents' dark bedroom. Using the light spilling in from the hallway to navigate, she walked around the bed and past the dresser until she reached the door of her parents' walk-in closet.

As slowly as she could, Sophie turned the knob and pushed the door open. She slipped inside and closed the door behind, sealing herself in darkness.

After she had been there for a few seconds, she became aware of the sound of another person breathing.

S is for Slasher

***

When Cindy reached the end of her count, she opened her eyes, threw her head back and shouted, "One hundred!" The sudden movement made her dizzy and she nearly fell over backwards, but she grabbed the back of a nearby recliner and managed to keep herself upright.

She looked around the empty room and sighed. Cindy had hoped, against all odds, that Mallory was just playing an elaborate prank on her, and that everyone would be standing behind her when she finished counting. It would have been startling and embarrassing, but at least then she wouldn't have had to play this stupid game. No such luck.

While Cindy was considering where to begin, she heard a single knock on the sliding glass door. She turned towards the sound, still expecting to see one of the others, but the lights in the basement were so bright, and the night outside so dark, that it was impossible to see anything beyond the glass but her own reflection.

"Of course," Cindy mumbled as she crossed the room to the door. She went to unlock the door and found that it had already been done. Had Jared and Iris left out of this door? She couldn't remember.

Still bracing herself for Mallory or Cat to jump out at her and scream, Cindy pushed open the door. The air outside was cool and crisp. The light from the basement shining through the doors and windows cast a row of block-shaped bright spots on

S is for Slasher

the patio and grass outside, but outside of those rectangles, everything was pitch black.

"Very funny, guys," Cindy called out. "I'm pretty sure going outside is against the rules!" She was surprised by how quiet her voice sounded, how weak. She imagined the others standing just out of sight, giggling about the whole thing. Laughing at her. At her weakness.

Determined to prove them wrong, Cindy took a step forward, landing inside one of the patches of light. She hesitated, but then pushed on through and took another step into the night.

"Whatever you're doing, just don't lock me out of the house, okay?" Cindy said. "That's a dick move."

Cindy listened for any signs of movement, but there were none. Just the gentle rustling of a breeze in the branches of the trees.

A faint smell reached her nose, carried on the air. It was sharp and slightly metallic. Almost like blood.

Cindy was suddenly aware that she was standing alone, in the pitch-black darkness, at the edge of the large and dark woods. She decided to turn back and go inside. Whoever was out there messing with her would have a laugh at her expense, but there was some satisfaction in knowing that they would be stuck outside for the rest of the game.

This is what Cindy was thinking about when the knife pierced her throat.

***

After a few agonizing seconds sitting in the dark, Sophie broke the silence. "Is someone in here?" she asked, her voice small and timid.

In response, the person in the closet let out a sigh of relief. "Jesus Christ, am I glad it's you. I thought Cindy had found me and I just about shat myself."

"Oh," Sophie said. She relaxed a bit. "Chase."

"The very same," Chase said. "I guess we're buddied up."

"What are you doing in my parents' bedroom?" Sophie asked.

"Pretty sneaky, huh?" Chase said. "I figured no one would find me here. I guess I wasn't quite right, but I can't say I'm upset about how it worked out." He paused. "Hey, I hope this wasn't off-limits, or anything. Is it cool that I'm in here?"

Sophie didn't like the idea of someone else sneaking around her parents' bedroom. It felt taboo, like a violation of some ancient law from childhood. But she was glad to have someone to talk to – and anyway, it was a silly thing to be worried about at this point.

"It's cool," she said. "I was just surprised. I didn't think anyone but me knew about this spot."

"It was Cat's idea," Chase added quickly. He seemed genuinely nervous. Was it because they were sitting together, alone, in the dark, only a few inches away from each other? Sophie had been so put off by Mallory and Cindy's accusations that she never considered the idea that Chase might actually have a crush on her, but now that she did, she found

S is for Slasher

it oddly exciting.

"That's too bad," Sophie said. "I was almost impressed for a second there, but I guess Cat deserves the credit."

"What…" Chase trailed off, and for a moment Sophie worried that her flirtatious tone didn't translate – she didn't have much practice. But when Chase spoke again, she could tell that he was smiling. "I mean, sure, it was technically Cat's idea, but she only had the idea because of me."

"Really?" Sophie asked. She was smiling, too. "How did that work, exactly? You went to Cat and said 'hey, come up with a good place for me to hide,' and this was her suggestion?"

"That's right," Chase said. "I'm like a… a director, or something, and Cat's the location scout. So, even though she's the one that found the spot, I'm the one that gets credit."

"Wow, look at you with the movie talk. Jared would be so impressed."

Chase groaned. "Just what we all needed, more reason for Jared to talk about movies."

Sophie giggled but was hit by a sudden wave of self-consciousness. "Don't make me laugh."

"Why? Afraid you'll piss your pants?"

"Don't be gross," Sophie said, with mock offense. "I just meant, we're hiding, and we don't want Cindy to find us, which she will if we keep making noise. And besides, you're not nearly funny enough to make me wet myself."

"Well, just wait," Chase said. "I'm just getting warmed up. You'll be soaking wet in no time."

S is for Slasher

Sophie gasped.

"Too much?"

Sophie held back from answering right away. The juvenile double entendre didn't actually bother her, but the sound of apprehension in Chase's voice, like he was worried he had gone too far, was proof that he wasn't just making his usual dumb jokes – he was actually flirting with her.

It was a satisfying feeling, made all the more pleasurable by the power she held in denying him relief – not to mention her increasing awareness of the closeness of their bodies.

"Not at all," she said.

***

Cat was hiding in the shower of the first-floor bathroom when the door creaked open.

She was sitting in the tub, behind two layers of shower curtain, so all she could see was a shadowy figure standing backlit in the center of the door. Cat held her breath, hoping that Cindy would move on without investigating further.

When the door shut again, plunging her back into darkness, Cat thought she had pulled it off, but it didn't take long to realize that someone was still in the bathroom with her.

First, they hit the switch that turned on the exhaust fan.

Then, they turned the sink on, full blast.

When the shower curtain suddenly moved toward her, pushed forward by a pair of large hands,

Cat realized that the person in the room with her wasn't Cindy, after all.

The hands gripped tight around her throat, and when Cat opened her mouth to scream, her attacker used one hand to wad up part of the curtain and shove it deep into her mouth while the other hand was pressed tight against her windpipe.

Cat quickly lost consciousness, sparing herself from what came next.

***

"Can I ask you a question?" Chase said. "It's about what you said earlier, about your neighbor."

Sophie felt her heart skip a beat, but she managed to keep herself steady. "If you want," she said. "I pretty much already told the whole story."

"Pretty much? So... there's more?"

Sophie wasn't sure how to answer.

"I should've asked earlier," Chase said after a moment. "But you seemed sort of uncomfortable with everyone around... I didn't want to make you more uncomfortable."

Surprised by Chase's consideration, Sophie relaxed once again. "You're right," she said. "The truth is, he... he really scared me. He was so tall and so wide, and the muscles around his neck and arms were crazy. I'd never met someone so... big."

"He sounds hot," Chase said, quickly adding. "Kidding, sorry. And you said you heard noises coming from his house?"

"From behind his house," Sophie corrected.

"I think you know why," she said.

Chase reached out and gently put his hand on the back of Sophie's head. He gave it just the tiniest bit of pressure and Sophie did the rest of the work, seeking out his mouth in the darkness and pulling him into a deep kiss.

Neither of them heard the footsteps as they grew closer to the closet, or the sound of an ear being pressed against the door as a hand gripped the knob, waiting for the perfect moment to strike.

***

The flash hit Sophie before she knew that the door had been opened. She'd been kissing Chase with her eyes open, so when the white light filled her vision, it lingered for a long, disorienting moment. When the blindness began to clear, Sophie found that she and Chase's bodies were no longer touching. Shortly after that, she became aware of the sound of laughter.

The scene around her resolved itself: Chase was halfway out of the closet, still sitting on the floor, while Mallory stood over him, holding Chase's digital camera in her hands. She crouched down to show him what was on the screen.

At first, all Sophie could think of was the game – was it over? Why was Mallory here instead of hiding? Had she and Cindy switched roles, somehow?

As she came back to herself, Sophie realized what had actually happened, and her confusion cooled into a dense, hard ball of anger.

"What the fuck?" Sophie rasped.

"Language!" Mallory said with mock outrage, causing herself to burst out laughing again.

"What is wrong with you?" Sophie asked. She looked to Chase for an explanation, but all he did was grin back at her and shrug.

"Oh, come on," Mallory waved her hand. "That was classic."

Sophie unsteadily rose to her feet. "You think this is funny?"

"What are you complaining about?" Mallory said. She had stopped laughing and seemed genuinely annoyed at Sophie. "You're always talking about how much you like Chase. I pretty much set you guys up!"

"For what it's worth," Chase said as he shuffled all the way out of the closet and propped himself up against the side of the bed. "You're actually a really good kisser."

"See?" Mallory said. "I just did you a favor. Plus, everyone knows how bad you need to get some."

Sophie raised her eyebrows. "Get some?"

"Oh!" Mallory squealed. She put the camera's viewfinder up to her eye. "That was great, say that again."

"Get some," Sophie said as she knocked the camera out of Mallory's hands.

"Whoa, calm down," Mallory said.

Sophie shoved Mallory in the chest, hard enough that she stumbled backwards a few steps.

"What the fuck is your problem?" Mallory said.

"Yeah, Sophie," Chase said. "Chill out."

Sophie stepped forward and pushed Mallory again.

"Cut it out," Mallory yelled. "You fucking psycho virgin!"

Sophie shoved her again, harder this time, causing Mallory to stumble backwards through the bedroom door. She stepped forward, hunched down a bit to center herself, then pushed a final time with all of her strength.

Mallory took two steps backwards and hit the banister with enough force to send her toppling over the edge of the mezzanine. She fell screaming into the living room, where her head slammed against the coffee table hard enough to crack the glass. After that, she was silent.

"Mallory?" Chase called out. When there was no response, he stood up and shouted her name. He ran out to the mezzanine and looked over. "Oh my God," he whispered. He looked at Sophie with a shocked expression. "What did you do?"

Sophie was pleasantly surprised by her own feeling of detachment. She looked at Chase and shrugged.

Chase ran downstairs to the living room, where a single lamp cast a dim light. Sophie watched from overhead as he awkwardly searched for a pulse, then pressed his ear against Mallory's mouth.

"She's not breathing," Chase said. "She's not breathing!"

As Chase awkwardly began to perform CPR on

Mallory, a hulking figure emerged from the shadows. He stood there for nearly a full minute, standing over Chase, before producing a knife and plunging the seven-inch blade into the side of Chase's neck.

Chase fell to his knees and clutched the wound, gurgling nonsense as his blood spurted across the floor, covering Mallory's face. The knife pierced him a second time, just above the left cheekbone, and when it was removed, Chase collapsed on top of Mallory.

Sophie watched all of this with her hands resting calmly on the mezzanine. When Chase stopped twitching, she turned away, picked his digital camera off the floor, and began to walk deliberately down the stairs. As she did, she heard the sound of two gunshots, both muffled by a silencer.

By the time she got to them, Chase and Mallory had both been rolled over onto their backs. Both of their bodies had been shot in the forehead, splitting open the top of their heads and exposing bits of brain matter.

Standing over the bodies was Nathaniel, six-foot-four, broad-shouldered and thickly muscled, wearing a green, brown and beige desert camouflage uniform.

Sophie already knew what to do. Nathaniel had explained it all to her, in the messages he left on her bathroom mirror. It was hard to believe that the first one was two years ago. Hard to believe everything that had happened since then, and everything that was yet to come.

S is for Slasher

Sophie, breathing steadily through her nose, brought the camera's viewfinder up to her eye and snapped three photos: one of Mallory, one of Chase, and one that captured both of their lifeless bodies in one frame. When the flash had died down from the final shot, Sophie offered the camera to Nathaniel.

"Come on," she said. "Let's go do the others."

Watch Me

Aisling Campbell

Taylor ducks down behind a fallen tree, and finally she has a moment to catch her breath.

Casey's gone, skewered and hanging in the trees. She was still moving, twitching, when Taylor ran but she's gone. You don't come back from something like that -- especially not out here with no cell phone signal and a psychopath on their tails.

Taylor knows it's not exactly PC to call the guy a psychopath -- she's not really qualified to analyse his goddamned mental health. For all she knows he's a well-adjusted member of society most days of the year and this is just his cheat week. Those few days when he gets to purge himself of all his nasty impulses by putting on a mask and killing girls in the woods.

Her side hurts.

She thought she'd dodged, but maybe the fucker got her anyway.

When she looks down she sees red against the white of her tank top. Not loads, not 'oh great I'm bleeding out' amounts. But enough to make things complicated.

She peels back her top to get a look at the

wound.

It's hard to tell if there's anything in there, or if the shotgun pellets had just grazed her. It's definitely better than the full-on shot Megan took to the chest.

She'd be pissed, if she'd lived. Those tits had been expensive. It'd taken her over a year of extra waitressing shifts to pay for them.

There's nothing Taylor can do now, crouching in the forest. She's got vague ideas of making a dressing out of strips of fabric and holding it together with panty elastic, but she's not that desperate, and the bleeding isn't that bad.

She tries to think.

The last she saw of Zoe, she was running the other way with the psycho right behind her. Zoe does track, she's fast and with stamina in spades, so Taylor figures she's got some breathing room before the bastard comes after her again.

She tries to summon up the image of the map from the cabin, but she'd barely had time to glance at it before she'd had to run.

If she doesn't pick the right direction, she's got a pretty good chance of dying of exposure out here -- assuming the psycho doesn't get her first.

There's a river, and a lake, and if she can make it to that then it's just a matter of following along the water until she makes it to civilisation -- she remembers seeing the stream through the car window on the way up here.

But he'll probably be expecting that.

He may have an all-consuming passion for gore,

but he's not stupid. The traps are testament to that.

No, if she wants this to end then she's going to have to end *him*.

Just like last time.

***

The old camp buildings should still be around here somewhere -- from back when this place was a summer camp for kids. Before all the deaths and the lawsuits shut it down.

They'll probably be booby-trapped, but that's a risk she'll have to take.

There might still be a first aid kit somewhere -- bandages don't go out of date, right? -- and maybe something to use as a weapon.

And if she waits long enough, he'll come back. It's probably where the sicko hangs out in between murders -- maybe he even lives there? A long-lost kid leftover when the camp closed down.

Maybe he's been out here all that time, snacking on squirrels. Taylor doesn't really care what the origin story is, what his deal is. She just needs to know that he bleeds like she does.

Like she *is*.

She pushes off from the tree, swallowing back the groan as a fire flares up in her side. There aren't any footsteps right now, no snapping twigs, so she's pretty sure she's alone, but it doesn't hurt to be careful.

If she was in better shape she could climb a tree, try to get a sense of where she was. But for now

S is for Slasher

she'll have to trust her memory, and luck, as she starts walking.

She can almost imagine Casey in her ear, saying "How are you not *freaking* out right now?"

It would be too hard to explain. How the calm just settles. She's been here once before already.

She was thirteen. Body just starting to change. Long-legged and happy, in short-shorts and a t-shirt.

When she felt him staring, she liked it. Felt powerful. Should've known to walk away. To be wary.

She led him on -- and that's not what her therapist would tell her, she'd tell her that she was innocent, a child, a victim. But Taylor didn't see it that way -- too much guilt and shame. The wink she threw, the way she bounced so her growing boobs bounced too, all an invitation. Not to what he did, sure. But to something. Stupid. Stupid. Stupid.

But maybe he should have known to be wary of her too.

She's not thinking about her friends.

It's partly a conscious decision -- she doesn't need distractions -- and partly because *friends* maybe isn't the best way to describe them.

She knows Emily was the one to start the rumours -- even though she knew *everything*. Taylor had told her, had cried in front of her, had panic attacks in front of her.

Bitch, she thinks. But with a touch less venom than usual. Everyone always says you can't speak ill of the dead, after all. She'd been the first to go, and

S is for Slasher

it had been quick. Maybe a minute of pain and fear, before her head hit the ground while her body stayed standing until *he* let go of it.

It's been just under two hours since then, but it feels like longer.

It'll be dark in two more.

The guy hadn't even waited for the cover of night. He'd probably been ready and waiting since the moment they'd arrived.

He'd probably been watching from somewhere that first night, while they got drunk and complained loudly about their lives. Smug, knowing he'd soon be giving them something to *really* complain about.

He'd probably watched while Megan fucked the warden.

Probably killed him first once the poor man headed back to his hut, tired and happy after his time with her.

After Emily died, they'd all gone running to the warden's hut, practically falling right on top of the whole bloody scene.

Taylor really hoped the slit throat came first. But the way the guy's teeth had clamped down on the severed dick in his mouth kinda answered that question.

She notices the tripwire seconds before she stumbles into it. Follows it with her eyes up the tree to a container of kerosene and some kind of lighter.

The fact that it's here means she's getting somewhere.

There hadn't been a ruse. No lost dog or promise

S is for Slasher

of weed. Just violence.

She didn't expect it, and that was the point.

He'd lifted her up, slammed her into the van before she'd even thought to scream. Stuffed a rag into her mouth and covered it with duct tape. Bound her hands and ankles. Ripped her shirt and--

The door is rigged with a shotgun and some string.

She enters through a window after she sets the bear trap under it off with a stick. There are nails, sticking out of the window frame and over the sill. She manages to get inside with only a few extra scratches on her thighs and ass.

There might be poison on them -- he seems like the kind of douchebag that would do something like that -- but if so there's nothing she can do about it now.

The cabin she's in looks like an office of some kind.

When the organisers cut ties, it seems like they didn't bother to clear out. There are ornaments on the bookshelves -- a little china bear, a faded photo in a carved wood frame.

The dust is thick, which means it's probably safe. Even so, it doesn't hurt to be cautious.

There's string left out on the clutter of the desk, and she ties it around the handles on the drawers, using it to pull them open.

Nothing springs out, apart from a large spider which skitters for cover. She checks for wires, for any kind of trigger -- if not for a trap, then maybe for an alarm system, but it's clear.

S is for Slasher

There's a small first aid kit, and a bottle of cheap vodka at the back of a cupboard. Apparently the former occupant had a bit of a drinking problem.

She pulls up her shirt and inspects the damage.

"I think it's infected. Please. Please help me."

He'd looked at her like she wasn't even speaking English. Like he was looking at an animal, a dog, rolling around on the floor. Like it wasn't his fault, or his problem, and he was just going to let things play out. Watch her get sick, watch her suffer and die.

She sniffs the alcohol before she pours it over the wound. Wouldn't put it past him to switch out vodka for acid, anticipating exactly this circumstance.

Maybe she's overestimating, but that's safer than the alternative.

She's proof enough of that.

She has the foresight to strip off the tank top and bundle the non-bloody bits of it into her mouth. Before the vodka hits her skin.

It felt like fire before.

Now it's like a star, exploding with heat, so bright she can't think for a moment.

There are painkillers in the kit, but they're decades out of date. At best they're useless, at worst they'll mess her up.

Once she gets to a hospital it'll be okay.

She just needs to avoid sepsis until then. It'd suck to fight her way free only to fall victim to bacteria.

Which is why she needs to act.

S is for Slasher

I'm going to die here.

She wraps the gauze around her middle. The bleeding has almost stopped, so at least she won't have to burn herself to cauterise it. She'd been dreading that, not sure if she'd have the stomach to smell her own flesh cooking.

Once the gauze is secured with surgical tape, she puts her top back on. It's damp, from the saliva and the blood, but comfort isn't exactly top of her list right now.

Getting up hurts, but not a lot doesn't right now. The adrenaline from before is wearing off, now she's not in immediate danger of being blasted to pieces, so she's starting to feel everything so much more clearly.

He's going to watch me die.

There are the cuts on her legs from getting in the window, a mild sprain in her left ankle, scuffs on her knees. There's a cut on her cheek, maybe from running through the woods. Her palms feel rough.

There'd been something broken in her left knee. It was swollen, the leg below it felt wrong -- numb. But she'd told herself she'd walk on it, if she needed to. She couldn't move most of the fingers on the left hand, but that was okay. She wouldn't need them for what she had planned.

The infection was where he'd cut her. She hasn't been able to see what he'd done -- her bruised ribs wouldn't let her bend enough -- but she could remember the touch of the scalpel. It burned whenever she needed to pee, enough to make her sob.

But the upside was he wasn't touching her there anymore.

He was using her mouth instead.

She remembered doing homework at the kitchen table, reading textbooks and calling over her shoulder at her mom, "Did you know the human jaw can apply 200 pounds of pressure per square inch?"

It sounded like a lot. Taylor hoped it was enough.

There's not much of use in the office, until she finds the trapdoor.

It's under a rug, and obvious as hell.

When she first walked over it, she thought it was a trap. She still thinks maybe it's a trap. That once she descends, that'll be it -- like a fly in a spider's web.

But if it's his lair, there'll be weapons.

She's hoping for a gun, but she'll take what she can get.

She couldn't see much in the way of pockets on his outfit, so he's limited in the amount of ammo he can carry, which is good for her. If she can get him without the gun, then she might stand a chance.

Of course, a chance is all it is.

She pulls back the rug and grabs the ring on the door, angles herself away from the opening so if something pops out she might be able to avoid it.

There's nothing, and that fact is starting to play on her nerves. There are plenty of traps around this cabin -- the bear traps, the tripwire, the shotgun behind the door. It only makes sense for there to be

S is for Slasher

more, unless the guy is arrogant enough to believe no one would make it this far.

Her phone makes a shitty flashlight, but it's the best she's got. It's also the only thing the hunk of plastic is good for right now.

She scans carefully over each step before she puts a foot down. Every creak makes her want to scream.

The cellar is full of junk, detritus from the camp's brief life. There's equipment for games, chairs stacked against the wall, even a few spare bed frames.

It smells like something curled up and died in one of the corners, and she's really hoping it's just a raccoon, but she's not holding her breath.

All she can do is keep moving forward. One step at a time.

The second trapdoor is hidden in an alcove made up of damp, disintegrating cardboard boxes.

There's no lock, no bolt -- on this side at least. And when she pulls on the handle it lifts.

The damn thing is heavy though, and the muscles in her arms and down her side -- where the wound is still sending out licks of flame -- burn.

But she gets it open.

Nowhere else to go but down, and there's no way she's getting that thing shut behind her without breaking an arm, or at the very least some fingers. So she leaves it, and hopes like hell he doesn't come back any time soon.

***

S is for Slasher

The comfort level drops another ten points at the bottom of the shitty, home-made ladder. There's concrete on every side of her, bare and rough. Light too, so she can put her phone away, caged bulbs running along the walls.

She can't stand up, only crouch, and it's hard to imagine the psycho crawling through here on his belly like a rat.

The concrete is cold against her knees as she shuffles forward, further into the tunnel. Her left knee aches a little in a way which makes her damaged nerves tingle.

She crawled most of the way up the stairs. When she got to the top she braced her back against the wall.

She could see him on the floor down below.

The blood was still flowing, spreading out from under him like a big black hole eating away at the concrete floor.

She hadn't expected so much blood. It made sense though. All that blood, rushing downwards, spurting out of him like from a faucet.

She remembered him fighting her, trying to strangle her, punching her as she'd hung on like a dog with a toy. Once flesh began to tear, he hadn't lasted long before shock set in. Weak as a kitten as Taylor spat his manhood onto the floor.

Taylor laughed, as she levered herself up off the floor. Maybe he could still hear her, or maybe not. The aches and pains are all still there, but she was above them all.

S is for Slasher

he's got his arm, she may not get the chance for a single disabling strike like she'd hoped.

If only she knew how to operate a cutting torch, she could burn the asshole's face off.

She wishes for stairs, like there were in her kidnapper's basement. Then she could fix a tripwire across the top and wait for the bastard to fall. Strike while he's disorientated.

But wishing never solved anything.

She pours out a volume of lighter fluid at the base of the ladder. She's tempted to go all around the room, drench it all and set it alight now -- so when he returns his nest will already be a little concrete box of ashes.

Instead, she draws a trail back to her hiding place, a fuse for her to light when the time is right.

She crouches down with the machete in hand and waits.

Manages a few minutes of alertness before her eyes close, brain trying to rest despite, or perhaps because of, all the blaring chemicals running through her body.

She'd forgotten how this kind of waiting felt.

At first she thinks maybe she's imagining the scraping, the clang of metal up above. Then she hears someone breathing hard in the passageway, clothes rustling against the floor as they crawl.

The jolt of adrenaline is like a kick to the stomach. She picks up the lighter, holds it ready with her finger on the striker.

She hears heavy boots on the ladder and more panting. She waits, counting the rungs in her head, counting down to the right moment.

There's a splash as his boots hit the pool of lighter fluid. Taylor pushes the striker down.

The lighter explodes in her hand.

It takes a second for the signals to reach her brain, for the pain to hit. In that second she has time to look at her hand. To see the shards of plastic embedded in it. The glove of fire over her palm and fingers.

Shit. This should hurt like--

It all rushes in at once, and Taylor moans, cradling her hand to her chest. Trying to protect it even as she longs to cut it off, to separate the pain from her body.

She can't think.

It's just *there*.

She's shaking, sweating. Making a noise she's never heard before.

A gloved hand comes down over the tool tray and grabs a handful of her hair. Pulls. And the pain of that is still nothing next to the pulses running up and down from her blasted hand, but the fear is…

She doesn't want to die here. Not going to give the bastard the satisfaction, not going to fill whatever sick need it is he has.

She twists as she feels the heat on her back, the flames licking up from the floor.

He's dragging her through the pool of burning lighter fluid, and as she struggles she can see his coat. Stubborn, flame-resistant fabric.

She pulls again, manages to get onto her front. Puts her hand down to support--

S is for Slasher

I won, motherfucker.

***

She takes a moment to spit the blood out of her mouth. Her nose is trickling away like a loose faucet, over her lips and between her teeth.

Her knee feels damp where it's still nudged up against the guy's crotch.

"Shit," she mutters, pulling it back and wiping it on his pant leg. She climbs off him, giving the knife another twist. It doesn't hurt to be thorough. She's not giving this asshole his shot at a sequel.

There's just one thing left.

The mask.

It's a cheap Halloween thing, all garish green latex -- a plastic monstrosity which will outlive them all. Taylor grasps it by the nose and tears it away.

As she lifts, a coil of greasy auburn hair comes loose, and the mask lifts to reveal rounded cheeks, a small, pointed chin and cupid's bow lips.

Taylor begins to wrestle with the overcoat, heart beating quick. She takes the knife out and starts to saw at the thick fabric, punches through by accident and almost embeds it into the unmasked killer's sternum.

When she gets through to a jumper she just tears, ripping like an overeager lover.

Another layer gone, and she stops and stares.

"Oh, you fucking *bitch*."

S is for Slasher

***

The clues are in the room all around her. Pieces of a puzzle and she has time on her hands -- well, hand.

The lair has internet -- how else to look up all those nifty trap ideas and find hardware advice? -- and a call to the authorities means rescue is coming. No need to retrace her steps back to the warden's hut and attempt to drive a car one-handed back down that winding road.

After downing a couple of painkillers with a few mouthfuls of water from the sink, she goes back to the corkboard.

Taylor finds her would-be murderer soon enough, in a group shot taken on the lakeshore. Camp counsellors, ankle-deep in gray-blue water. There's seven of them, and right in the middle is the boy from the other photo -- on one side is the blonde (face scratched out again) and on the other a heavy-set girl with auburn hair and an adoring smile turned upwards to the boy like he's Jesus himself.

Taylor wants to reach into the picture and throttle her, to slap the self-absorbed stupidity right out of her.

She finds a diary, and that just makes her madder. She has to take a break from reading just so she can breathe the pulsing, migraine mass of anger away.

Dear diary, the boy I like doesn't love me. I know he'd fall for me if only that blonde slut wasn't here. Yeah, it's totally all her fault. All. HER.

S is for Slasher

It's stupid. Too stupid.

Dear diary, the boy I like killed himself. If I'd been there, instead of that whore, I could've saved him. It's her fault, I know it. If she'd only loved him properly, like I would've loved him...

Dear diary, I'm not coping well. I think I know what'll make me feel better though... Not therapy, not trying to move on, but murder. Yeah, murder. I'll kill girls just like that blonde bitch who took away my one true love. Skinny girls. Pretty girls.

Taylor wants to scream. To kick some sense into the dumb, dead corpse. To show her her scars, because Taylor's already paid that debt to society.

But the corpse is long past listening.

***

Taylor strips slowly, sensuously.

Jimmy isn't into it, she can see on his face. He thinks he's made a mistake coming back to her dorm room.

The missing fingers he could deal with, but *this* is a whole different ball game. The lumpy scar down her side, the burns. She's still wearing panties so he hasn't seen the worst of it yet -- she knows he'll run when she gets to that part.

But the striptease isn't for him.

It's for the creep watching from the bushes outside the window. She left the curtains ajar just for them because she wants him to *see*. See her.

She's burnt brightly here -- she's popular, smart, pretty. So of course someone's just waiting to snuff her out.

She flips her hair back, turns and twists, so the creep can see when she starts to peel down her panties. Wishes she could see their face as they realise she's not the untouched canvas they thought.

Imagines their face as she tells them what happened to the people who left those scars.

It's making her excited in a way poor, dull Jimmy could never manage.

She leans down to kiss him, kiss away the shell-shocked look on his face, and as she does she glances out the window.

Makes contact with two eyeholes in a cheap plastic mask.

She smiles.

Game on, asshole.

A Dying Art

Adam Holloway

"I takes her head, fingers digging in real deep, and Bubba says - what you say Bubba?"

Kane was starting to wonder why he came to these reunions. He'd been feeling like he had very little in common with his peers for some time, and this party was certainly cementing the sentiment. The old redneck standing before Kane and the rest of the audience clustered around the dining table was stood on his chair, the four creaking wooden legs acting as a stage for his sub-par performance.

Kane had zoned out for much of the routine because he'd seen it before - many times in fact. The redneck's name was Cletus Abattoir (surely not his birth-name, though none in their club had ever gotten the man to admit it), and he was acting as this year's host. He had told some version of this story at last year's reunion, and the one before that, too. This year he'd mixed it up a little bit by making the use of props and assistant, like a dime store magician.

The prop in question was a skull - still flaked here and there with the same kind of tight leather skin that Cletus favoured as general home décor. He had laughed at Kane when they'd first sat down for dinner and - leaping straight back out of his chair with surprise - had found several teeth embedded in the chair's leather seat cushion. Cletus had laughed that same old cackle as far back as when they'd first met in '72. His old mouth drawn wide, skin stretched not much less than the leather on the old skull, and no one was surprised to find that Kane's chair had more teeth than Cletus himself.

The two men were close in age - a fact not lost on Kane as he watched the old fool regale the room with his own twisted take on Hamlet. But they could not be more different - at least in the mind of the lithe, soft-spoken Kane. Kane had spent his life in constant training and preparation: engaging in cardio exercise every morning, sticking to a strict diet and engaging in intellectual pursuits of the mind and body. The redneck cannibal meanwhile had indulged in just about all there was that life offered to the seedy and immoral. There were other differences too, that Kane did not feel as happy about. One of them was standing next to Cletus, involved in his storytelling in a slightly stronger capacity than the skull.

The man (Kane assumed it was a man, though it was hard to tell the thing was even human with all the layers of fat, hair and muck the beast was caked in) wore a muzzle-like contraption about his face, so spoke with a muffled and grisly quality. Since they'd sat down to dinner the words most often coming out of the boy's mouth were "Yes, paw," and with his wearable speech impediment even that

S is for Slasher

was difficult to understand.

He was the "Bubba" (probably was the kid's real name, as Cletus wasn't too creative) which Cletus was emphatically praising the virtues of - as if the person was an appliance Cletus was selling and not, in fact, his own son. It seemed since last year's conference he had taken the boy to work with him, teaching his trade. Kane had protested this, albeit quietly. It was not just Cletus's trade, it was all of their trades; every one of them sat around the room was charged with the same calling. Bringing in an apprentice was frowned upon - or it used to be, anyway.

Kane didn't like sharing the table with a novice - someone who had no spirit of their own to pursue the hunt, so had to mimic and essentially steal someone else's. It went against everything their society stood for, though even he had to admit calling it a society was a bit of a stretch. It was more like a little boys club.

Every year they would meet up at a destination hosted by one of the members and talk shop. Last year was the good doctor's turn to host, and they'd met in a morgue. The doc had found this morbidly funny (the best kind of funny, as per club rules), but Kane had spent the whole weekend shivering. By the time Cletus was found rifling through body bags, gnawing on old limbs like popsicles, all humour had left the situation. This year was Cletus's turn to host (much to the chagrin of just about every person at the table).

So they'd all trekked out to the middle of

S is for Slasher

Nowhere, Texas, and found themselves lodging in a dilapidated farmhouse. It was exactly what they'd all expected. Cletus living in a hick place, surrounded by dumb yokels, running a moonshine distillery in his basement. The only thing unexpected was the hillbilly's son, Bubba, taking in their bags and looking like humanity's "missing link". But no one had protested, likely because things were changing in their world - and they all knew it.

Over recent years there was less talking shop at the annual reunion, and much more drinking and talking about the good old days, which Kane thought never really were all that good in hindsight. It was depressing. What was more depressing was that each year there were less of them. The good doctor himself, Baron Blood (actually was the guy's name, which Kane approved of wholeheartedly) was no longer in attendance. Seems, so far as it had been whispered around the old farmhouse, the good doctor got himself into a spot of bother.

After last year's disaster of playing host, the Baron decided he needed some excitement in his life. They'd probably call it a mid-life crisis if the doc wasn't already well into his seventies. He'd set out to relive some of those glory days they were all always talking about, like it was some kind of comeback tour. But the doctor wasn't as spry as he used to be, in body or mind. He'd set up shop tormenting some teens out in Elmsfield, Illinois, plying his trade as a psychotherapist. In truth, Baron Blood's doctorate was in the veterinary sciences,

S is for Slasher

He stopped creating and so stopped recounting his creations. He had no desire to carry on his work before tonight, so what was it about the evening that had him so maudlin? Why did Cletus and Bubba's relationship sting him so? Why was he suddenly feeling as though he wished some of his work was still around? Not in a mundane gallery somewhere, of course. But somewhere it might be seen or, at the very least, remembered...

He realised he had supped the entire glass of moonshine - a concerning thing to not notice oneself doing. Turning the empty glass over in his hand, he wondered if this was why the other members of the group had been giving him a wide berth these past few years. It's true he was quiet - though not the quietest member of their circle by far. That particular prize went to Glenn.

Glenn Mullins - the silent stalker of Maryland. The scourge of babysitters everywhere. That man could sneak up on even the twitchiest teenager like nobody else in the business. So, when a full glass of moonshine appeared in the corner of Kane's eye, held out by a strong and yet comforting hand, Kane had to admit he was a little surprised. How many people had witnessed that hand as the bringer of their demise? Hundreds, if the stories are to be believed. Though Kane knew better than anyone not to believe everything you hear - though in Glenn's case, he made an exception.

"Evening, Glenn." Kane took the glass from his old friend, not expecting much else in the way of conversation. He could hear the breathing from behind Glenn's mask - that rhythmic, hoarse pattern that struck fear into the hearts of kids and adults alike. Glenn had asthma. Pair that with the rubber mask he wore and it made for a chilling effect.

"Nice night isn't it?" Though Glenn wasn't a talker, it still felt rude for Kane to not make any attempt at conversation. Over the years Glenn and Kane had become good friends. They'd both come up in the Eighties - the wildest time for their profession - and they both treated their work like professionals. The only thing they didn't see eye-to-eye on was the term "slasher", actually. Glenn cherished the term - adopted it, made it his own - even Kane had to respect what he'd done with it.

Even with all that history, Kane could count the conversations the two of them had held together on one hand (his hand with the missing finger, no less). As Glenn slowly dragged up a chair next to him on the porch, Kane twisted the glass around in his hand. The moonshine was making him a little drowsy, and the drowsiness was making him even poorer company than usual, so he appreciated the company of the quiet man. Which was why he became even more upset when caught sight of Glenn removing his mask. "Yeah," replied Glenn, and the silent spell was broken.

"You know, I haven't seen you without your mask on in a spell. You feeling okay?" Kane was hoping his friend might have just been a little warm in the Texas heat, maybe having supped some 'shine himself, and was just removing his mask for comfort and not conversation. Taking a moment to

S is for Slasher

look over Glenn, to see if he could read some intent on his face, Kane wished he hadn't. That he hadn't looked and hadn't opened a dialogue.

"Feeling fine, Kane. Fine as ever." He didn't look fine. He looked old. The mask he wore was bland - some rip-off dime-store mask of a white-toast actor from a TV show in the seventies. It had aged over the years, sure. Blood stains are hard to get out, and so are bullet holes. It wore the hallmarks of a life well spent, that was for certain, but it still looked good. The mask was crumpled up on the floor, where it had been dropped. It was wheezing itself back into shape, the way rubber does. But the owner of the mask was a different story.

Glenn's expression was contorted in such a strong and stern way that Kane thought it might never bounce back to shape. It was like the man was dealing with some internal thought so powerful that it was affecting his whole being. He'd never seen his friend look like that before, but the most upsetting thing was that he'd never realised just how old his friend looked. They were the same age, more or less, and Kane didn't spend much time worrying over his own reflection. Seeing Glenn like this though, maskless and yet somehow still hiding something under the skin on his face, it made him uneasy.

"You see that?" Glenn gestured over to the window of the house, where inside they could see Cletus and Bubba entertaining their remaining guests. Cletus was hocking the same skull from earlier (or perhaps it was a new skull, the man certainly had a surplus) around the room and Bubba - now without his muzzle - was catching it in his mouth and bringing it back. It was like a man with a dog, and boy were they making a show of the whole thing. Kane saw it, and he nodded, but he couldn't help but feel like the two of them were looking at different things.

That exchange brought about another quiet spell, wherein the two old killers could just sip their drinks and enjoy their limited company. But Kane knew from his earlier look at his friend's face that that wasn't the end of it. So he sat in silence, waiting in intense anticipation for the levee to break once more. And then it did.

"I don't need a legacy. I've been thinking about it, and it just doesn't feel right to me. We deal in death, Kane. You know that, I know that, every idiot in this whole world knows that."

Kane shifted uncomfortably in his chair. Glenn was pretty astute - it's one reason he was so damn good at what he did - but he couldn't have guessed, could he? Had he figured out what was on his mind, when he wasn't even sure about it himself?

"So why do we try and fight it? If we're bringing it, why do we expect no one is going to bring it back to us? You understand that, like I do. You always did. I liked your art, and I liked it more knowing it wasn't forever. You going to get an apprentice, Kane?"

This was uncomfortably new territory. Conversations between them were sparse, but the

Mullins's hunting grounds - it was where he grew up. If he was going out of this world, he'd be the kind of man to go out the way he came in. Kicking, screaming, and on familiar dirt.

Looking closely at the body, it was hard to tell who it was. The resolution on the photograph was blurry, which was likely intentional. Newspapers get by selling the morbid and grotesque, and they can get away with slapping it right on the front page if it looks just a little censored. But Kane knew who the body was all the same, as would anyone else looking at this photo with an accompanying headline - which he imagined would read *The Accident Assaulter Apprehended!*, or perhaps *Silent Stalker Slaughtered At Last!*, or some other sensational drivel.

The second photo wasn't like a newspaper cutting at all. It was a family photo - original instant-print, not from a negative or copy. In the picture a young boy wearing a mask, dressed as a mime, holds a balloon, and stares dead into the camera. Kane could feel that stare even from beyond the print, the years and the grave - it was Glenn all right. Young Glenn Mullins, not yet a stalker of much beyond the stray cats in his neighbourhood. Glenn had once told Kane about half-a-dozen ways to skin a cat, and Kane had modelled an art-piece on it, using homeless people with tinfoil cat ears. Glenn had actually laughed at that one, which felt like winning the lottery.

Turning the photo over in his hands, expecting some sort of written message, he found himself

S is for Slasher

surprisingly disappointed to find the other side blank. After a few more moments of returning the photographed boy's stare, he placed the picture back on the coffee table and turned his attention to the letter. He unfolded the page to find exactly what he had expected: a eulogy (of sorts). This had become a custom for the club over time, but in recent years it had begun to feel like a routine occurrence.

Glenn Mullins, the Stalker of Maryland, is no more. Glenn was a prominent member of our hunting society, popularising and even enjoying the term Slasher.

Glenn met his end after returning to his childhood hometown of Accidental, Maryland, and, after laying waste to the majority of the town's limited inhabitants, was burned alive by his first victim's granddaughter - who luckily also perished in the fire.

He will be missed by few, but remembered by many through the bodies he left in his wake. He is survived by none, except for his fellow hunters receiving this letter.

It was all pretty standard fare, Kane knew, except for the handwritten note attached to the bottom:

Kane, Glenn wanted you to have these photographs. He had asked me to hold onto them for you at this year's meeting but refused to tell me why or when to send them. I assume now is the appropriate time. I would also like to extend my sincerest apologies - I know you two were close.

Horace Rapture,

S is for Slasher

Club Secretary

Horace's penmanship needed work, Kane thought, as did his assumptions. Killers were close to no one, and he should know that. It was a lonely life, and the only person left to remember Glenn Mullins whole life now was a man whose longest conversation with him was four minutes total, and just happened to be about his upcoming intentions to die. If that made them close, then who would there be to remember Kane's life?

This was the moment Kane had decided to get himself an apprentice. It was sad, given the conversation with Glenn and how loaded it had been with implied disdain for the idea. But there was nothing to be done. Kane needed something permanent, and through which he would build a legacy. He looked to the rubber mask in the corner he was saving - the one that had been Glenn's. He was certain he needed more from his life, to give it all meaning.

He was a little unsure where you go to find a successor, especially in a field such as murder, but he had gleaned enough of the modern world through the news broadcasts he intermittently caught to make a start. Kane headed down to his local library and leapt into the world-wide-web to catch himself a like-minded spider.

***

As it turned out finding a candidate on the internet was not a difficult task - it was actually incredibly easy. The time-consuming part was weeding through the insanely large quantity of responses. Kane spent a good deal of time down at the library in the evenings, combing through "applications" from would-be killers to try and find the right one.

The first messages had come in a trickle, mostly expressing disbelief. *ChuckM69* said "this is fake right?", followed by *LP420* who'd sent "wuu2? I'm calling the cops". But then, as he continued to post on forums and message boards, the responses became a tidal wave. *Matty611*: "Can you help me kill my stepdad?" *F-Hunter6969*: "Kill 'em all! Frag Em Biiiitch". Most messages were more of the same, with the odd sincere application thrown into the bunch.

There were multitudes of momma's boys looking to settle scores with the world, and angst-driven middle-aged men looking to grasp some semblance of power. But very few actually showed any promise, and most just caved after the slightest bit of pressing. Kane had begun to wonder if this method of killer courtship would ever prove successful, or if he was stumbling into a trap of his own making.

This trap was not a literal one, though. Not one that would lead to him getting caught. It would be easy for someone to trace these messages, but he knew they never would. Hunters like him never got caught the easy way. They died on a hunt or they didn't die at all. Besides, from what he could gather from his short foray into the virtual world, the entire

S is for Slasher

world is full of fucked-up people saying they're going to do something terrible. If, through sheer force of will, someone decided to actually tackle any or all of these people, Kane's name would be pretty low on the list - at least chronologically speaking.

The trap that Kane worried he had stepped into was the dangerous and ensnaring feeling of hope. He had gone against everything he believed in about his craft in even beginning to consider raising and training an apprentice, a successor. If that were all for nothing, then Kane would have done worse than die, retire or fade away - he would have besmirched all of his work that he had ever created.

This feeling of failure pervaded his days at his lair (a rather nice loft apartment downtown) and plagued his nights at the library, frantically clicking and scrolling his way through hate filled wannabes screaming for a hand-out. But it was there, at the library, after about a week of trying, that he finally found results.

The night librarian was an old coot by the name of Janice. Kane had never thought to catch her last name and had only spoken to her once. When he'd first arrived at the library, she'd caught him. Hunched over a desk, face cast in the sickly blue light of the screen, she'd grilled him about being a homeless man. It had taken a good deal of restraint for Kane not to make something of her - a feeling he hadn't felt in quite some time. The lust for violence had felt good, unrequited though it may be.

In the nights since she had left him alone,

seemingly content that he was not a transient but - as she had whispered when he walked into the building most nights - "just another old pervert." He had no love for Janice, true, but he barely acknowledged her existence. Until that last night in the library, the night he was going to give up. The night when he was forced to notice her - the night she wasn't at the desk when he arrived.

He'd received a message not long after he'd got set-up (technology was very much still not his forté, and it often took multiple attempts and the occasional reset to get his passwords right). This one stood out from the usual spam of hate and encouragement. It caught his attention in part because it was sent exactly the minute he had logged on, but also because it was just three simple words, asking him a question he hadn't been asked before.

"Where Are You?" The sender was anonymous, which was not unusual - the names people use online are all anonymous in a sense - but it gave him a peculiar feeling. Anticipation perhaps, or dread? It was exciting. Kane put the message aside, thinking he'd get back to it - but then the chat pinged up on the screen again. Three more words, this time a statement.

"I See You." Kane reflexively looked around - he hadn't been surprised since Glenn had approached him on the porch nearly two months ago. And that was Glenn - a master of surprise - so who was this thinking they could do the same now? Kane was no longer excited - he was insulted, and a

S is for Slasher

little angry.

He began to type out a response, but another incoming message interrupted his flow. "I Want To Show You Something." Kane leaned back from his computer. Angry as he was, he was still intrigued. If this person thought he could out-shock Kane, then he best be bringing something particularly spectacular. He stared at his screen intently, waiting for something, a video, an image, a particularly dirty limerick - anything, really - to pop up. But then the screen went black.

All of the screens in the library went dark - and the lights with them. Someone had cut the power. This was getting serious now. It seems like this person did actually know where he was and was trying to toy with him. But Kane was prepared - he'd spent a lifetime preparing, after all. Then he heard it.

Music - classical music. Someone, from the other side of the library, was playing classical music. It had a tinny quality, like it was being played from a low-quality speaker, but Kane could still recognise the track. One of his favourites - Chopin's *Fanaisie-Impromtu*. The posthumously released piece, which takes great skill to replicate, had been a song that he had listened to while undertaking some of his greatest works. Kane followed the song, all at once becoming unprepared but totally willing, to the other end of the darkened hall.

It was there that he found the source of the music - a little portable device, plugged into a little docking station placed on the receptionist's desk.

S is for Slasher

And it was there that he beheld the receptionist - at last truly seeing her. She was strung up to the ceiling with wires embedded through the palms and running down the full length of her arm under the skin. These ran through the whole length of her body, re-emerging from the skin at the base of her ankles and wrapping around a spike - a metal tool, surely hand-crafted and smelted for this purpose alone - which was fixed to the floor and impaled the woman. The spike entered Janice from between her legs, and protruded from her mouth - her face locked in a permanent fixture of agony and surprise - gasping at the skies in fear as her life abandoned her.

It was beautiful - a little crude, but beautiful. Kane recognised the work immediately. He had gone through a phase of impalement in the nineties, when the idea of new and exciting tools and methods of death inspired him. This particular posing of the victim, with the pooling of blood directed to an engraved spiral beneath the corpse, was a mirror image of his first attempt at impalement as an art form. He was lost for words. Fortunately, someone from the shadows filled the silence for him:

"So, do I have the job or what?"

***

Mitchell Lawrence Hannigan was a small man - in size, but not mentality. He could talk a great deal - often filling in both sides of a conversation. Kane had hoped, in their early meetings, that this nature could be trained out of him - like a yappy dog.

Since their meeting in the library six months prior, they had met several times. At first in public, clandestinely. Kane had arranged for them to encounter each other like strangers, at art galleries and photography exhibits. He was still sounding the man out - despite how promising their early encounters were.

Eventually they had agreed to meet at Hannigan's apartment for the first time - which was, in itself, a gallery of sorts. Though in truth not one that Kane openly cared for. It had been overwhelming enough to walk into the finely furnished (and frankly far too expensive) space. Worse still when he had realised that the artworks - photographs, sketches and paintings - adorning the walls were all Kane's own works.

There were, of course, none of the original sculptures here - though his host kept insisting it wasn't for lack of trying. But there were paintings by Kane, the ones he had left by his crime scenes and (as far as he knew) burned or locked permanently in police evidence lockers the country over. There were sketches of his more intricate pieces - some were crude designs by him, but others must have been by professional police sketch-artists - framed and protected by glass like the Mona Lisa.

The photographs were perhaps the most jarring to Kane. These were not publicly available images. None of Kane's works were available online (he'd checked in a moment of search-engine weakness),

S is for Slasher

and the newspapers were only allowed to get their fill after the scenes had been cleaned up. Which meant removing the bodies, which also meant dismantling the art - both of which was very much still present in these photographs.

Hannigan had taken a great thrill in explaining the content of the photographs to Kane, seemingly ignorant (either truly or wilfully) of his guest's disdain.

"This is the *Forming of the Self* from '82. You can see here that the heads are actually stitched together with barbed wire *through* the mouth, causing the cheeks to swell and distend slightly."

Kane wasn't sure if the police or media had been naming his artworks, or if this was something Hannigan had come up with himself. What he was saying was actually partly true, though the real reason the cheeks looked so full is that Kane had fed them their own kidneys - while they were alive - and then sewed the mouths shut while he worked on the rest of the piece. Still, points for effort.

"Over here is *Reflections* from '91 - it's more modern, but still has a lot of substance. You can really get a feel for the insides of the victim, with the placement of the glass so perfectly held."

Kane didn't care for the way he'd apologised for the "modernness" of the piece, or how he'd used a word like "substance" without truly explaining what he meant, but still. It was a good feeling to see the work again - glass was a difficult tool to work with. His early attempts with it had been disastrous, leading to some improvised "people-mosaics", which had been messy - but admittedly fun.

"Ahh, and my favourite part of my whole collection - *The Inside - Number 9*. The way the subject seems to dance in the frame, the muscles and sinew forced to contract by the wirework in death. Truly, there are no words."

There were words, Kane was sure of that because Hannigan was using far too many of them. The Inside series, as it had apparently been dubbed, were intermittent occurrences in Kane's career. Between bigger, more intricate pieces, it was just nice to take someone and show the world who they were on the inside. And it was quite easy too, but time consuming to take off all the skin in a way that kept the victim conscious.

Hannigan continued to talk as Kane continued to be overwhelmed by his surroundings. Apparently this strange, small man had decided he should be the artist's successor even before the artist had decided he needed one. He claimed he felt a "strong affinity" from a young age to Kane's work. He avidly read and collected every article he could find on the killer, eventually curating his own personal gallery. He was well funded thanks to his family, who were "no longer in the picture". He'd said this last part with a wink that made Kane's stomach churn with clichéd pain.

But in spite of the man's sycophantic nature, Kane had to admit he had talent. Since they'd first met, Hannigan had recreated several more of Kane's original pieces, each time regaling him with a forced art critic's review on the work. If Kane

S is for Slasher

wanted a legacy, this man was likely his best candidate. Sad though it may be.

"So?" Hannigan asked, his lips curled into an impish smile. Apparently he was waiting on an answer which he seemed certain of - though as to the question Kane had no idea. Hannigan shuffled nervously in his seat, a little unsure of himself now. "Look dude, what more do I need to prove? You're not getting any younger and let's face it -"

He snapped his fingers and a young woman emerged - Kane hadn't noticed her in the room before now, though they had met several times. "- you're not making any new work. You're washed up. Let me fix that."

The girl brought over a crystal decanter filled with ruby red liquid. Kane had yet to determine the relationship between the two. If it was romantic then it was definitely one-sided, because her behaviour suggested more of a servant than a lover. She poured a glass for Hannigan before awaiting the approval to do the same for Kane.

"Let me be your legacy."

The words stung Kane more than he anticipated. It was not that he wasn't expecting it - it was the reason the two had met to begin with. It wasn't the definitive nature of the statement - Kane truly did feel he was done with slaughtering for art. The exact nature of Kane's hesitation actually came down to two things.

The first was that he still didn't trust Hannigan's commitment to the art form. Kane had been insisting for months, each time Hannigan had taken

S is for Slasher

him to a new crime scene, that he wanted to see Hannigan create something - truly create. To make something new, something inspired - something personal. And at first Hannigan had nodded, with a face that feigned understanding, and insisted he'd do better. But then the next piece would be unveiled, and it would be another replica of something Kane had done himself years prior. The remakes were all pale in comparison to the originals, and the flattery had grown insulting.

The second thing was actually much more simple than assessing Hannigan's ability to create art - Kane just simply didn't like the man. He was one-part bootlicker, two-parts snake, and finished off with a garnish of petulant child. He would heap praise upon Kane and his life's works without ever saying anything of substance. Then, when Kane would try to impart wisdom, or correct him on a misconception he made about Kane's work, he would grow sullen and insolent. He would snap and snipe, grow bitter and inflate his own sense of superiority. More often than not he would take this out on the girl, who never said a word in response.

Kane had no time for women, unless they piqued his artistic sensibilities as they used to in his prime, but he didn't care for the way Hannigan treated his. Many a hunter had been brought low by underestimating the women they preyed upon - it was rare they met their end at the hands of men. It was always a woman, usually the last woman standing, who brought them low. This arrogance didn't bode well for a long and lustrous career.

S is for Slasher

The girl had been at all of the scenes Hannigan had taken him too. She was often covered in more blood than Hannigan, more tired from whatever tasks he'd set her about to than he himself. It aroused suspicions in Kane, and suspicions kept him safe. So when Hannigan grasped the girl's arm, stopping her from pouring Kane a glass until he got his answer - Kane decided to give him one.

"No."

And he left the flailing imitator there, floundering and - for once – speechless.

***

It had been a wasted year for Kane. That was how it felt. True, he hadn't killed anyone for many years before this point, but this was different. In the year following the last reunion, he'd actually set himself a goal. He was to find a worthy successor. He had failed at this, and so even though technically the year was about on par with the rest of the recent years in terms of activity, this one felt much worse.

He hadn't heard from Hannigan since he left his apartment. This was aided in part by Kane moving his lair, hoping to get away from any spite the man might misplace in his direction. He had made sure that when he moved, he updated Horace, the club secretary. He wanted to be certain that he received any and all due correspondence, be they obituaries or the next reunion's location.

This year, as it turns out, was to have been Glenn's year to host. It was decided that, in his

S is for Slasher

honour, the event would be held in Accident, Maryland, at the house in the woods Glenn used to use as a lair. It felt like it was going to be a sombre affair for Kane.

He felt as though he'd betrayed the understanding his old friend had assumed in him by seeking out some sort of avoidance of death, and then he had failed. But still he came. He even brought along Glenn's mask with him, though exactly why he was not sure. Perhaps he'd bury it.

He tucked the mask into his coat as he approached the house - only realising when the light from the porch struck him that he'd been handling it during the walk. He'd heard the conversation from the tree line and thought he could recognise a few voices in attendance this year. But only when he stepped into the light of the house's front yard did he realise the full extent of the guest list. There, on the porch, clinking a glass of ruby red port with Horace and laughing with Cletus, was Mitchel Lawrence Hannigan.

***

The evening had passed by in a blur of simmering anger. Hannigan had not taken no for an answer - and given the fool's privileged upbringing, Kane was not surprised. But forcing his way into the hunter's club was a step too far. The insult compounded to the injury were the stories he regaled the others with - tales of recreating Kane's works and, in his words, *surpassing them in magnitude and craft.*

Kane had said nothing in response. Horace and the others had shifted uneasily. They were polite to new blood, but not ignorant to the respect of the old. The only one who truly seemed to enjoy Hannigan's antics was Cletus - the redneck was practically encouraging the little upstart.

The evening came to boiling point when, seemingly incensed at not getting a rise out of Kane, Hannigan decided to dig his nails into the wound. "Oh Kane, you simply must lighten up - your friend Glenn sure did!" And then he mimicked setting himself ablaze - imitating the violent end for a violent legend. Cletus fell out his chair laughing, Bubba alongside him. Kane left the room - once more grabbing a drink and excusing himself to the porch.

Out there in the night air he found the girl, swinging her legs off the edge of the wooden porch, a beam between her legs, her hands draped over the broken railing, not a care in the world. Kane sat beside her in an old rocking chair, presumably one his dead friend had enjoyed an evening or two of quiet contemplation in. *It figures*, Kane thought. *Every time I seek the quiet, I am surprised by company.*

But this time he was not bombarded with conversation and noise. He was surprised by getting what he wanted. They sat there in silence for a good while, taking in the night air and drowning out the noise from the dining room with whisky. He looked out to the trees, and for a moment he pretended he was prey - looking out into the woods for the killer. *The Slasher of Maryland*, hunting him down, moving quietly and never being seen. He liked the thought.

He was disturbed from this quiet revelry by a hand on his shoulder. The girl had gotten up and moved back inside - he'd never even noticed her stand - and then there she was, at his side, with his coat in one hand, his shoulder in the other. And she had done it all with the stealth of a professional. "It's cold," she said, and then she left. He watched her leave, noticing the mud on the undersides of her feet, and the scars on her arms and legs - the hand that was on his shoulder had all the marks and calluses of someone who worked - truly worked - on their craft.

Kane rocked back in his chair, holding his coat over his lap. He looked back to the darkness of the trees as he ran his hands over his coat pocket. It was empty.

***

Kane was awoken by the sound of laughter coming from outside the house. It was Cletus's signature cackle. Kane got up and slowly made his way over to the window. There, in the wooden tree line of the forest, was a statue. Formed of barbed wire, blood and guts, and pure grit and determination. The primary material used in its construction was Hannigan, his body twisted and broken into pieces, no two of which touched another

S is for Slasher

and none of which touched the ground. It resembled a fractured spider, stepped on by something bigger than it could comprehend. It was art - somehow holy and profane all at once. The girl stood beside Kane as he wept and offered her silence.

Also from Red Cape Publishing

Anthologies:
Elements of Horror Book One: Earth
Elements of Horror Book Two: Air
Elements of Horror Book Three: Fire
Elements of Horror Book Four: Water
A is for Aliens: A-Z of Horror Book One
B is for Beasts: A-Z of Horror Book Two
C is for Cannibals: A-Z of Horror Book Three
D is for Demons: A-Z of Horror Book Four
E is for Exorcism: A-Z of Horror Book Five
F is for Fear: A-Z of Horror Book Six
G is for Genies: A-Z of Horror Book Seven
H is for Hell: A-Z of Horror Book Eight
I is for Internet: A-Z of Horror Book Nine
J is for Jack-o'-Lantern: A-Z of Horror Book Ten
K is for Kidnap: A-Z of Horror Book Eleven
L is for Lycans: A-Z of Horror Book Twelve
M is for Medical: A-Z of Horror Book Thirteen
N is for Nautical: A-Z of Horror Book Fourteen
O is for Outbreak: A-Z of Horror Book Fifteen
P is for Poltergeist: A-Z of Horror Book Sixteen
Q is for Quantum: A-Z of Horror Book Seventeen
R is for Revenge: A-Z of Horror Book Eighteen
S is for Slasher: A-Z of Horror Book Nineteen
It Came from the Darkness: A Charity Anthology
Out of the Shadows: A Charity Anthology
Hot off the Press: A Charity Anthology
Castle Heights: 18 Storeys, 18 Stories
Sweet Little Chittering
Unceremonious
The Nookienomicon

Short Story Collections:
Embrace the Darkness by P.J. Blakey-Novis
Tunnels by P.J. Blakey-Novis
The Artist by P.J. Blakey-Novis
Karma by P.J. Blakey-Novis
The Place Between Worlds by P.J. Blakey-Novis
Home by P.J. Blakey-Novis
Short Horror Stories by P.J. Blakey-Novis
Short Horror Stories Vol.2 by P.J. Blakey-Novis
Keep It Inside & Other Weird Tales by Mark Anthony Smith
Everything's Annoying by J.C. Michael
Old Tales Reborn by J.C. Michael
Six! By Mark Cassell
Six! Volume 2 by Mark Cassell
Monsters in the Dark by Donovan 'Monster' Smith
Barriers by David F. Gray
Love & Other Dead Things by Astrid Addams
Bone Carver by Gemma Paul
Shadows of Death by Dee Caples

Novelettes:
The Ivory Tower by Antoinette Corvo
By His Hand by William R. Perry

Novellas:
Four by P.J. Blakey-Novis
Dirges in the Dark by Antoinette Corvo
The Cat That Caught the Canary by Antoinette Corvo
Bow-Legged Buccaneers from Outer Space by David Owain Hughes
Spiffing by Tim Mendees
A Splintered Soul by Adrian Meredith
Scavengers of the Sun by Adrian Meredith

Novels:
Madman Across the Water by Caroline Angel
The Curse Awakens by Caroline Angel
Less by Caroline Angel
Where Shadows Move by Caroline Angel
Origin of Evil by Caroline Angel
Origin of Evil: Beginnings by Caroline Angel
Exist by Caroline Angel
The Vegas Rift by David F. Gray
The Broken Doll by P.J. Blakey-Novis
The Broken Doll: Shattered Pieces by P.J. Blakey-Novis
South by Southwest Wales by David Owain Hughes
Any Which Way but South Wales by David Owain Hughes
All Roads Lead to South Wales by David Owain Hughes
Appletown by Antoinette Corvo
Nails by K.J. Sargeant
The Eternal by Timothy Friesenhahn
Lead Me to the Dark by James Twyman
196 Days Later by Chisto Healy

Art Books:
Demons Never Die by David Paul Harris & P.J. Blakey-Novis
Six Days of Violence by P.J Blakey-Novis & David Paul Harris

Magazines:
Cauldron of Chaos

Follow Red Cape Publishing

www.redcapepublishing.com
www.facebook.com/redcapepublishing
www.twitter.com/redcapepublish
www.instagram.com/redcapepublishing
www.pinterest.co.uk/redcapepublishing
www.ko-fi.com/redcape
www.buymeacoffee.com/redcape

Printed in Great Britain
by Amazon